TROUBLE AFTER DARK

GANSETT ISLAND SERIES, BOOK 21

MARIE FORCE

Trouble After Dark
Gansett Island Series, Book 21
By: Marie Force
Published by HTJB, Inc.
Copyright 2019. HTJB, Inc.
Cover Design: Diane Luger
E-book Layout: Holly Sullivan
E-book Formatting Fairies
ISBN: 978-1950654659

marieforce.com

View the McCarthy Family Tree here. marieforce.com/gansett/familytree/

View the list of Who's Who on Gansett Island here. marieforce.com/whoswhogansett/

View a map of Gansett Island. marieforce.com/mapofgansett/

THE GANSETT ISLAND SERIES

More new books are alway in the works. For the most up-to-date list of what's available from the Gansett Island Series as well as series extras, go to marieforce.com/gansett.

CHAPTER 1

*D*eacon didn't wake up that morning planning to crash a wedding and steal a bridesmaid. In fact, he didn't wake up expecting much of anything on his fourth day on the boring remote island where his older brother was holding him hostage for the summer. What the hell was he even doing on Gansett, the island he'd grown up on, where his brother was now the freaking police chief?

Deacon was a grown-ass man and could do whatever the hell he wanted. Why was it that Blaine had such power over him, even now? It was infuriating, but he didn't need to think about that while he had a hot babe holding on tight to him as he drove his motorcycle toward the bluffs on the island's north side.

Since she was wearing his only helmet, he could hear the ends of her sexy red dress whipping in the wind as he accelerated around a curve, dodging a family of four on bicycles who were smack in the middle of the road. He, who didn't have much trouble attracting female companionship, could honestly say it'd been years—perhaps a lifetime—since he'd met a woman as stunningly gorgeous as the one wrapped around him at this moment.

He'd first seen her the other night at the island's clinic after one of the craziest nights in recent memory—when Finn McCarthy's ex had stabbed Finn and his new girlfriend, Chloe Dennis. Half the island had ended up at the clinic, along with the cowboy strippers who'd been performing at Katie Lawry's bachelorette party when the stabbings took place.

Deacon didn't recall Gansett Island being that interesting when he'd lived there as a kid.

His bridesmaid had long, silky dark hair that fell nearly to her spectacular ass, flawless, lightly tanned skin, bluish-gray eyes fringed with extravagant lashes, large breasts that were barely contained by the halter-style dress and lips made for kissing.

The last thing Deacon needed, especially right now, was any more female complications. However, he'd dare any red-blooded man to take one look at the sexy bridesmaid on the back of his bike and not want her riding shotgun. Downshifting, he turned into the lot at the bluffs, pulled into a parking spot and killed the engine on the vintage Harley he'd bought off a buddy on Cape Cod, where he used to live before being banished to freaking Gansett by his goddamned brother.

Despite his displeasure at being back on the island, Deacon had to admit that Gansett had a kind of wild, untamed beauty that he'd forgotten about during his years away. He wanted to hate everything about being there and how Blaine had issued the ultimatum to Deacon, as if he were a recalcitrant teenager—*come home with me or face major charges*. Hell of a choice.

He got off the bike and helped his stolen bridesmaid remove the helmet. First order of business would be finding out the name of the goddess he'd run away with. Wait till Blaine figured out that she'd left with him. He'd pop a nut. Deacon choked back a laugh at the thought of Blaine's nuts popping because of him. It had given him great pleasure all his life to irritate his brother and vice versa. Why? He couldn't say. That's just how it was between them.

Blaine was such a Dudley Do-Right, and Deacon, well, he was a Dudley Do-Whatever-the-Fuck-He-Wanted.

With his passenger free of the helmet, Deacon took another

long look at one of the most exquisite female faces he'd ever beheld. It didn't take a rocket scientist to see that while she was stunning, she was also troubled, and he'd had more than his share of troubled females. The most recent one had landed him in jail, which had led to his ex-communication to Gansett, the last place on earth he wanted to be. Although, the godforsaken island was looking pretty damned good to him at the moment.

She ran her fingers through her hair, attempting to straighten the damage done by the helmet. A light breeze ran through it, and he was struck dumb by the sight of her standing on the cliff like a goddess in red.

Deacon Taylor didn't stare at women.

They stared at him.

His unprecedented reaction to her should've been cause for concern in light of his recent troubles, but he wasn't going there today. He opened the compartment on the bike where he'd stashed a six-pack of beer and some ice before leaving the apartment Blaine had assigned him, located behind the house Blaine shared with his wife, Tiffany, and their daughters. Getting to know his nieces was one of the only goals he had for his summer in exile.

After twisting off the cap on one of the beers, he handed it to the goddess.

"Thanks."

"What's your name?"

"Julia."

He touched his bottle to hers. "Nice to meet you, Julia. I'm Deacon."

"I've never met anyone named Deacon before."

"It was my grandmother's maiden name."

"It's cool."

"Thanks. I like it." He took a deep drink from the bottle. Blaine would pop the other nut if he knew Deacon was riding around with a makeshift cooler on the bike. Deacon took pleasure in thinking up new ways to aggravate his brother. "Are you sure it's okay that you left the wedding?"

"It's fine. Katie is so wrapped up in Shane that I doubt she's even noticed I'm gone."

He wondered if she felt as sad as she looked and sounded. "Are you okay?"

"Never better." She forced a smile and then chugged half the beer in one long gulp.

"Do you not like him?"

"Who?"

"Your sister's husband?"

"Oh God, I *love* him. He's great. He saved Katie's life when she got caught in a rip current outside the Surf."

"*Whoa.*"

"Trust me, our whole family will love him forever for saving her. Not to mention, his sister, Laura, is married to our brother Owen."

Deacon took a minute to do that math in his head.

"A brother and sister married a brother and sister," Julia said. "Nothing illegal about it."

He laughed. "If you say so."

"Laura and Shane are awesome. Owen and Katie got lucky. They married into an amazing family. Do you know the McCarthys?"

"Sure. I grew up with them. My sister-in-law's sister is married to Mac McCarthy."

"My family loves your brother. He was good to my mom during a very difficult time in her life."

"That sounds like him. He's a saint."

"You don't like him?"

"He's okay, if you like the holier-than-thou type."

"I take it you're not holier than thou?"

He laughed. "Ah, no, not exactly." Deacon wondered what she'd think of him if she'd known he spent a night in jail five days ago or that his saintly brother had gone to the mainland to bail him out. His alleged "crime" had been for a good cause, but when a woman like Julia heard the word *jail*, she wouldn't stick around to hear the story. She'd be long gone, and he wouldn't blame her. "How about you?"

"I try to do the right thing, for all the good that does me."

"What do you mean?"

"People suck."

"All people, or certain people?"

"Most people, especially the male variety. Present company excluded, of course."

He laughed again. "Of course. What happened?"

They wandered over to a massive log that acted as a curb to keep cars from driving off the cliff and sat next to each other.

"It would be easier to tell you what *hasn't* happened."

"Okay..."

She didn't say anything for a long time as she stared out at the ocean.

Deacon thought she wasn't going to tell him, but then she began to speak.

WHY WAS SHE ABOUT TO AIR OUT HER PROBLEMS WITH A TOTAL stranger? Not to mention another guy who was so hot, he probably had women throwing their panties at him to get his attention? What was the point of talking about it? How would that fix anything? It wouldn't, but she found herself telling him anyway.

"People take advantage of me."

His brow furrowed, possibly with a touch of outrage that she appreciated. "How so?"

"Guys... They take one look at me and think they have me figured out. I must be easy. I must be a slut. I must be gullible. I attract all the wrong guys, especially the most recent one." Her heart was like a cement block in her chest when she thought about Mike, the promises he made, the things he said to her, the hopes she'd pinned on him, only to find out he was far worse than the others.

"What did he do?"

"He played me for a total fool. Made me fall in love with him. Promised me everything. We were going to have a life together and have babies and a house." To her fierce annoyance, a tear slid down her cheek. She brushed it away angrily. The last thing she wanted was

5

to spend any more tears on him. "Then his mom got sick with breast cancer. He was freaking out because she didn't have insurance and needed treatment. I loaned him money."

Deacon winced. "How much?"

"Fifteen thousand. Almost everything I had."

"Let me guess—his mom's not sick?"

"Ding-ding-ding. You win the grand prize. His mom is fine, but his *girlfriend* is pregnant, and he needed the money to get prenatal care for her because *she's* the one who doesn't have insurance."

"What a scumbag."

"So now she has my money, my man and a bouncing new baby. I heard they're buying a house together. They probably used my money for the down payment." She couldn't help but laugh at the sheer madness of it all. "Ridiculous, right?"

"I'm sorry that happened to you."

"I am, too, because now I'm flat broke and stuck here for God knows how long until I can make some money to get home to Texas and get the stuff I had to move into storage after I got evicted from my apartment. If the storage place doesn't sell it since I missed a payment."

"What's in Texas?"

"A job I used to love until I got a new boss who called me Sugar and asked me to do personal errands for him."

"Seriously?"

"Yep. It was awful, and after I loaned Mike the money and then figured out what he was really about, I called out sick for a few days because I was too upset to leave my house. The boss from hell told me not to bother coming back. That led to me losing my apartment when I couldn't afford to renew the lease."

"I'm sorry. That sucks."

She shrugged. "I brought it on myself by being stupid with Mike and then handing my boss a reason to get rid of me. I tried to find another job, but nothing materialized that would pay me enough to cover my expenses."

"So there's no reason to go rushing back, then?"

"No." Julia kicked at a rock with one toe of the sandals she'd bought with the last of her credit card limit. She'd been sleeping on a coworker's sofa since she got evicted from the apartment she used to share with Katie. She'd been unsuccessful in landing a roommate, thus her basically homeless status. That word *homeless* struck fear in her heart the way few things ever had since she left her violent childhood behind. "Not anymore."

"I'm stuck here for the summer, too."

"How come?"

"Doing a favor for my brother."

"What kind of favor?"

"He needed a harbor master. I'm certified, so he asked me to come do it."

"What about your regular job?"

"I'm between jobs at the moment, so the timing worked out for both of us." The Cape Cod town he'd worked for last year as the harbor master had invited him not to return after he spent a night in their jail.

"What'll you do after the summer?"

"Find something else, I suppose. How about you?"

"Same, I guess. Although the thought of starting over, *again*, is exhausting."

"You've done it before?"

"Too many times to count. My father was in the military. We moved a lot."

"We grew up here on Gansett. I *hated* it."

"My siblings and I spent summers here with our grandparents, who owned the Sand & Surf. It was our favorite place on earth." It was also the only break they got from their abusive father. They'd lived for those blissful summer days on Gansett, where they were safe and loved and away from the monster, as they'd called General Mark Lawry.

"Really? You loved it?"

"We loved everything about it."

"Huh. I couldn't believe when my brother moved back here will-

7

ingly to become the police chief. He hated it as much as I did when we were kids. But then he met Tiffany, who's now his wife, and he's happier than a pig in shit with her, their kids and a job he loves."

"Do you like his wife?"

"I barely know her, but he sure as hell likes her."

"Some people get lucky. Like my brother and sister." Julia, Katie and Owen had been a team for so long that she wasn't sure how she was supposed to function now that they'd found new lives for themselves. Julia was lost without them, not that she'd ever say as much to them. She'd never do anything to undermine their hard-won happiness.

But God, she missed them. Especially Katie, who'd lived with Julia until Katie had come to Gansett for Owen and Laura's wedding, met Laura's brother, Shane, and decided to stay for a while that turned into forever.

Julia glanced at Deacon, wishing he wasn't hotter than the sun. He had messy dirty-blond hair the color of honey, golden-brown eyes, a muscular body and the perfect amount of scruff on his jaw. But whatever. Who cared if he was hot? She'd had more than enough of good-looking guys who were beautiful on the outside and assholes on the inside. "How old are you?" she asked, to make conversation more than anything.

"Thirty-five. You?"

"Thirty-three."

"I wonder if we ever crossed paths as kids. Although, I'm sure I'd remember you."

Another line from another pretty mouth. Julia had heard such things so many times, they barely registered anymore. Just once, she wished a man would see her for who she was on the inside, but they never got past her packaging to discover what she was really made of.

She looked out at the gorgeous scenery, wishing Gansett could have the usual effect on her. As a kid, she'd come alive the minute she stepped off the ferry. This time, she was just dead inside. "Did you think you'd have it all figured out by now?"

"Have what figured out?"

"Life."

He shrugged. "I never had a timeline for figuring things out. Maybe that's why my brother finds me so annoying. He's a police chief at thirty-seven. Not that he didn't have his rocky times, but he's married with two kids and a dream job. He's got his shit together."

"I thought I'd be married with kids in school by now. I had a definite timeline. But nothing has worked out the way I hoped it would, and now…"

"What?"

"Nothing. It doesn't matter."

"Sure it does. What were you going to say?"

She crossed her arms against her knees and rested her head on her forearms while continuing to look at him. "Maybe it's time to give up on the dream."

"Don't say that. You never know what's coming right around the next corner. Anything can still happen."

She shrugged. "Doesn't matter."

"You know what I'm thinking?"

"What?"

"You're stuck here for a while. I'm stuck here for a while. Maybe we can hang out and make it more fun than it would be otherwise."

Sitting upright, she eyed him with skepticism that was hardwired into her DNA after so many disappointments. "Is 'hang out' a metaphor for sex?"

He laughed. "You don't pull any punches, do you?"

"What's the point of pulling punches? I've had enough of the bull-shit. If you're asking me to have sex with you, the answer is no. I'm on a man diet, which also means a dick diet. If you're looking for someone to hang out with and have some fun this summer that doesn't in any way include sex, then sure, why not?"

Deacon sputtered with laughter. "A dick diet?"

"Yes, as in no dick."

He shook his head as his gorgeous eyes danced with amusement. "How long have you been on this so-called diet?"

"Four months now."

"Gotcha. Just to be clear—I wasn't coming on to you. I was legitimately looking for a friend to make my summer in exile more bearable."

Julia didn't believe him, but she kept that to herself.

"What's your number?"

She recited it and watched him tap the numbers into his phone and add her name to the contact.

"I'll hit you up."

"Cool." She couldn't care less if she ever heard from him. "I should probably go back to the wedding."

"How come?"

"I'm the maid of honor. I have to give a toast after dinner."

"You want a plus-one?"

"It's kind of late for that at this point since you already crashed."

His wolfish grin revealed a sexy dimple in his left cheek and did wondrous things to his gorgeous face—and she had no doubt he knew that. "I won't eat."

Julia had to admit that soldiering through the rest of this night would be more fun with a companion than it would've been on her own. Besides, Katie was so in love with her new husband that she wouldn't even notice if Julia brought a last-minute guest. "Sure. Let's go."

CHAPTER 2

*J*t was refreshing to meet a woman who didn't immediately want something from him, Deacon thought as he drove them back to the Wayfarer. He remembered the venue from when he was a kid on the island, but in recent years, it had fallen into disrepair until the McCarthy family bought it, renovated it and reopened it in time for Julia's sister's wedding to Shane McCarthy.

At a briefing he'd attended at the police station as part of his new job, he'd been told the grand reopening of the Wayfarer would occur during Memorial Day weekend, with several days of events planned, including the wedding. Evan McCarthy, who'd become a big star in the last few years, would be back on the island to headline the entertainment at the actual opening.

Deacon had gone to school with Evan and looked forward to seeing him again.

He followed Julia through the main doors of the Wayfarer and encountered chaos at the reception.

The bride came rushing over. *"Oh my God!* There she is." Katie promptly broke down into tears as she embraced her sister. "Where've you *been*? We've been looking everywhere for you!"

"Oh, I, uh… I took a break."

Deacon jerked when someone roughly grabbed his arm and dragged him out of the fray.

"What the *fuck*, Deacon?" Blaine's low tone was full of condemnation. "What're you even doing here, and where did you go with her?"

Deacon wrestled his arm free of his brother's tight hold. "I stopped by earlier to check out the new place, and she asked me to get her out of here for a bit. Not that it's any of your business what I do."

"*Everything* you do on my island is my business."

"Fuck off with your police chief act."

"It's not an act. It's a fact."

"Yeah, yeah, whatever. Your wife is looking for you."

"You have no business here."

"Actually, I do." He winked at his brother. "Julia asked me to be her plus-one, so maybe we can turn this wedding into a double date, brother dear." Deacon relished the fury that flashed across Blaine's face before he schooled his features and stormed off.

Good riddance.

When had his brother become an even bigger drag than he used to be? Was it when he became the chief? Or had marriage done that to him? Deacon brushed off the unpleasantness with Blaine to focus on his "date."

Julia was surrounded by people, including the bride and groom, so Deacon made his way to the bar, where he ordered a beer.

"Way to make off with the maid of honor, dude." The young male bartender flashed a silly grin. "People were freaking out looking for her."

Deacon took a sip of his beer, keeping his gaze fixed on Julia. "She didn't think anyone would notice."

"Oh, they noticed. Even had the DJ make an announcement."

Deacon cringed. "Yikes."

"Those are her brothers and sisters." He wiped down the bar as he shared intel with Deacon. "From what I hear, they're all close. The dad, who was a general, was a total bastard. Beat them up, beat up the mom. He's doing time now."

Shock reverberated through Deacon. She'd been *abused* as a kid?

Oh God... Deacon hoped there was a special place in hell reserved for people who abused kids and animals. And men who abused the women they supposedly "loved." He would never understand that kind of love. In fact, that very issue was what had put him in jail. He'd come to the defense of a woman he'd casually hooked up with when her ex-husband showed up at the bar where she worked, despite the restraining order that was supposed to keep him far away from her.

Deacon had gotten in the middle of their dispute, fought with the ex, landed in jail and gotten himself exiled to Gansett for his trouble. As much as he didn't want to be on the island with Blaine breathing down his neck, he'd do it again to protect Sherri, who'd lived in fear of her ex long enough. Before the cops had shown up, Deacon had put a serious hurt on him. Word was that he'd broken his nose and ruptured a testicle.

Excellent.

Only thanks to Blaine intervening with the local police had Deacon avoided felony assault charges, so for that, he probably ought to be thankful to his brother. However, gratitude toward Blaine made him feel a little nauseated. He took another swig of beer, filled with bitterness that Blaine hadn't wanted to hear the details behind the fight. He'd just heard the words *Deacon, fight, potential assault charges* and jumped to his own conclusions.

If Deacon had to guess, Blaine probably would've done the same thing under similar circumstances. His brother had no patience for bullies. That was one thing they had in common. He'd never forget the time that Blaine had jacked up Darren Tuttle after he found out Darren had been hassling Deacon in school. Blaine had dispatched Darren, who'd never again looked in Deacon's direction.

At times, having Blaine around had been fortuitous. Now was not one of those times, Deacon thought as he caught his brother glaring in his direction.

Deacon ignored him and returned his focus to Julia and her family. From what he could tell, there were three sisters and four brothers. Some were blonde like Katie, and others were dark-haired like Julia. An older woman he assumed was their mother stood with them, a fierce-looking, tattooed dude by her side. Deacon would bet they had a good story to tell.

People fascinated him. Why did they do the things they did? Why did they hurt the people they supposedly loved? Why did one person appeal to him when another didn't? What motivated them? In his career in law enforcement, he'd seen the worst of humankind—and the best.

He liked to think there was more good than bad in this world, but ten years as a Boston cop had given him reason to wonder. A knee injury had led to a medical retirement from the BPD, which was when he'd started over as harbor master in Harwich. That job and that town had suited him, until the night he'd stepped up for a friend and had his life upended once again.

Whatever. He'd survived upheaval before, and he'd survive it this time, too. Hopefully, he could get through this summer without doing something really stupid, like punching his brother or falling for Julia.

JULIA HATED THAT EVERYONE WAS UPSET WITH HER, EVEN AFTER SHE'D apologized for worrying them.

"What's going on with you?" Owen asked when the others had dispersed from the impromptu family meeting in the middle of the dance floor.

"Nothing is going on. I just needed a break."

"In the middle of Katie's wedding?"

How could Owen possibly understand what it felt like for her to see him and Katie happily settled with their true loves while she recovered from being screwed over by yet another in a long string of losers? The three of them had been a team for so long that Julia wasn't sure how to go on without them available to her at a moment's notice.

Intellectually, she knew they'd still be available to her, but emotionally... They didn't come first with each other anymore, and that was the part she was having trouble accepting.

How many times had they had to rally around their mother or one of their younger siblings or each other during the decades of hell they'd endured at the hands of their father? Too many to count.

Long after they'd become legal adults, the three of them had moved when their family relocated with the military so they could continue to be available to their younger siblings. It'd been madness, and even now that the monster was in prison, it was still hard to believe the nightmare was really over.

"Jule?"

She glanced at Owen, whose brow was furrowed with concern for her. "Sorry. What did you say?"

"I asked why you needed a break in the middle of Katie's wedding."

"I... I'm not sure. I just felt a little overwhelmed and needed some air. Deacon offered to take me for a ride, and I thought Katie was set with Shane for the next little while. I didn't mean to upset everyone."

"I think you hurt her feelings by leaving."

Julia certainly hadn't intended for that to happen. "I'll smooth things over with her. Don't worry."

"I am worried. You're not yourself this weekend. Whatever's going on, I wish you'd just talk to me about it."

There was no way she could tell her older brother about being taken for a ride by a man who'd used her to set up his life with another woman. She'd withstood enough humiliation since she'd put those pieces together. She didn't need more. "It's nothing you need to worry about, O. You've got your hands full with Laura and the kids."

"That doesn't mean I don't have room in my hands for you, too, if you need me."

His sweetness brought tears to her eyes, which, of course, he noticed. Owen had been primed since early childhood to be on the lookout for trouble in his family and knew it when he saw it. He put his arm around her. "Julia... Please talk to me."

"I will. When I'm ready to."

"Promise?"

She nodded and leaned into his embrace, drawing strength from him the way she had her entire life. "You know what I do need?"

"What's that?"

"A job. You know of anyone on Gansett who's hiring?"

"Why do you need a job?"

"Things went south with mine when the new boss came in and ruined everything. I figured I'd stick around for the summer on Gansett."

He didn't need to know she was flat broke and couldn't afford the flight back to Texas. Before she lost her job, she'd bought a one-way ticket to Gansett, hoping she might get some vacation time to spend on the island after the wedding. She'd also booked the cowboy strippers for Katie's bachelorette party. Both had been nonrefundable.

"I'm sorry about the job, but thrilled you'll be spending the summer. I'll ask around. We'll find you something."

"Thanks, O. I'm also looking forward to getting to know my niece and nephews, my brother- and sister-in-law and the man our mom has fallen so hard for."

"Charlie is awesome. You'll love him."

"That's what everyone says. Plus, I'm excited to spend time with Gram and Gramps."

"We're so glad that they've moved back to the island. They said they want to be with their great-grandchildren, and we're all for that." Their grandparents, Russ and Adele, had turned over ownership of the hotel they'd owned for more than fifty years to Owen and Laura as a wedding gift. "Did you hear that Cindy is thinking about sticking around, too?"

"What? No, she hasn't told me." Julia hadn't had five minutes alone with her younger sister since they arrived on the island for the wedding festivities.

"I guess it all came about last night when she met Chloe Dennis, who owns the Curl Up and Dye salon. The woman who usually helps Chloe at the salon in the summer is pregnant and not coming this year. Cindy jumped at the chance to spend the summer on Gansett. And with Finn McCarthy moving in with Chloe, Cindy snapped up the place where Finn had been living. I think it's got two bedrooms. You should check it out if you're going to stick around."

"I will. Sounds like Cindy has it all figured out." Julia was glad someone did.

"She's excited to spend the summer."

"None of us has forgotten our Gansett summers with Gram and Gramps," Julia said wistfully, longing for those simpler summer days even if she wouldn't go back to that time in her life for anything.

"Best days of our lives."

"The only peace we ever got."

"Don't forget Gram is hosting a brunch at the hotel for Katie and Shane tomorrow."

"I haven't forgotten."

Owen nudged Julia. "You ought to ask your friend Deacon to come. He's been watching you the whole time we've been over here talking."

"What? He has not."

"Yes, he has. If he's anything like his brother, he's good people."

In the past, she would've liked hearing that he'd been looking at her while she talked to her brother. Not anymore. In a moment of recent self-awareness, she'd come to the conclusion that she'd put far too much value on the attention of men. Now? He could be the best guy in the world, and Julia wouldn't care. She'd lost faith in all men.

Deacon was fine to hang out with, to have some fun with. Beyond that? No, thanks.

KEVIN MCCARTHY WAS COUNTING THE HOURS UNTIL HIS NEPHEW'S wedding was done so he could get Chelsea to the mainland to deliver their baby. Her due date was still two weeks off, but he wasn't leaving anything to chance. Tomorrow, they were moving to his brother Frank's house in Providence, which was right near Women & Infants Hospital.

Chelsea wasn't old by any stretch of the imagination, especially in comparison to him. He was *actually* old. But her pregnancy counted as high risk because she was nearly thirty-seven. The phrase *high risk* was enough to send his blood pressure into the danger zone every time he heard it applied to Chelsea's pregnancy. After what'd happened when his nephew Mac's wife delivered their daughter during a tropical storm on the island and his niece Janey had nearly died having her son, Kevin was leaving nothing to chance.

They were getting the hell out of there. In fact, they'd be long gone by now if it hadn't been for Shane's wedding. Neither of them had wanted to miss that.

Kevin's medical school training was a long time ago, and his rotation in labor and delivery had taught him that anything could happen. The only thing that was going to happen to Chelsea was the delivery of the beautiful baby she longed for.

Sitting at a table with his son Riley, Riley's fiancée, Nikki, and Kevin's younger son, Finn, and his girlfriend, Chloe, Kevin had to marvel at the notion of starting over as a father twenty-seven years after Finn was born. A couple of years ago, he would've scoffed if someone had told him he'd be expecting his third child in his fifties. But that would've been before his wife left him, forcing him to find a new life—and a new love, who hadn't yet had the chance to be a mother.

He'd been shocked when Chelsea told him she wanted a child. For a few days, he'd pondered the very real possibility of ending his relationship with her. But his brothers and sons had helped him see that a baby would be someone new to love, and he would be a great dad in his fifties. Besides, he'd gotten to the point where living without Chelsea had become unimaginable.

She nudged his hand with hers. "What's up over there?"

"Huh?"

"You're a million miles away."

Chelsea had her feet up on a chair that Nikki, general manager of the Wayfarer, had gotten for her to take the pressure off her swollen ankles. Her belly seemed to get larger by the day, and the baby was active almost all the time.

"Just thinking about the plans for tomorrow. It's going to be an early morning with the car on the eight o'clock boat."

Chelsea groaned. She still suffered from queasiness in the mornings.

"Sorry, hon. I tried to get a later time, but they were sold out."

"Isn't your nephew-in-law the owner of the ferry company?"

Kevin flashed a grin at her. "Yes, but he can't bump other people who actually pay him."

Her sour look told him what she thought of that.

"Who's gonna take care of us while you're on the mainland?" Riley asked.

The others laughed.

"They do require significant adult supervision," Nikki said.

"From my experience," Chelsea said, "all McCarthy men require significant supervision."

Kevin scoffed at that. "On behalf of my sons, brothers and nephews, I'm offended."

"It's kinda true, Dad," Finn said, smiling. "We're a handful."

Chloe leaned into him. "Yes, you are."

"*Ew*." Riley made a disgusted face at her. "You'd better not be talking about his package."

Finn puffed his chest out. "You know she is, bro."

Chloe elbowed him, causing Finn to choke out the extra air in his lungs. "Don't be disgusting."

"There's nothing disgusting about it. Last night, you said—"

Her hand covered his mouth just in time to thankfully stop whatever outrageous thing his son had planned to say.

Chelsea laughed helplessly until an odd look came over her face as she clutched her belly and looked down at the floor.

"What?" The word came out of Kevin in a frantic shout that put his sons and the girls on full alert.

Chelsea looked over at him, her eyes big with shock. "I think my water just broke."

"No, it didn't." Kevin wasn't having it. Their baby was *not* being born on this goddamned island. That wasn't happening. Uh-uh, no way. Joe would get them on the boat tonight, and they'd drive to Providence, where they'd have the baby at the top neonatal hospital in the area, and that would be that.

"Dad."

Kevin looked up at Riley, who stood with his brother on either side of Chelsea.

"Chelsea needs you."

Riley's words permeated the panic and denial.

"Call for the rescue."

"I don't need the rescue, Kev." Chelsea reached for him. "I just need you."

"I'm here." She didn't need to know that he was panicking on the inside. She'd never know that. "Let's get you to the clinic. Finn, can you please let Victoria know that we're going to need her and David?"

"I'll get them there."

David and Victoria worked with Katie and had been partying all day. Had they been drinking? Would they be able to help Chelsea? What if they couldn't? For a brief, paralyzing moment, he feared he might pass out, until Riley grasped his arm, gave him a little shake and a look that had him getting his shit together.

Kevin bent to lift Chelsea out of her chair. "Hold on to me. Everything will be okay."

"I'm scared, Kev."

"We've got this." He was an MD, for Christ's sake. If it came to it, he could deliver the baby himself. As he carried her from the wedding reception, past the curious gazes of the happy couple and their guests, Kevin could only hope it wouldn't come to that.

CHAPTER 3

"What do you suppose is happening?" Katie asked her husband.

Shane was her *husband*. She had a *husband*!

He kissed her forehead. "Let me find out."

While Katie waited for him to return, she stood on the side of the dance floor, trying to find Julia in the crowd. She still wanted to know why her twin sister and maid of honor had *left* during her wedding. Katie didn't want to be bothered by it, but she couldn't help feeling hurt that Julia had taken off that way.

Katie refused to let it ruin an otherwise perfect day for her, but she wanted to know what was going on with Julia. Katie made her way over to where her mother and Charlie were seated, heads together, discussing something. She hated to interrupt them, but hey, it was her big day.

"What's going on?" she asked her mom.

"We think Chelsea just went into labor."

"Oh my God! They were going to the mainland tomorrow."

"Seems like the baby might have other plans," Charlie said in his usual gruff style.

Katie adored him. He was the father she wished she'd had growing up. She'd never forget the way he'd wiped away a tear when she asked him to dance earlier during the father-daughter and mother-son dance. Shane had reduced his aunt Linda to tears when he'd asked her to fill in for his late mother. They'd talked about skipping that dance but had decided to honor the people who'd stepped up to fill those roles for them. It had been an amazing moment, and Katie was glad they'd done it.

Charlie stood. "How about a drink, ladies? More champagne?"

"Sounds good to me," Katie said.

Her mom nodded in agreement. "Me, too. Thanks."

"You got it."

Charlie went off to get their drinks, and Katie stole his seat, grateful for a moment alone with her mom.

Katie watched Charlie stop to talk to people as he made his way toward the bar. "He's so great."

"He really is. You made a mess of him when you asked him to dance."

"I really love him, and more than anything, I love the way he loves you."

"He loves you, too. He's like a dream. I keep thinking it can't possibly be this way forever, but I'm starting to believe that maybe it will be."

"You've earned every second of happiness you've found with him, Mom."

"We've all earned the right to be happy." Sarah leaned in a little closer to Katie. "Can I bring you in on a secret?"

"Uh, *yeah*."

"At the brunch tomorrow, while everyone is still here, Charlie and I are going to get married."

"Oh my God! That's amazing! Why didn't you tell us?"

"I didn't want to take anything away from your wedding by tossing mine in. But it's so rare to have all my kids in one place at one time, and Stephanie's back for the season." Charlie's stepdaughter, Stephanie McCarthy, had waged a fourteen-year battle to get her beloved stepfather out of prison after he was wrongly accused of abusing her.

"I couldn't be happier for you and Charlie and for us to be getting him as our stepfather."

Sarah dabbed at the tears that suddenly flooded her eyes. "I'm sorry to steal a piece of your big weekend."

"You can't steal something that's given willingly." Katie hugged her mom, holding on tight to the woman who'd been their anchor in the storm of their childhood. It had taken far longer than her children would've preferred for Sarah to finally leave her abusive husband, but now she had only good times and happiness ahead with Charlie.

He returned with drinks for all three of them that he placed carefully on the table.

Katie stood to hug him.

"Oh, hey, what'd I do to deserve this?"

"You've made my mom so incredibly happy."

He flashed a grin. "Ah, so she told you our plans, huh?"

"She did, and I'm thrilled."

"We were hoping you wouldn't care if we did it this weekend while everyone is here. I don't want to wait any longer to make Sarah my wife."

Katie stepped back from him and fanned her face. "That's the sweetest thing I've ever heard."

From behind her, Shane slid an arm around Katie's waist and drew her into his embrace, kissing her bare shoulder.

"How's Chelsea?" Katie asked, leaning against him.

"On her way to the clinic. She seemed fine, but Kev is a mess."

"I can understand that. He was adamant about her delivering on the mainland. Victoria and David will take good care of her." She looked over her shoulder at him. "In the meantime, I have some big news from my family."

"What's that?"

"Mom and Charlie are getting married tomorrow at brunch."

"Oh, damn! That's awesome news."

Sarah's face flushed with happiness. "We figured while all the kids were here..."

"It's the perfect time, for sure."

"We should keep it a secret from everyone else," Katie said. "Let's surprise them."

"That'd be fun." Sarah beamed at Charlie before her gaze shifted to Julia, who was on the other side of the dance floor, standing by herself, looking pensive and unsettled. "What do you suppose is going on with your sister?"

Katie had wondered the same thing. "I don't know, but I intend to find out."

JULIA WANTED TO ENJOY HER SISTER'S WEDDING, BUT THE LONGER THE festivities dragged on, the more depressed she became. Watching happy couples slow-dance made her yearn for someone of her own to dance with, someone she could count on, who didn't lie, cheat or steal. Was that too much to ask for? Apparently so, if her track record was any indication of what was out there.

She recognized Evan McCarthy, who'd become a bit of a star in recent years, standing with a group of people he had to be related to. The men shared a similar look, with dark hair and distinctive blue eyes. Julia wondered if any of them was still single and then chastised herself for even having the thought.

"What do I care if they're single?"

"Talking to yourself, darlin'?"

Deacon had snuck up on her, startling her when he spoke. He was close enough that she felt his breath skim over her neck, resulting in an outbreak of goose bumps that irritated her. She didn't want him giving her goose bumps or anything else.

"Didn't your mother ever tell you it's not polite to sneak up on people?"

"She probably did, but she told me so many things I did were wrong that I started to ignore her after a while."

"I'm sure you missed all the important stuff."

He laughed, and she tried not to notice the way laughter made him even hotter than he already was thanks to the damned dimple that appeared only when he was truly amused.

"You want to dance?"

"With you?"

"Well, yeah, I guess. Unless you have a better offer on the table."

"I don't."

"So yes? You want to dance?"

"Not really."

He nudged her. "Come on. It's your sister's wedding. You should have some fun. If not for your sake, then for hers."

She didn't want to dance. She especially didn't want to dance with another handsome charmer. Been there, done that, had the empty bank account to prove it. But she also didn't want to be a drag at her sister's wedding. "Fine."

He took her hand and gave a gentle tug toward the dance floor. "The excitement and enthusiasm are overwhelming."

"I'm not going to be good for your ego."

"Thanks for letting me know so I can prepare my fragile ego for the hits he's going to take from you."

"I'm sure he's not used to difficult women."

Of course, the DJ chose that moment to slow things down. When the opening notes of "Can't Help Falling in Love" played, Julia wanted to groan.

Deacon took her into his arms and held her with a respectful distance between them that she appreciated. Most guys would've used that opportunity to demonstrate the size of their attributes. "My ego is used to nice, easy, pliable women who tell him how awesome he is every minute or so," he said, picking up the thread of their conversation.

Julia didn't want to laugh, but the sound gurgled out of her anyway.

"Now we're talking." He grinned down at her, looking far too pleased with himself.

"Where'd you learn to dance?"

"My mom taught us. She danced in high school and college and was on her way to a career as a dancer when she tore her ACL."

"That's so sad. She worked all those years…" Julia swallowed the lump in her throat that appeared out of nowhere and blinked back tears. What the hell was wrong with her that she was trying not to cry for a woman she'd never met?

"Her physical therapist was my dad."

"Really?"

"Uh-huh. She says all the time that injuring her knee was the best thing to ever happen to her because she met him and found her true calling being a wife, a mother and a business owner."

"What was her business?"

"She taught dance on the island for twenty years until she sold her business. It later went defunct. Blaine's wife, Tiffany, started a new studio years later, although she's not teaching very much these days."

"It's really cool that she's able to see how getting hurt turned out to be a good thing."

"She's a big believer in things happening for a reason. Sometimes it takes a while to see the reason, she says, but it's always there."

"What do you think she'd say the reason is for men taking advantage of me?"

"She'd probably tell you the nonsense is leading you to the one you're meant to be with, and you'll recognize him as a truly good guy because you've seen the worst of mankind."

"How will I recognize him?"

Deacon seemed to give that significant thought. "You'll know when you meet someone who treats you right, who respects you and doesn't ask you for money or other things he has no business asking for."

The song ended, and the DJ played "Love Shack." Later on, Owen would perform a set with Evan McCarthy. Julia was looking forward to seeing her brother play. Some of her fondest memories involved Owen and his guitar.

While people flooded back onto the dance floor, Deacon took Julia by the hand and led her outside to the patio that overlooked the beach. He was turning out to be surprisingly good company.

"The thing is," he said, "you have to be willing to put yourself out there if you're going to meet that good guy."

"That might be a problem in light of recent events."

"Have you reported him to the authorities?"

"What? No, I haven't reported him."

"Why not? Are you just going to let him get away with stealing fifteen grand from you?"

"The cops aren't going to do anything."

"How do you know that if you haven't filed a report?"

Julia shook her head. She'd grown up watching people in authority turn a blind eye to what was happening in their home and had lost faith in justice. She was still half-waiting for her father's guilty plea to be overturned on a technicality that would set him free. "I'd rather not go that route." The thought of reporting it made her anxiety spike.

"That's what he's counting on. You know that, don't you?"

"Know what?"

"He thinks he knows you so well. Julia would never report me to the cops. She's not that kind of girl, which makes her the perfect girl to steal from."

When he put it that way, Julia couldn't deny the truth of it. "I wouldn't know the first thing about how to go about reporting him."

"I know how to do it, and I'd be happy to help you."

Julia bit her bottom lip and tried to organize her thoughts. "What would it entail?"

"First of all, you'd want to review his social media to prove his mother isn't sick. Take screenshots of everything he posted around the time he was telling you his mother was desperately ill. Next step would be to document the baby, the house, the setup with the other woman. How did you give him the money?"

"Venmo."

"That's awesome. There's a digital footprint. That helps tremendously—you can prove you gave him the money. Do you have text messages or anything that shows him talking about his mom being sick?"

"I think we talked by text about her having had cancer before, which I now know isn't true." It burned her ass that she'd believed him, but he'd been so sincere with her, so caring and considerate. Now she knew he'd been setting her up for a scam.

"You've got a solid case against him, Julia. You just need to put it together and pull the trigger. Your local police would probably act on something like this. I know I would have if this had come across my desk when I was on the job. It's a clear-cut case of fraud."

"You were a cop?"

"Uh-huh. Ten years in Boston."

"Oh." She crossed her arms. "How come you aren't a cop anymore?"

"I got injured."

"Did you get shot?"

"Nah, nothing that dramatic. I tore my ACL chasing a perp, and after I had surgery, I didn't regain full range of motion, so they medically retired me. When you're a cop on the beat, you have to be able to run fast and climb and jump over stuff. I can't do that anymore."

"Just like your mom, you had to change your plans."

"Yep, but unlike her, I'm still looking for the reason for what happened to me. I loved being a cop. It was my 'calling,' if you believe in such things. Since I left the force, I've been kind of floundering."

"I know what that's like." At times, Julia felt like she'd been floundering her entire life. Unlike most of her siblings, she'd never found a profession that particularly interested her, so she'd used her organizational skills to fashion a career as an office manager. That, too, had turned to shit when a new boss had arrived to make her life a living hell. "If I file a report, would I get the money back?"

"Maybe, maybe not. It's hard to say. Depends on whether he still has it."

"It's probably long gone."

"Possibly, but you'd give him some serious heartburn if you filed charges, and you'd put him on notice that he can't treat people this way and get away with it."

"Would he get arrested?"

Deacon's sinfully sexy lips curved into a smile, and his golden-brown eyes glittered with delight. "Yep, and searched, fingerprinted, booked, charged, possibly held overnight and then arraigned. The whole nine yards."

Julia had to admit that the idea of Mike being arrested and charged for what he'd done brought her a perverse kind of pleasure.

"What do you say? You want me to help you get him in some trouble?"

"Yes, please."

He cracked up. "So polite."

"Well, you're offering to do me a favor. The least I can do is be polite."

"I'll trade you a favor for a favor."

Disappointment flooded her. Of course he was just like the others.

"Not that kind of favor," he said, laughing again. "Get your mind out of the gutter. I'm talking about the kind of favor where you have dinner with me in exchange for my professional services. I don't have many friends here, so it's kind of lonely."

She rolled her eyes at him. "I'll have dinner with you, but only if it's not a date."

Deacon considered that, rubbed at the stubble on his chin and gave her a calculating look. "No deal. I want a real date."

She shook her head. "I told you I'm done with all that."

"Forever?"

"Maybe."

"If you take that stance, then he *wins*, Julia. If you deny yourself the chance to be happy with someone else, he wins. Are you going to let him win?"

"It's not just him. It's all of them."

He cocked his head adorably. "You want them all to win?"

"No, I don't want that, but I also don't want to date anyone. Can't we just go as friends?"

"Hmmm, I'll have to think about that."

"Hey, Julia!" Her sister Cindy's voice had Julia turning toward the party. "It's time for more toasts, and Katie is looking for you."

"I'm coming." To Deacon, she said, "I'll see you later?"

"Save another dance for me."

Now that she knew he was interested in dating her, she didn't want to dance with him anymore. He was too tempting, and she was determined to stick with her man diet for the foreseeable future.

CHAPTER 4

She's coming around, Deacon thought as he watched Julia walk inside to tend to her sister. She'd gone from not wanting to talk to him at all to telling him her problems, dancing with him and agreeing to let him help her. He fucking hated bullies and men who preyed on women and children. He'd seen far too much of it as a member of the domestic assault intervention unit while on the job.

The depraved shit that people did to the ones they supposedly loved never ceased to amaze and disgust him. He had no patience for that kind of crap. That's why he'd ended up in a bar fight, defending a woman who'd been nothing more than a casual hookup to him.

What gave a man the right to raise his fists toward a woman? Nothing gave him that right, but too many felt entitled to take whatever they wanted. The guy who'd stolen from Julia would live to regret it. Deacon couldn't wait to help her put together the facts and file a report. He'd help her regardless of whether she ever agreed to go out with him.

Deacon stayed off to the side and out of the wedding fray, but close enough to the action that he could watch Julia do her maid-of-honor speech.

His gaze traveled around the room, settling on his brother Blaine, who was beaming at his pretty wife. She looked at him like Blaine had hung the moon. Next to them were Mac McCarthy and his wife, Maddie, who was Tiffany's sister, and Mac's sister Janey and her husband, Joe Cantrell.

Deacon had kept up with island gossip thanks to his mom, who passed along the latest news during their weekly phone calls. Deacon hadn't had the heart to tell her he didn't care who married who on Gansett. But it gave them something to talk about, so he'd let her tell him. Now he was glad he knew the basics—and he was glad his parents were traveling in Europe this summer and wouldn't be up in his business while he was home.

Big Mac McCarthy hadn't changed a bit since the days when he'd led their Boy Scout troop, and his wife, Linda, was as youthful as ever. You'd never know the two of them had raised a bunch of kids and run several businesses for decades. Deacon had always looked up to Mr. McCarthy and hoped he'd get the chance to say hello before the day was out.

Julia looked adorably uncertain as she stepped into the spotlight. "Katie, you and I go way back."

Seated at the head table, Katie laughed while Shane kept a protective arm around her.

"I can't imagine life without my twin sister, my best friend from the minute we were born. You're one of the best people I know, and no one deserves more than you do to be happy."

Deacon wanted to stop her and tell her she deserved to be happy, too, but he kept his mouth shut so he wouldn't cause a scene at her sister's wedding.

"We've been through almost everything together, good and bad. Watching you get married feels like the end of an era in a way. It's the end of our era and the start of your life with Shane."

His heart broke for her. She was trying so hard to be strong about her twin moving on without her, but he felt her sadness as if it were his own.

Julia cleared her throat and sent a teary-eyed smile in the direction of her sister and new brother-in-law. "Please join me in raising your glasses to Katie and Shane. May you enjoy a long and happy life together."

"My kids have been through so much."

Deacon hadn't seen Julia's mother approach him, so her softly spoken comment took him by surprise.

"This is terribly difficult for Julia, seeing Owen and Katie settling down. The three of them… They were always a team, and now she must be feeling like she's been left behind."

Deacon didn't say anything, because he wanted her to keep talking and providing insight into what made Julia tick. Why he cared about what made her tick was something he could try to figure out later.

"She's struggled to find her way."

He already knew that much just from the short time he'd known her.

Her mom looked up at Deacon. "You must be wondering why I'm telling you these things."

"Maybe a little."

"I asked around about you. I found out you're Blaine's brother."

"That's right."

"He's one of the finest men I've ever met."

Deacon had to force himself not to roll his eyes. "That's nice to hear."

"He was there for me during the lowest moment of my life. He'll always have a special place in my heart." She placed her hand on Deacon's arm. "If you're anything like him, you could be so good for my Julia."

Whoa…

"I'm sorry. I know it's wildly inappropriate for me to intervene like this, but I figured you wouldn't mind after you kidnapped her and then danced with her."

"It doesn't count as a kidnapping if the alleged victim goes will-ingly with her captor."

She laughed. "I take it you're a police officer, too?"

"Former. Now I'm a harbor master."

"I don't mean to be a pushy matchmaking mother, and if you knew me at all, you'd know how out of character it is for me to be having this conversation with you. But Julia… I worry so much about her. She tries to show the world how tough she is, but on the inside… Inside, she hurts."

Deacon had already figured out that much for himself. "She's a beautiful woman." Her mother was, too. She was an older version of Katie and their other sister, whose name he didn't know yet. Julia must look like her father.

"She is, and that's actually been a problem for her. People see her beautiful exterior and think they know what kind of person she is. They have no idea how she's struggled or what she's been through."

Listening to her mother talk made Deacon want to know everything there was to know about Julia—the good, the bad, the ugly. He could honestly say he'd never wanted to know everything about any other woman before. That level of involvement had never interested him. Only a few days ago, he'd been telling Blaine how the idea of being committed to one woman forever was not for him.

If that one woman was someone like Julia, however… She was the kind of woman a man changed his plans for.

"I'm sorry," Sarah said with a nervous laugh. "Weddings make me sappy, and clearly, champagne makes me chatty. I don't mean to make you uncomfortable."

"You haven't. Not at all."

She glanced at Julia at the head table and then at him. "Deacon, I'd like to invite you to the brunch we're having tomorrow at the Sand & Surf at ten in the morning, if you're available."

"I'd love to come. Thank you." Julia probably wouldn't want him there, which was all the more reason to go.

Her mother patted his arm. "I'm so glad we had a chance to talk."

"I am, too. It's nice to meet you, ma'am."

"Please, call me Sarah."

"Thank you, Sarah." He felt like she'd trusted him with something precious, and he was determined to treat it with the respect it deserved.

"I'll see you in the morning," Sarah said as she left him.

"See you then."

Julia had touched him with her sweetness, her sadness, her vulnerability and her beauty. He could only hope she'd give him the chance to show her that not all men were assholes. Some of them could be trusted. *He* could be trusted. It should've terrified him that he was having such thoughts only hours after meeting her. But after hearing what she'd been through, he wanted to show her something better.

She looked over at him, and when her gaze connected with his, she offered a small smile that filled him with an unreasonable feeling of hope.

With her around to keep things interesting, spending the summer on Gansett Island didn't seem quite so dreadful.

KEVIN WAS LOSING HIS MIND ONE VICIOUS CONTRACTION AT A TIME. He'd been through this twice before, but that was nearly thirty years ago. He didn't remember it being this difficult for his former wife.

Chelsea was truly suffering and had resisted Victoria's suggestion that she have an epidural before it was too late. She was determined to have a completely natural birth, but the longer this went on, the more convinced Kevin was that she needed to do something to take the edge off the pain.

"Sweetheart," he said between contractions as he bathed her face with a cool cloth. "Let them give you something."

She shook her head. "Not good for the baby."

"Chels… They wouldn't give you anything that would harm the baby. And I'd never suggest you try it if I wasn't totally sure it was safe."

Tears rolled down cheeks that were red from exertion. "Are you sure?"

"I'm positive. Everything will be fine, and you'll be so much more comfortable."

"Okay."

He leaned over the bed rail to kiss her. "I'll get Victoria." Kevin moved quickly so he wouldn't have to leave Chelsea alone any longer than necessary. He found Victoria at the desk in the hallway. "Chelsea would like to have the epidural."

"We'll be right in."

"Thank you."

"Take a breath, Kevin. She's doing great. Most of our first-time moms take a long time to get through transition."

Her assurances helped to settle him somewhat, but he wouldn't breathe normally until their baby had arrived and both mom and baby were safe.

Riley and Finn joined him in the hallway.

"How's it going, Dad?" Riley asked.

"She's having a tough time, but Vic says it's normal."

"Totally normal," Victoria said as she went by them on her way to Chelsea's room.

"Anything we can do for you guys?" Finn asked.

"Not that I can think of. You don't have to stick around."

"Of course we're sticking around," Riley said. "Where else would we be when our baby brother or sister is about to be born?"

Their support had Kevin blinking back tears. "Thank you." He hugged each of his sons before returning to Chelsea's room.

Victoria and David had her sitting up for the epidural.

Chelsea looked up at him, her eyes wild with panic.

"I'm here, love." He took her hands and sat next to her bed, careful not to jostle her. "Hold on to me."

"A little pinch," Victoria said.

Chelsea winced and grasped his hands tightly.

"All done," David said a minute later. "You should start to feel much better almost right away."

They helped to get her settled back in bed and adjusted the monitor that was wrapped around her belly.

"You'll be ready to push before too much longer," Vic said. "Try to get some rest while you can."

When they were alone, Kevin kissed the back of Chelsea's hand. "I wish I could do this for you, sweetheart."

Her soft laughter had him looking up at her. "If men had the babies, the population would be extinct."

He was relieved she was able to joke again, even if it was at his expense. "Very true."

"It'll be worth all the pain when the baby is here. I can't wait to meet him—or her."

"Neither can I."

"Thank you for this, Kev. I know it's not what you had planned for this next chapter of your life."

"Plans change. I'm as excited as you are to welcome our little one. And the boys are, too. They're both here. They said they wouldn't be anywhere else when their baby sibling was about to be born."

"That's so sweet of them."

"They're going to be awesome big brothers. They'll want to spoil him or her rotten."

"And we'll let them."

"Of course we will."

Chelsea's eyes closed, and while she napped, Kevin kept a close watch on the monitor that recorded each contraction as it happened. He noticed when they started coming closer together. It'd been decades since his OB/GYN rotation in med school, but he remembered enough to know that meant it was almost time to push.

Victoria came in and checked Chelsea again before declaring it go time. She went to get David, and the two of them hustled around the room, making preparations for the delivery.

Kevin focused on staying calm so he could help keep Chelsea relaxed and in the zone for the final stage of labor. The next hour passed in a blur of pushing, resting, tears, excitement, anxiety, hope and finally, at the end of Chelsea's heroic effort, a seven-pound, five-ounce baby girl.

They had a *daughter*.

Kevin couldn't contain his tears at the first sight of her adorable little face, her tightly fisted hands and long legs that immediately had him thinking of Chelsea's long legs. He crawled onto the bed with Chelsea, who held the baby against her chest as she gazed up at Kevin.

"We did it."

"*You* did it. You were incredible. She's absolutely beautiful, just like her mother."

"She's got your blue eyes."

"For now. Sometimes they change."

"They're the same shape as yours."

"Should I go get the boys?"

"Yes, please do."

Kevin kissed her and the top of the baby's head. "I'll be right back." He went out to the waiting room. "Riley, Finn… Would you like to meet your baby sister?"

They jumped up and came over to hug him.

"Congratulations, Dad," Finn said.

"We have a *sister*," Riley said. "Holy crap."

"Come meet her." Kevin led them back to the room, where they stood on either side of Chelsea's bed.

"What's her name?" Finn asked as he gently caressed the baby's light dusting of blonde hair.

Kevin looked to Chelsea to share the name they'd chosen.

"Meet Summer Rose McCarthy."

"Summer," Riley said. "I love that. It's the best time of year."

"That's what we thought, too." Kevin had loved the name from the first time Chelsea suggested it to him. It conjured up days at the beach, warm ocean breezes and long nights under a star-filled sky.

Surrounded by the four people he loved the most in the world, Kevin could finally exhale. Everything was all right. The baby was here, she was beautiful, and Chelsea… He'd always known she was a goddess, but after watching her give birth to their daughter, he loved her even more than he had before.

CHAPTER 5

*J*ulia slept fitfully, infuriated by strange dreams about Deacon Taylor, of all people. Why in the hell was she dreaming about a man she'd known for all of one day? Granted, it had been a rather awesome day, which she hadn't expected when she'd arrived for Katie's wedding. She'd anticipated another difficult, sad, emotional day, like Owen's wedding had been for her. Yesterday had been all those things until Deacon showed up.

He'd been surprisingly… nice and insightful. In addition, he was a great dancer, a fun companion and a gentleman. At the end of the evening, he'd walked her back to the Surf and left her at the front stairs with a hug and thanks for a fun time.

As she'd gone inside, aware of him watching her, she'd felt strangely let down, which was ridiculous. She wanted nothing from him or any other man. So what possible reason could she have for feeling deflated by the way their awesome day together had ended? She'd told him she was on a man diet, a *dick diet*, for crying out loud. She cringed when she recalled telling him that. What did she think was going to happen after he had that information?

And what exactly had she hoped for?

"Ugh," she said in a growl that thankfully only she could hear. She was so frustrated by everything lately. And now she had to get up after sleeping like shit, pull herself together and pretend to be fine in front of her family for one more event before the wedding weekend was finally over.

She'd perfected the fine art of pretending to be okay so they wouldn't be up in her business. That'd been easier since Katie moved to Gansett. Without her nurse sister watching over her, Julia had been able to relax somewhat. Enough to let some old bad habits back into her life.

She had that under control.

Mostly.

This weekend had been a test, but she was determined to get through brunch and then figure out her next move.

She sat up and groaned. Her head hurt from too much champagne and not enough food. The story of her life. When her emotions were in an uproar, she found it all but impossible to eat. As her emotions had spent years in an uproar while she was growing up with an abusive, domineering father, she'd worked her way into anorexia by the time she was in middle school. She'd graduated to bulimia in high school. Even after Katie had sounded the alarm and gotten her into treatment—twice—followed by years of intensive therapy, the old fiends still reared their ugly heads often enough to remind her she had control over nothing.

Stress, anxiety and depression exacerbated her disorders, and she'd been suffering all three lately. As a result, eating had been a chore, and she'd lost weight she didn't have to lose. She had to be careful until Katie left on her honeymoon. Her twin knew the signs of trouble in Julia better than anyone and was always vigilant when they were together. Julia hadn't told her sister the latest about what Mike had done to her. The last thing Katie needed was her maid of honor showing up to her wedding dragging a suitcase full of drama.

There'd been a time when Julia's problems had been Katie's and vice versa. Although Katie had fewer problems than Julia, or so it seemed. All the Lawry kids walked around with emotional scars from their tumultuous childhood. Some were better at hiding them than others. Katie had coped by never dating—at all—until she met Shane. Julia had taken the exact opposite path, and look at where that had gotten her.

Lonely, broke and basically homeless.

Her stomach grumbled at the same instant a wave of nausea hit. That happened far too often. She'd feel hungry and nauseated at the same time. Doctors had told her over and over to feed the nausea, but that was so much easier said than done when a lump the size of a grapefruit basically lived in her throat during times of distress.

Most of her life had been a time of distress, thus the eating issues.

Julia got up, showered, washed and dried her hair and brushed her teeth. She studied her reflection in the mirror with the usual feelings of inadequacy. Her eyes were too close together, her nose too prominent, her cheeks sunken. All she saw were flaws. Others told her she was beautiful. She didn't see it. She'd never been able to see what they saw in her.

She put her long dark hair up in a bun and got dressed in a lightweight summer dress since the brunch was being held on the hotel's deck. The forecast was for a warm, sunny day.

A knock sounded at her door, and Julia went to answer it. As usual, the sight of her beloved grandmother, Adele, raised Julia's spirits. Adele and her husband, Russ, had been a lifeline to Julia and her siblings. She hugged her grandmother.

"Good morning, my love. I hope you slept well."

Julia tried to respond, but she couldn't get the words out as her emotions overtook her. Being around her grandmother often had that effect on her.

"Julia, honey, what's wrong?" Adele released her and stepped into the room, closing the door.

"Everything is wrong. Every single thing."

She guided Julia to sit with her on the unmade bed. "Talk to me."

Julia was too ashamed of what'd happened with Mike to tell even her grandmother about it. "Things in Texas are a mess."

Thankfully, she didn't ask for specifics. "So stay here for a while. Spend the summer in your favorite place."

"I honestly don't have a choice. I lost my job, I'm broke and all but homeless since I didn't have the money to renew my lease."

"You'll never be homeless as long as I'm around. Why didn't you call me? I would've sent you the money."

"You're the best, Gram, but I'm not taking your money."

"Why not? I gave your brother a hotel. The rest of you are our heirs. Why wouldn't I take care of you now rather than after I'm gone? Your mother has come into a fortune through Charlie, and they'd happily give you whatever you needed." The state had given Charlie half a million dollars for each of the fourteen years he'd spent unjustly imprisoned. "You have a lot of people who love you and would do anything for you."

"I appreciate that, but I'm not taking charity from you or Mom or anyone else. I'll figure it out. I didn't tell you this because I wanted you to fix it."

"You've always been my sweet, stubborn girl." Adele's pretty, lined face lit up with a smile. "I admire that about you. You've been so fiercely independent from the time you were a little one. No one could tell our Julia what to do or think. She had her own ideas about everything." Adele put her arm around Julia. "I've always wished that you could see what I see when I look at you."

Julia leaned her head on Adele's shoulder. She liked the way she looked to her grandmother.

"Spend the summer here with us. We'll make everything that's wrong better."

"You always do."

"That's what grandmothers are for."

"I need a job. You know of anyone who's hiring?"

"I heard about something just yesterday at bridge that might be perfect for you. Let me make a phone call and see if it's still available."

"Thanks, Gram."

"My pleasure, love. I know that sometimes it takes more than a summer on Gansett to fix what ails you, but a couple of months in your favorite place is a good place to start."

"Yes, it sure is."

. . .

DEACON SHAVED AND TRIED TO FIND A SHIRT NICE ENOUGH FOR THE occasion so he wouldn't embarrass Julia—or Sarah, who'd been kind enough to invite him. As he rifled through the clothes he'd thrown into a bag while Blaine had waited impatiently for him to pack what he needed for the summer in exile, he seethed all over again at the memory of his older brother standing over him, telling him what was going to happen.

"You're coming home to Gansett with me for the summer," Blaine had said, "and that's the end of it. Otherwise, I'm going to let them charge you with assault."

Blaine hadn't wanted to hear the reason for the fight. After he got the call that his younger brother was in trouble, Blaine hadn't heard anything but the sound of his own voice. Deacon had been a bit of a troublemaker as a kid, getting caught drinking, smoking pot, doing what kids did when they were trapped on an island with nowhere to go and nothing to do. Because their father had worked on the mainland during the week and their mother had younger kids to care for, Blaine had responded to the calls when Deacon screwed up.

Once, while still in high school, Deacon had been caught screwing the mayor's daughter out at the bluffs. They were both sixteen at the time, and that might've blown up into a nightmare if it hadn't been for Blaine agreeing to personally ensure that Deacon would never go near the girl again. He'd liked that girl a lot and had resented Blaine for years for making such a promise on his behalf.

Every time he got Deacon out of one of his scrapes, good old Blaine had acted like Deacon had robbed a bank or committed murder. However, putting up with his sanctimonious brother had been far preferable to the wrath of his parents. For all his faults—and he had many faults—Blaine had never ratted Deacon out to their parents. He'd cleaned up Deacon's messes and kept his secrets.

After the bar fight, Deacon had told the local cops he was retired from the job in Boston, which had gotten him a cell with no one else in it. During the long night he'd spent alone in that cell, he'd debated

43

whether he should tell them that his brother was the police chief on Gansett Island. When Deacon heard he might be looking at a felony charge, he'd played the brother card.

Blaine had come in loaded for bear, as their father used to say, agreeing to remove Deacon from the area for the time being and to personally see to it that he stayed out of trouble. It had taken about four minutes for Deacon to regret calling him. As he'd followed Blaine's truck to the ferry landing on his motorcycle, he'd had to resist the urge to turn the bike and head west, away from everything and everyone.

Deacon pulled a rumpled light blue dress shirt from the bag, smelled it to determine if it was clean—it was—and held it up for inspection. No question it had to be ironed before he could wear it to brunch.

Shit.

Moving to the apartment door, he looked out to see if Blaine's police department SUV was gone. Seeing that it was, he went down the stairs and across the driveway to knock on the back door of his brother's home.

Tiffany came to the door with baby Addie on her hip. "Hey, Deacon. What's up?"

"I wondered if I could borrow your iron."

"Of course. Come in." Tiffany had her dark hair up in a bun on top of her head and wore a tank top with yoga pants. His brother's wife was a beautiful woman. "The iron is in the laundry room off the kitchen. Or I'd be happy to do it for you if you wouldn't mind watching Addie."

"I couldn't ask you to do that."

"You didn't, and I don't mind."

Deacon eyed the baby warily. "Will she mind hanging with her uncle Deacon?"

"She'll love it." Tiffany handed over the baby and took the shirt from him. "Did you sleep in this thing?"

He laughed as he tried to figure out how best to hold the

squirming baby. "Despite how it might seem, I didn't actually sleep in it."

"You're in luck. I've got a good iron."

"Excellent." He looked down at the baby, who watched him with a serious expression, as if she wasn't sure what to make of this man who looked a little like Daddy. A much *younger* version of Daddy.

While Tiffany got out the ironing board, Deacon stood awkwardly in the doorway to the laundry room. "What's up, Addie?"

"You know she can't talk yet, right?"

"Duh, of course I do." He had no idea when babies started talking.

Tiffany laughed, which meant she knew he was full of shit.

Deacon offered a sheepish grin and a shrug. "I think it's awesome that you named her after our grandmother. She's the best."

"I absolutely love the name Adeline, and I love your grandmother. She's a firecracker."

"Yes, she is." She lived in Connecticut in a senior community that kept her busy and entertained. Deacon had heard rumors of a "boyfriend," but thankfully she didn't bring that up during their weekly chats.

Tiffany got busy ironing his shirt with a ruthless efficiency that impressed him.

"You're good at that."

"I iron Blaine's uniform shirts for him."

"He's a lucky man."

When she smiled, her whole face softened. "We're both lucky. He and my girls are the best thing to ever happen to me."

"Huh, you really feel that way about boring old stick-up-his-ass Blaine? My brother?"

She laughed again. "I really do, and PS, he's the farthest thing from boring."

Deacon responded with a barfing sound that made Addie laugh, so he did it again and again when he kept getting the same reaction from her. Making his baby niece laugh, he found, was a rather delightful way to pass the time.

"What the fuck are you doing in my house?"

Deacon rolled his eyes at Tiffany and turned to face his surly jackass brother. "I came to borrow an iron."

Blaine took Addie from him, which hurt Deacon's feelings, not that he'd let on to Blaine.

"Then why is my wife ironing for you?"

"Knock it off, Blaine. I offered to do it."

Deacon wanted to kiss Tiffany for coming to his defense, but he had a feeling that would earn him a knife through the heart, so he kept his appreciation—and his lips—to himself.

"I'm happy to have the chance to get to know my brother-in-law," Tiffany added with a pointed look for her husband. She finished the shirt in half the time it would've taken Deacon and tugged it off the ironing board to give it a thorough inspection before handing it back to him.

"Thank you so much for this."

"Any time."

"No," Blaine said, "not any time."

"Don't mind him." Tiffany put her hand on Deacon's arm. "You're welcome here *any* time, and you don't have to knock."

"Yes, he does have to knock."

Deacon ignored his brother and smiled at Tiffany, who was his new best friend. "Thanks a million."

"Hope you have fun wherever you're going."

"I was invited to the brunch the Lawry and McCarthy families are having at the Surf."

"Who invited you to that?" Blaine asked.

Deacon wanted to tell him to fuck off and that it was none of his business, but he took the diplomatic approach instead. "Mrs. Lawry."

"How do you know her?"

"I met her at the wedding."

Blaine eyed him with suspicion that Deacon should've been used to by then. "And she suddenly asked you to come to a family thing?"

"Yep." He made a face at Addie that had her cracking up again. Her laughter was his new favorite sound.

"What's up with that?"

"It may come as a shock to you, but I'm a rather nice guy. People tend to like me, present company excluded, of course."

"I like you," Tiffany said. "And Addie does, too."

He winked at Tiffany. "I like you, too. I can already tell you're much too good for my brother."

The low growl from Blaine made Deacon's day, and it was only nine thirty. "Have a good one, everyone."

"Don't be late for work on Monday."

Blaine had wanted him to start right away, but it had taken a few extra days to transfer his license from Massachusetts to Rhode Island, which had postponed his start date. "I wouldn't dare be late for my first day. I've heard the boss is a stickler for punctuality."

Blaine muttered something under his breath, but Deacon didn't hear it and didn't care enough to ask him to repeat it. He headed for the back door with his ironed shirt in hand, a new friend in his lovely sister-in-law and a baby niece he couldn't wait to see again.

CHAPTER 6

"What the hell is wrong with you?" Tiffany asked her husband the second Deacon was through the screen door that led to their back deck.

"Why was he in our house when I wasn't here?"

"Are you seriously implying that you have something to worry about? That the minute your back is turned, I'd go running into the arms of your brother?"

"I'm not worried about you. It's him I don't trust."

"News flash—it takes two to tango, and neither of us is interested. He's my *brother-in-law*, for crying out loud. He asked to borrow an iron. I offered to do it for him. He was entertaining Addie. Unless you're spoiling for a really big fight, stop making it into something it wasn't."

She took Addie from him and headed for the stairs to change the baby and put her down for her morning nap. Sometimes she thought baby Addie understood everything that went on around her. Addie gazed up at her mother with wise eyes and a furrowed brow, feeding off Tiffany's annoyance.

How could Blaine even hint at such a thing? Deacon was his *brother*. Why did Blaine have to be so intense when it came to him? He seemed like a nice enough guy, and he'd been nothing but polite and respectful toward her and Addie.

"Your daddy is in bad need of an attitude adjustment." Tiffany picked Addie up off the changing table and snuggled her for a few minutes before putting her in her crib with a light blanket over her. As always, the baby popped her thumb into her mouth and rolled onto her side, as ready for her nap as her mommy was. Ashleigh had fought the naps, but Addie was a big fan.

When she was certain the baby was settled, Tiffany left the room, closing the door behind her. She had monitors strategically positioned around the house so she'd hear her if she woke early. Tiffany went into her own room and stopped short at the sight of Blaine stretched out on their bed, hands behind his head, the picture of relaxation at a time of year when he almost never fully relaxed.

She eyed him suspiciously. "What're you doing?"

"Taking a break. Care to join me?"

"No, I'm mad at you."

He propped himself up on an elbow and gave her an imploring look. "Please?"

Tiffany found him irresistible, even when she was mad at him. She sat on the bed and wrapped her arms around her legs. "I'm here."

"Not close enough."

"As close as I'm getting until you explain to me what that was about downstairs." The familiar scents of sandalwood and citrus coming from him would normally have her snuggling up to him. Not today.

"He irritates me."

"Okay, but what's that got to do with you basically accusing me of being inappropriate with your brother?"

"I didn't do that."

"Ah, yes, you certainly did."

"Well, that wasn't my intention. My ire was directed at him, not you."

"And why is that? You invited him to stay with us. Did you expect him to never venture across the yard? He has nieces here that he'd like to get to know. Addie took to him immediately."

Blaine scowled at that news.

"If you didn't want him here, why'd you invite him to stay in the apartment?"

"I didn't exactly invite him."

"Huh?"

"So when I had to go to the mainland last week?"

"What about it?"

"It was because he'd gotten arrested after a bar fight. I made a deal with the local chief not to press assault charges against him if I made him disappear for the time being. That's why he's here—and trust me, he doesn't want to be here."

"Why didn't you tell me that when it happened?"

"Because I didn't want you to know my brother is a fuckup before you even met him. If I had a dollar for every scrape I got him out of when we were kids, I'd never have to work again. I'd sort of hoped those days were behind us."

"I thought he was a cop, too?"

"He was. In Boston for ten years. He was medically retired after he blew out his knee on the job."

"If he's such a fuckup, how did he keep that job for so long?"

"Like I said, I thought he'd finally grown up. Clearly, I thought wrong." He reached across the space between them. "Are you going to forgive me?"

"Not yet. Did you ask him what the fight in the bar was about?"

"Does it matter? He got himself arrested and run out of town."

"Yes, it matters. Why would he get into a fight over nothing?"

"It was over a woman, or so he said. I don't want to talk about him anymore. Is Ashleigh still at Maddie's?"

"Yes, but I'm not done talking about him or what you implied downstairs. I understand that your brother irritates you for whatever reason, but that's no excuse for acting like a jackass when you came home to find him here."

"I'm sorry."

"Are you really, or are you just horny?"

"Can't I be both?"

"I'm hurt that you'd suggest I'd be unfaithful to you."

"I'm very sorry I hurt your feelings. I know you'd never do that."

"I wouldn't. Not ever. Especially with your brother, who I only just met. Just because I sell frisky stuff at my store doesn't mean—"

He kissed her deeply, thoroughly. "I'm profoundly sorry, baby. It was shitty for me to even hint at such a thing."

"You owe your brother an apology, too."

His nose wrinkled. "No, I don't."

"Yes, you do. And until you apologize to him, we're shut down for business."

"By shut down, you mean…"

She got right in his face, her nose touching his. "No sex until you apologize to him—and you'd better mean it, because I'm going to ask him." When she started to get up, he stopped her with his hand on her arm in a light grip.

"By no sex, you mean…"

"No. Sex. Of. Any. Kind. Until. You. Apologize. To. Deacon. Am I clear?"

Blaine moaned and fell back on the bed. "I can't believe you're doing this to me."

"You're the one who started it by making absurd accusations. Once you clean up your mess and do a *good* job of it, I'll consider reopening for business. Until then, your hand can be your new best friend."

He groaned dramatically, and Tiffany had to bite her lip so she wouldn't laugh at his pathetic performance.

She pulled her arm free and got up to spread her yoga mat on the floor to get her workout in while Addie was asleep. If she put on one hell of a performance for her horny husband, well, he had only himself to blame for her performance—and the large bulge in his shorts.

JULIA MADE HERSELF PRESENTABLE FOR THE BRUNCH, DETERMINED TO get through the last of the family obligations before she'd be free to figure out her own shit. Another meal to suffer through while her stomach was so agitated that eating would be a chore. Anxiety was a bitch on a good day, and she hadn't had many good days since Mike had cleaned out her bank account and broken her heart.

Hopefully, her insightful family members wouldn't be monitoring too closely what she ate—or didn't eat. Ever since she'd first landed in the hospital, her struggles with food and eating had become a family matter, when she'd have preferred to keep her problems private. When they were together, she felt like everyone was always keeping tabs on her, which meant forcing herself to eat, even when she had no desire whatsoever to do so.

She'd learned to give them just enough to keep them off her back. Her food issues were nowhere near as severe as they'd once been, but during times of extreme stress, the old issues came roaring back to remind her she was powerless against them.

Julia was the last one to join the party on the deck, and her mom greeted her with a hug.

"How'd you sleep?"

Awful. "Great. You?"

"I was awake half the night."

She looked amazing to say she didn't get much sleep. In fact, Julia didn't think she'd ever seen her mother looking prettier than she did today, in a flowing white summer dress that offset her deep tan. Her chin-length blonde hair curled at the ends, and her makeup made her blue eyes pop. "How come?"

"Have a seat, and I'll tell you."

Julia slid into one of two remaining seats and greeted her siblings, including Katie, who sat with Shane across from her. Charlie's stepdaughter, Stephanie, was also there with her husband, Grant McCarthy. Julia was about to ask Owen if he knew what was up with their mother when Deacon came up the stairs to the deck, wearing a pressed light blue dress shirt and khaki shorts. For a moment, she was struck dumb by the sight of his handsome face.

And then he smiled.

Ah, that damned dimple is so sexy.

"Deacon," Sarah said. "I'm so glad you could join us. Have a seat next to Julia."

What the hell was her mother up to?

Deacon sat and leaned in to whisper to Julia, "Morning."

"Hi."

"Your mom invited me. Hope it's okay."

"Sure. Why wouldn't it be?"

"Now that you're all here," Sarah said, reaching for Charlie's hand, "Charlie and I have a very special announcement to make." She glanced at Charlie, who looked at her with such a fierce kind of love that Julia was actually a little jealous, which immediately made her feel small and petty. "We're going to be married this morning while you're all here!"

Sarah's announcement was met with applause, excitement, tears and an outpouring of love from Sarah's seven children and Charlie's stepdaughter.

"If Owen and Stephanie wouldn't mind joining us up here," Charlie said gruffly, his voice wavering with emotion he couldn't begin to hide.

Shane's father, Frank McCarthy, a retired Superior Court judge who'd also married Katie and Shane, came onto the deck to do the honors for Sarah and Charlie.

Sarah kissed Charlie on the cheek. "Be right back."

"Hurry."

Sarah went into the hotel and reemerged a few minutes later, escorted by her parents, Russ and Adele, who were beaming with happiness. What it must mean to them to see their only child finally settled with a man who loved and respected her the way Charlie did.

Julia watched the proceedings with a feeling of detachment even as her heart swelled with happiness for her mother.

Sarah held out a hand to Owen, and Charlie did the same to Stephanie, who was sobbing. He hugged her, whispered something in her ear that made her laugh and then hugged her some more.

Their story had touched Julia deeply when she first heard it, and as she watched them together now, their deep bond was obvious.

Next to them, Owen stood with his arm around Sarah, the two of them survivors of the hell Julia's father had put them all through. Without Owen and their mom, the rest of them wouldn't have gotten through it intact. Or as intact as anyone could be after what they'd endured.

Julia glanced toward her youngest brother, Jeff, who'd attempted suicide while still living at home. Their grandparents had intervened and moved with him to Florida to get him into intense therapy that had helped to put his life back together. He and the other Lawrys were all smiles and tears as they watched their mom exchange vows with Charlie.

When they had recited traditional vows, Frank turned to Sarah. "You and Charlie have indicated that you each have something you'd like to share. Would you like to go first?"

Sarah nodded and took a deep breath. Happiness radiated from every part of her, and Julia realized she had never seen her mother truly happy before now.

"I swore I wouldn't cry today, because this day isn't about tears. It's about hope and second chances and love like I never knew existed until I met you, Charlie. For so many years, I lived without the love and joy and hope that you give me every minute of every day. I'm so thankful we found each other on this tiny island in the middle of the ocean. There's nowhere else I want to be for the rest of my life than wherever you are. I love you so much."

Charlie released his hold on Sarah's left hand only long enough to wipe tears from his face. "You certainly know how to get to me," he said. "You have from the start, with your lovely blue eyes that saw through to the heart of me. The best thing I ever did was come to work at the hotel during the renovations, where I met Owen's beautiful mom and found my happy beginning. I don't like to call it a happy ending, because today is just the start for us. I can't wait for everything that comes next with you, your children, your parents, my daughter, our family. There is nothing you could want or need that I wouldn't find a way to get for you. All you have to do is ask, and it's yours. I'm yours."

By then, everyone was wiping up tears, even Julia, who was unreasonably moved by their heartfelt words. Would anyone ever look at her the way Charlie was looking at her mom? Across the table, Shane had his arm around Katie, who leaned into him. What might it be like to have someone she could truly count on to have her back? Would she ever meet anyone she could trust the way her mom trusted Charlie or Owen trusted Laura or Katie trusted Shane?

She'd looked high and low, and all she'd found were the dregs. Were there any good guys left out there for her to find?

Deacon chose that moment to lean in, his arm on the chair behind her. "Are you okay?" He kept his voice down so only she could hear him.

She shot him a look, still wondering why her mother had invited him. He'd been a stranger to both of them yesterday. "I'm fine."

He studied her intently, as if he could tell just by looking at her that she was lying. She wasn't fine, and she couldn't actually remember the last time she'd been fine. Had she ever been? The thought sent her mind spiraling through memories that were better left in the past where they belonged.

Her mom and Charlie exchanged rings, and then Frank declared them husband and wife. "Charlie, you may kiss your bride."

Charlie wrapped his arms around Sarah and looked at her for a long, intense moment before he kissed her gently but with so much feeling that it brought new tears to Julia's eyes. She stood abruptly, and her chair fell over, making a loud clatter as it landed on the deck. When everyone was supposed to be looking at her mom and Charlie, they were looking at her, once again wondering what was wrong with Julia.

Everything was wrong.

"I'm sorry. Excuse me." She had to get out of there before she broke down in front of her entire family. The last thing in the world she wanted was their full attention. That belonged to her mom and Charlie today, not her.

Julia went down to the street and walked a short distance to the stone breakwater that made up the northern end of New Harbor. Choosing her steps carefully, Julia made her way out to the end where she sat, removed her sandals and let her feet hang low enough to be splashed by waves breaking gently over the huge stones.

When she was a kid visiting her grandparents and needed to get away from the crowd, she'd come out here to sit and think and breathe. The first time she'd done it, they'd gone into a panic looking for her, and when her grandfather found her at the end of the breakwater, he'd told her to please let him know the next time she needed a break so her grandmother wouldn't be worried. She'd told him every time after that, and he'd always understood and supported her need for solitude.

Thank God for the two of them. Julia could still close her eyes and go right back to how dreadful it had felt to return to the reality of their hellish life at home after those blissful summers. She could easily recall the painful desire to tell her grandparents the truth about life with their father, despite the dreadful consequences he'd promised to anyone who "told tales out of school."

She could remember the way her stomach would all but seize up when it was time to leave Gansett, making it impossible to eat for days. Her issues with food started during those chaotic years, when she'd had no control over anything in her life, least of all the violent, unpredictable outbursts that were so much a part of their childhood. It'd been the worst for her, Katie and Owen as the eldest three. Their father had directed most of his rage at them and their mother, but the others had suffered right along with them. John stuttered until he was twenty, and it suddenly disappeared. Cindy had awful headaches, Josh had turned to booze and Jeff to drugs before he'd nearly succeeded in ending his own life.

For Julia, the pain had fueled eating disorders as well as her almost pathological need for attention from men, which she'd mistakenly thought would bring her solace. It had done the exact opposite.

Julia picked up a handful of stones and threw them one at a time into the sea below, watching them disappear beneath the surface.

She'd once sat in this very spot, the night before they were due to return home for another endless school year, and contemplated whether it would be easier to slip beneath the surface of the water and never come back up. In that moment, slipping beneath the sea had been preferable to going home to her father.

"Your grandfather told me I might find you out here."

Julia looked up at Deacon, shocked to see him standing there.

"May I join you?"

She shrugged. "It's not my jetty."

He sat next to her on the same massive rock. "I'd forgotten how beautiful this island can be."

"How could you forget that?"

"I've been gone a long time."

"Didn't you come home to visit your family?"

"Not very often. Mostly, they came to see me when I lived in Boston."

"You aren't close to them?"

"Not really. I made a point to talk to my mom and grandmother every week, but other than that, not so much."

Julia couldn't imagine life without the close bond she'd always shared with her brothers and sisters. It was how they'd survived. "Why?"

"I don't know, really. We've just never been particularly tight. My sister is the oldest, then Blaine and then me. Our other brother and sister are much younger than the rest of us. I was long gone by the time they hit high school."

"Where do they live now?"

"My older sister is married with two kids and living in Connecticut. You know Blaine's story. My younger brother just graduated from college in Boston and my younger sister lives in Newport."

"Funny how we both come from big families."

"I know, right?"

For a long time, they stared out at the captivating ocean vista, the sight of which never got old to Julia. "When we spent summers here, I would curl up on the window seat in my room and stare at the ocean for hours. My gram knew how much I loved that seat, so she always gave me and Katie the same room." Julia had no doubt Adele had ensured she'd gotten their old room this weekend.

"You love it here."

"I really do."

"Funny how I hated living here when I was a kid."

"What? Why? How could anyone hate it here?"

"It was so *confining*. We couldn't go anywhere or do anything but what was on the island. I left the day I turned eighteen, and I've only been back a handful of times since. It's just not my scene."

"So why are you here?"

"That's kind of a long story, and you need to get back to your mom's wedding before she thinks you're upset that she married Charlie."

"I'm not. He seems great, and he's clearly crazy about her."

"Then what're you doing out here when the rest of your family is celebrating?"

"I needed a break."

He nudged her shoulder playfully. "From what?"

"The outbreak of happiness in my family. It's making me feel like I have poison ivy all over me." She rubbed her arms. "I can't take it."

Deacon laughed—hard.

"It's not funny!"

"Yeah, it kinda is." He stood and brushed off his shorts. "Let's walk back before your mom gets her feelings hurt. After the brunch, I'll take you for a ride in my boat, and you can be miserable where no one but me can see you."

She took the hand he held out and let him pull her up. When she was standing, she withdrew her hand, folded her arms and gave him an assessing look. "Why did my mom invite you to her wedding?"

"I honestly don't know. Maybe she suspected you might need a friend?"

"Is that what you are? My friend?"

They began the walk back, choosing their steps carefully on the enormous rocks that made up the jetty.

"If you want me to be."

"I told you, I'm not going to sleep with you or do anything else with you."

"Ew, we're friends. I don't do that stuff with my *friends*."

Julia laughed at the outrage in his tone. "I'm glad we understand each other."

"Oh, we do. For sure."

"You're not playing games trying to be my friend, thinking you'll wear me down and get me to sleep with you, are you?"

"I'm really offended that you'd suspect me of something so devious."

She gave him a gentle shove that he didn't see coming and had to grab his arm to keep him from taking a bad fall.

He gave her a wide-eyed look. "You saved my life."

"Whatever."

"No, it's true. That would've been a bad fall."

"I fell off this jetty once, when I was twelve."

They continued to work their way back toward the shore. "Were you hurt?"

"I was black and blue and scabby for weeks. It really scared me— and my grandfather, who saw it happen and got to me before I could be smashed against the rocks. Took me a long time to come back out here after that, but every day, he and I would walk a little farther out until I got past it. He said he didn't want me to lose something I loved because of one random incident."

"He sounds pretty great."

"He's the best man I've ever known."

When she tripped over a raised rock, Deacon grabbed her arm and kept her steady.

Julia looked over at him. "I guess now we're even."

"I guess so. So about that boat ride I promised you… I was going to take the boat out, get familiar with the harbors and the layout of things before I officially start the new job on Monday. You want to come along?"

"Are you allowed to take someone with you?"

"As long as I have a life jacket for you, which I do."

"Sure, that sounds like fun." It sounded like more fun than trying to figure out what the hell she was going to do with herself now that Katie's wedding was over and she had no way to get home without bumming money off a family member, which was *not* going to happen.

CHAPTER 7

*B*ack on the sidewalk, they walked the short distance to the Sand & Surf and took the stairs to the deck, rejoining the brunch already in progress.

Katie cast her a questioning look that Julia ignored as she thanked the waiter who put a plate laden with more food than she'd eat in a week in front of her.

At the far end of the long table, her mom was talking and laughing and smiling, caught up in her new husband and her well-earned happiness. Maybe her mother hadn't seen Julia leave and didn't seem to have noticed when she came back. She could only hope.

Adele got up from her seat next to Sarah and came to speak to Julia, toting the iPhone she was addicted to. Her grandchildren teased her about being worse than a teenager with her phone. "I heard back from my friend Big Mac McCarthy. I saw him at a cocktail party last weekend, where he mentioned that his son Mac desperately needed office help for his construction business. His wife, Linda, mentioned it again at bridge this week. I texted Big Mac to ask if Mac was actually hiring, because my granddaughter would be perfect, and he said to have you come by the marina tomorrow around nine to talk to Mac. He said he'd make sure he's there."

"That's amazing, Gram. Thank you so much."

"I really hope it works out. The McCarthys are good people, as we all know. Big Mac is Laura and Shane's uncle, and Mac is their first cousin."

"Really appreciate the contact."

"My pleasure, honey." She glanced at the plate Julia hadn't touched. "Are you all right?"

"I'm fine. My stomach is a little upset from too much champagne yesterday. Nothing to worry about." Her grandmother would worry, despite Julia's assurances. Adele knew better than even Julia's own mother how bad her issues with eating and food had gotten.

They'd protected Sarah from so much while she'd still been with their father. Back then, she'd had more than enough to contend with trying to survive every day. The first time Julia had ended up in the hospital, Katie had called their grandmother, not their mother, and Adele had come running. No one knew about the other time she'd been hospitalized, not even Katie.

Adele squeezed her shoulder as if to say everything would be all right, even if it didn't seem so now. Just being around her grandmother made her believe that, despite evidence to the contrary.

"Are you going to eat something?" Deacon asked after her grandmother had returned to her seat.

She pushed her plate in his direction. "I'm not really hungry."

"Are you sure?"

"Yep. Have at it."

As he put her full plate on top of his empty one, Julia caught Katie watching her from across the table, her face set in a concerned expression.

Great. The last thing Julia wanted was concern from her sister the nurse, who saw too much. Her problems were her own, and she would deal with them.

Somehow.

DEACON HADN'T EXPECTED BRUNCH WITH PEOPLE HE'D MET ONLY THE

day before to be any fun and had come only because Sarah had asked him to. The Lawry family was an energetic, entertaining group, and he'd seen for himself that they were close to each other the way Julia had described them. But after spending time with Julia and observing the way her family behaved around her, he realized they worried about her.

He wondered why that was. As a former police officer, he was a keen observer of people. He enjoyed figuring out what made them tick and understanding relationships between siblings, partners, spouses. People intrigued him. Julia intrigued him. He found her to be an interesting mix of strength and fragility. It killed him to know that she and her siblings had been mistreated by their father. Would she ever tell him about that herself?

And he fully intended to investigate the guy who'd taken advantage of her and try to get restitution for her. During his career in law enforcement, he'd learned that bullies came in all shapes and sizes. Some intimidated with their strength, others with their words and still others by preying on people who would do anything for anyone, like Julia. She was the kind of person who'd give a stranger everything she had without asking for anything in exchange.

When her ex came to her and told her a sob story about his sick mother, of course she was going to do everything she could to help— even give the man her entire savings to save his mother's life. Deacon had known her for one day and already understood that much about her.

He looked forward to getting to know her better. It'd been a while since he'd made a new friend, especially a woman who'd already made it clear that friends was all they were ever going to be. That was fine with him. He'd had enough with romantic entanglements for a while.

His phone vibrated with a text. He pulled it from his pocket to read the message from Sherri, the woman he'd defended in the bar fight. Speaking of romantic entanglements.

Hey Deacon. Sorry it's taken me a few days to get in touch. Things have been kind of crazy since the other night. If you can believe it, Jerry fired ME because of the fight. As if I had anything to do with Roger coming in there and starting something. I just want to say I really appreciate what you did and I'm so sorry for the trouble it caused you. I heard you've left town?? Will you be back? I hope so!

Holy shit. She'd gotten *fired*?

"I need to make a call," Deacon told Julia. "I'll be right back."

"Okay."

He got up and left the deck, taking the steps to the sidewalk, where he placed the call to Jerry at the bar.

"It's Deacon."

"What do you want?"

"Why'd you fire Sherri? It wasn't her fault Roger showed up and started trouble."

"I don't need the drama in my place. She's nothing but drama with the ex and the custody battle and the fighting."

"None of that is her fault. She's got kids to feed, Jerry."

"Look, I know you're banging her—"

"Jerry! That has nothing to do with why I'm calling you. She's a good person who made the mistake of marrying an asshole. Why do you have to make things worse for her by taking her job? You know she's not going to be able to make what she does at the bar anywhere else."

"That's not my problem."

"You disappoint me."

"I'm pretty disappointed over the damage you did to my bar. Who do you think has to pay for the repairs?"

"I'm sorry about that, but what was I supposed to do? Stand by and let him kill her?"

"Don't be dramatic, Deacon. He wasn't going to kill her."

"You don't think so? You didn't hear what he said to her. I spent ten years dealing with domestic incidents on the job, and I know the signs of a situation about to explode. He threw her and their children out on the street and has done nothing but harass her ever since. Don't tell me you're okay with that."

"I'm not okay with it, but I have a freaking business to run, and I can't have this shit going on in my place. My business is down ten percent since the fight."

"If I send you the money for the repairs, will you hire her back?"

"It's ten grand."

Deacon felt like he'd been punched in the gut again, like he'd been in the fight. "I'll pay it. Will you hire her back?"

"I don't know, man. This isn't the first time her personal problems have impacted my business. I don't want anything to do with it."

"This isn't her fault. He's terrorized her for *years*. She needs to feed her kids, and she's not getting a dime in support from him."

"I feel terrible about what she's going through, but it's not my problem. I have to keep my business afloat so I can feed my own kids."

Realizing he was getting nowhere with Jerry, Deacon said, "Fine. Don't worry about it. She has plenty of friends who'll help her out."

"You're not being fair—"

Deacon ended the call. He'd heard more than enough. He knew some furniture had gotten smashed in the fight and some glasses broken, but ten thousand in damages? Jesus. Since Jerry was being a dick about giving Sherri her job back, Deacon called up the app he used to pay his bills and opened the account where he'd been stashing money in the hope of buying a new bike. There was twelve thousand five hundred in the account, and she needed the money far more than he needed a new bike.

He sent ten thousand of it to her with a note that said, *Jerry is a dick and so is Roger. Hope this helps to hold you over until you find something better. I'm really sorry for any trouble I caused by getting into it with Roger. Keep in touch, and let me know how you're doing.*

Not even a minute later, his phone rang with a call from Sherri. "Deacon! Oh my God! You don't have to do that! None of this is your fault."

"I know it's not, but I didn't have to tangle with Roger in the bar, which is what got you fired."

"Roger got me fired, not you. You were just trying to help."

"Take the money, Sherri. You need it more than I do."

"I wouldn't feel right taking your money."

"I won't take it back, so you'll have to figure out what to do with it."

She broke down into soft sobs that made him ache for what she'd been through. "Thank you so much."

"It's nothing."

"You have no idea what this means to me."

Deacon hoped he hadn't made a huge mistake by sending her the money. He didn't want to give her false hope that they'd ever be anything more than friends who used to hook up once in a while. "Has Roger been leaving you alone?"

"I wish."

The cop in Deacon went on full alert. "There's a restraining order in place. He's not supposed to be anywhere near you."

"He does his best work by text and email, and I can't block him because of the kids. It's a freaking nightmare that won't end."

"I can reach out to the local police and see what I can do."

"You don't have to do that. You've already helped me out so much. I'll never forget the way you came to my defense that night. No one has ever done anything like that for me before."

Deacon would do it again, even knowing what a shitshow it would turn into. He'd done what he'd do for any woman who was being harassed by a man who wouldn't leave her alone. He hadn't done it because of any special feelings he had for Sherri.

"I would've done that for anyone, Sherri. He was totally out of line."

"Still... It meant a lot to me. When will you be back in town?"

"Ah, maybe the end of the summer? I don't know exactly."

"That's a long time from now. I'll look forward to seeing you whenever you get back."

"Sherri, listen... I need to tell you—"

"I have to run. The baby is awake and screaming, and the kids are fighting. I'll talk to you soon? And thank you again, Deacon. So much. You're the best."

The connection went dead before he could reply or finish telling her that as much as he'd enjoyed the time they'd spent together, they were never going to be more than they'd already been. Shit. How did he get himself into these situations? It was what Blaine called his hero complex. According to his older and wiser brother, Deacon got himself into stupid situations because he had a burning need to play the part of the hero.

Whatever. If being a decent human being and stepping up for those who needed help meant he had a hero complex, well, he could live with that. Besides, before he met Tiffany, Blaine had been known within their family for taking on "projects," women who were in need of saving. But Blaine never remembered that when he was accusing Deacon of trying to be a hero.

He dashed off a text to one of the local cops he'd been friendly with in Harwich, letting him know that Roger was still hassling Sherri and they ought to keep an eye on that.

His friend wrote right back. *On it. Thanks for the heads-up. How's it going in Siberia?*

Fabulous...

"Everything all right?"

At the sound of Julia's voice, Deacon spun around to face her. His brain froze as he wondered if she'd overheard him on the phone with Sherri. And then he wondered why he cared if she'd overheard him. "Yeah, all good."

"Are you sure?"

"Yep. You still want to take a boat ride?"

"I'd love to. I just need to get changed."

"I'll wait for you on the porch."

"I'll be quick."

"Take your time. I'm not in any rush. This is one of my last days of freedom for a while." Blaine had warned that they'd be straight out until Labor Day. That didn't intimidate him. Deacon liked to be busy, and he loved being on the water. In that way, the job his brother had forced on him was perfect for him. At least that part of his summer in Siberia would be bearable.

Julia flashed a smile, went up the stairs and through the main door to the hotel.

Deacon followed at a more leisurely pace and returned to the deck to thank Julia's mother for brunch. He found her standing next to her new husband, who had his arm around her, the two of them fairly glowing with happiness. What might it be like to be that happy? Deacon wouldn't know. He'd never come anywhere close to what the two of them had clearly found in each other. "Thanks again for having me, and congratulations to both of you."

Sarah surprised him when she hugged him. "We're so glad you could be with us today, Deacon."

Charlie shook his hand. "Thanks for coming."

"Is Julia all right?" Sarah asked. "I saw her leave for a bit."

"She's good, I think. We're going to take a boat ride this afternoon."

"Oh, that's wonderful. She'll enjoy that." Sarah hesitated, seeming to decide if she should say more. "I worry about her."

"You worry about all of them," Charlie said with a smile for his new wife.

"That's true. But Julia..." Sarah shook her head and seemed to force a cheerful expression. "I'm sorry. I don't mean to unload on you."

"No worries at all. I'll let you get back to your family."

"Deacon..."

He turned back to her, his brow raised in inquiry.

"I know you've only just met Julia, but I think she could use a friend. Call it mother's intuition or what have you..."

"I'd like to be her friend, if she'll have me."

Sarah nodded and seemed satisfied for now. "It's so very nice to have our lovely Blaine's equally lovely brother on the island for the summer. Don't be a stranger. Pop in to say hello any time you're nearby."

Deacon had to force himself not to react to Blaine being called *lovely*. "I'll do that. Congratulations again."

"Thank you."

CHAPTER 8

*J*ulia went up to the third floor to the small room she'd shared with Katie two nights ago. Katie had been superstitious about seeing Shane before the wedding and had asked to stay with Julia for her last night as a single woman.

Although, technically, her last night as a single woman had been the day before Owen and Laura's wedding. Katie and Shane had been together pretty much from the moment he'd rescued her from a rip current at the beach outside the Surf, where the Lawry siblings had been swimming their entire lives. That'd been a close call, and it still made Julia shudder to think about how suddenly her sister could've been taken from them.

As she changed into a bikini, tank and denim cutoff shorts, Julia thought about that day and the roller coaster of emotions she'd experienced after hearing what'd nearly happened to Katie on the same day their beloved Owen had married Laura.

Julia had survived a lot in her life. She never would've survived losing Katie. Suffice to say that Shane had had her at hello with what he'd done for Katie—for all of them—that day.

After living in a state of perpetual disaster for most of their childhood, the Lawrys had already had more than their share. Certainly, in the grand scheme of things, they were due some good karma after everything they'd already been through.

Julia was ready for some good karma. Any time now.

A knock sounded at the door. She opened it to find Katie standing there.

"Hey, what's up?" Leaving the door open, Julia went back to tossing sunscreen, a hat, sweatshirt and hotel towel into a beach bag. "I thought you'd be off honeymooning."

Katie came in and closed the door. "We're not leaving until tomorrow."

They were going to Ireland, which was another reason to be envious of her twin. Julia had always wanted to go to Ireland. "You must be excited for the trip."

"We are. But I'm worried about you."

Julia glanced at Katie over her shoulder. "How come?"

"You left in the middle of my wedding without saying a word to anyone, for one thing."

"I'm sorry about that. I just needed to get some air."

"Because my wedding was so stifling?"

Julia closed her eyes, counted silently to five and then turned to face her sister. "Not at all. I was just feeling emotional and took a breather."

"Why were you feeling emotional?"

"Other than the fact that my twin sister and lifelong best friend was getting married?"

"Yeah, other than that."

Here was the one person Julia couldn't dodge, couldn't fool and couldn't escape. She sat on her bed, exhaling. "Things have been kind of complicated at home since you left."

Katie sat on the other bed. "How so?"

Julia bit her bottom lip as she tried to think about how to say it without making Katie feel bad for leaving. "It's just different."

"Stop hedging and tell me what you mean."

"I miss you, okay? Nothing is the same without you there, and I didn't want to say that because I don't want you to feel bad about leaving. I totally get why you stayed here after Owen's wedding. And look at you now. An old married lady."

Katie moved from her bed to Julia's and put her arm around her sister, leaning her head on Julia's shoulder. "Just because I'm married now doesn't mean I'm not still your sister, your bestie, your twin. I'm right here, Jule. Right where I've always been."

That wasn't true, but Julia wasn't about to say so, not when her sister was so happy in her new life. She would never want to say or do anything to detract from Katie's happiness. "I know."

"You didn't eat anything this morning."

"I wasn't hungry. Too much champagne yesterday."

"You didn't eat anything at the wedding either."

"I did, too."

"No, you didn't."

"Weren't you too busy being married to watch me all day?"

"What's going on? And don't say it's nothing. I know the signs by now."

Not only did Katie know her better than anyone, she was a family nurse practitioner and had been aware of Julia's eating disorders from the beginning. In fact, Katie had been the one to sound the alarm the first time Julia ended up in the hospital.

"I've had a rough couple of months. Nothing to worry about, but there's been some stress. I'm managing it."

"By not eating?"

"I've been eating. I promise."

"When? When was the last time you had something substantial to eat?"

Julia had to think about that and knew there was no sense in trying to hide the truth from her twin. "Yesterday before the wedding."

"That's almost twenty-four hours ago, Julia. You know full well that's too long." From her purse, Katie withdrew a banana and handed it to Julia.

Julia took it from her, reminded of the many times Katie had convinced her in the past to eat by giving her a banana, knowing how

Julia had always loved them. She peeled the banana and took a bite, forcing herself to chew and swallow. "It was one bad day. I promise to get back on track today. You should go be with your husband. He's probably wondering where you are."

"He knows where I am."

"Did you tell him your crazy sister was off the rails again and you had to perform an intervention?" Julia immediately regretted the harsh words, but it was too late to take them back.

"Not at all. I told him I wanted to spend some time with you before you have to leave."

"I'm sorry. You didn't deserve that. I swear I'm fine. There's nothing to worry about. Also, I'm not leaving right away. I was thinking I might stick around for the summer."

Katie's pretty face lit up with a huge smile. "Really? That's great news!" Then she sobered once again. "However… I don't believe you when you say you're fine. I've seen fine, and I've seen not fine. This looks more like the latter to me. Maybe Shane and I should postpone our trip—"

"No! Absolutely not!"

"Then I'm going to need you to do something for me."

"What?" Julia would do just about anything to not be the reason they postponed their honeymoon.

"Two things, actually. One, I want you to agree to see David or Victoria at the clinic for a full workup in the next few days, including blood work. And two, if you're going to be here for the summer, I want you to start seeing Shane's uncle Kevin. He's a brilliant psychiatrist with an office right here on the island."

Julia didn't want to do either of those things, but if it meant that Katie wouldn't postpone her trip because of her, she'd do it. "Fine."

"Swear to God?"

Julia fully understood the importance of Katie asking her to swear to God. In their family, there was no greater measure of assurance. "I swear to God."

"Good, because I'm going to check when I get back to make sure you were seen at the clinic."

"Are you allowed to do that?"

"To check on a patient? Absolutely."

"Go on your trip. Don't worry about me. I promise I'm okay."

"Don't fall down this rabbit hole again, Julia. You've worked so hard to get off the merry-go-round. Please, if not for yourself, then for everyone who loves you, please take care of yourself before it gets out of control again."

"I will. I am. It's under control."

Katie gave her a skeptical look that Julia knew she deserved. How many times in the past had she sworn to her sister that things were under control when they weren't? And they weren't now, but there was no way she was going to let her issues ruin this happy time for Katie.

Her sister withdrew her phone and started tapping away.

"What're you doing?"

"Logging into the appointment system to get you scheduled. You want David or Vic?"

Realizing there was no point in objecting, Julia sighed. "Vic, I guess."

After some more tapping, Katie said, "Tomorrow at three?"

"Okay."

She continued to tap away.

"What're you doing now?"

"Telling Vic that I made an appointment for you and to let me know if you don't show."

Julia bit back a stinging retort. "I said I'll go, and I will." She made an effort to keep from snapping at Katie.

"I just texted Shane's uncle Kevin about scheduling you. I sent him your number, and he'll get in touch when he gets a minute. He and his wife just had a baby, so it might be a couple of days. I expect you to respond to him, do you hear me?"

"Anything else?"

"You may as well know that I'm going to tell Owen to keep an eye on you."

"Come on, Katie! I don't need anyone keeping an eye on me."

Katie raised a brow. "No? Do you honestly think I'm going to stand by and allow this to happen again? If you want us out of your business, take care of yourself. That's nonnegotiable."

Owen and Katie had saved her life once before, and Julia knew there was no point in arguing with Katie. If Julia wanted her sister to leave on her honeymoon as scheduled—and she did—then she had to go along with Katie's demands. "Fine. Whatever. Go on your trip and don't worry about me."

Katie put her arm around Julia and leaned her forehead against Julia's. "I will *always* worry about you, and I'll always love you, and I'll always, *always* want you to be my very best friend, even now that I'm married."

The heartfelt words triggered a groundswell of emotion that Julia was powerless to contain.

"Please don't tell me you ever doubted that," Katie said softly as she held Julia while she wept.

"No, not really. It's just that everything is different now."

"Everything that matters is exactly as it has always been, exactly as it will always be."

Julia clung to her sister and her assurances. Did Katie have any idea how much Julia needed to hear that?

Katie pulled back from their embrace and wiped the tears from Julia's face. "So what's up with Blaine's smoking-hot brother?"

"Is he smoking hot? I hadn't noticed."

Katie laughed and nudged her with her shoulder. "Sure you haven't. What gives?"

"Nothing. I just met him yesterday. We had some fun at the wedding, which he crashed, by the way."

"I wondered where he'd come from. From what I hear, he and his brother don't get along."

"Yeah, he said that. But they're going to be working together this summer, so that ought to be interesting."

"Do you, you know… like him?"

"As anything more than a friend? Nope."

"Why not?"

"I'm on a man diet."

"Huh? A man diet?"

"Also known as a dick diet."

Katie cracked up laughing. "That's not really a thing, is it?"

"It is, and you'd know that if you'd ever dated anyone other than your husband."

"I was holding out for perfection."

Julia rolled her eyes. "For the rest of us mere mortals, there's nothing but frogs in the swamp, and I, for one, have had enough frogs to last me a lifetime. So I'm on a diet. No men, no dicks, no headaches, no heartaches."

"For how long?"

Julia shrugged. "Four months so far." Since the day she'd learned the full extent of Mike's betrayal. "Maybe forever."

"That's silly. What if Deacon turns out to be the one you're meant to be with and your so-called dick diet keeps you from something that could be really great?"

"None of them are really great, Katie."

"Shane is. Owen is. Charlie is. David is. I know lots of men who're amazing husbands, boyfriends, partners. Ask Mom how great Blaine was to her when she first arrived on the island, devastated and hurt from the last run-in with Dad. Mom adores Blaine, and I'm sure his brother shares a lot of the same qualities."

"He could be the best man in the whole world, and it wouldn't matter. All men are radioactive."

"Does he know that? Because judging by the way he was staring at you during brunch, he's not aware that he's off-limits."

Julia wasn't sure how she felt about hearing Deacon had been staring at her. "He knows because I told him."

"You came right out and told him you're on a dick diet?"

"Yep. I also said I'm not dating at the moment, so if he's hanging around hoping I'll put out, there's not a snowball's chance in hell of that happening."

"Huh."

"What does that mean?"

"It's just that I'm surprised. You love men—and dick. I never thought you'd actually give up either."

"I'm fed up with it all. Men are nothing but trouble, and since dicks are attached to men, I'm giving up both."

"Won't you miss it? The dick part, that is."

"Eh, not really. I've spent my entire adult life proving Dad right about me. It's time to prove there's more to me than how I look."

Katie went very still. "Proving Dad right about what?"

"You know. What he said about me."

"I don't know."

"Yes, you do." Julia's brain raced as she tried to recall telling Katie. "I'm sure I told you."

"I'm sure you didn't, so how about you tell me now?"

Julia didn't want to. She didn't want to say the hateful words out loud and give them new power over her—or Katie.

"Tell me."

With the genie out of the bottle, there'd be no stuffing it back in. "When I told him I wanted to go to college, he said there was no point. He said I'd spend my life on my back because when men look at me, they see I'm good for only one thing. You know how he was always commenting about my body and how I look."

Katie stared at her.

"I told you that."

"You most certainly did not." Katie blinked back tears. "I hate him so much, for so many things, but that…" Tears rolled down her cheeks.

Julia couldn't bear to see Katie cry.

"This is why," Katie said softly.

"Why what?"

"It's why you starved yourself."

"No, it isn't."

"Of course it is, Julia. You did it so you'd have control over something that mattered to him. He was so proud of how beautiful you are, and you did it so you wouldn't be beautiful to him anymore."

"That's not true. He had nothing to do with it."

Katie wrapped her arms around Julia and held on tight. "He had everything to do with it." After a long period of quiet, Katie released Julia to wipe tears from her face. "You know, when he called Owen after the trial and told O how he'd been abused as a child by his father and that's why he treated us the way he did, part of me wanted to forgive him. I mean, we all know what kind of damage abuse does to a child. But it's stuff like this, what he said to you, that I'll never forgive him for."

"It was a long time ago, and it doesn't matter anymore." Julia refused to give him any more power over her than he'd already exerted. Even with him in prison, locked away for years to come, the thought of him could still make her skin crawl.

Desperate to shake off thoughts of a man she'd much sooner forget than ever think about again, she pulled free of Katie's embrace. "I need to get going. Deacon probably thinks I got lost." Julia stood to run a brush through her hair and finish packing her bag.

Katie came up behind her and put her hands on Julia's shoulders, compelling her to turn and face her twin. "Will you do one more thing for me while I'm gone?"

"If I must…"

"Don't write Deacon off before you have a chance to get to know him. If he's anything at all like his big brother, he's one of the good ones."

Julia had already seen indications of him being a good guy but was wary enough to keep him firmly classified in the friend category. The last thing she needed with her entire life in an uproar was any sort of romantic complications.

Katie gave her an adorably imploring look. "Do it for me?"

"Ugh, why you gotta say it that way?"

"Because I know it'll matter to you."

Katie was well aware that there was almost nothing Julia wouldn't do for her or any of their siblings. "Fine. Whatever. Go away and have sex with your husband."

Katie waggled her brows. "Already did that this morning."

"Now you're just being a cocky bitch."

Katie's laughter sparked Julia's. It felt good to share a laugh with her sister after the tears.

Julia hugged her tightly. "Go on ahead. I promise I'll be fine. Enjoy every minute of your trip and the time with Shane. You deserve every happiness."

"So do you."

"If you say so."

"I say so, and I'm in charge."

"Easy, killer." Katie had been the leader and Julia the follower, and that dynamic had worked well for them. But now Katie had a whole new life with Shane, and Julia needed to figure out her own crap, without Katie leading the way.

The sisters walked downstairs together, where they found Deacon sitting on the front porch with Adele.

She brightened at the sight of her granddaughters. "There she is," Adele said, focusing on Julia.

Deacon stood, and when her eyes met his golden-brown gaze, a tingle of awareness overtook her. What the hell was that about? It was Katie putting ideas in her head, that's all. He was just another good-looking guy who was probably interested in one thing and one thing only. She'd be wise to keep their friendship strictly platonic. If she didn't let him get to her, there was no way he could hurt her.

"You ready?" Deacon asked.

"I am if you are."

"Let's do it, then." He surprised Julia when he bent to kiss Adele's cheek. "Thank you for the company."

Adele fanned her face dramatically. "It was entirely my pleasure."

Deacon laughed, and again the tingles electrified her, making Julia realize she needed to be very careful with this one.

CHAPTER 9

*E*very time he laid eyes on Julia, it was like he was seeing her again for the first time. When she came out the hotel's main door with her equally attractive sister, he'd noticed only her. She'd brushed her long dark hair until it fell in soft, shiny waves down her back and had a smudge of sunscreen on her cute nose.

She wore sunglasses, so he couldn't see her always-expressive eyes. He'd have to be dead not to notice how her cutoff denim shorts hugged her sweet ass or the way her tank top showed off a spectacular pair of breasts. While her physical attributes were hard to miss, he was far more concerned about her emotional well-being after their conversation on the jetty. Especially knowing what he did about her father and her family's history.

"Everything okay?"

She nodded. "Why do you ask?"

"You were gone awhile."

"Katie came up to see me, and we got to talking—as we do. Sorry to make you wait."

"I didn't mind waiting. Your grandmother found me, and we had the nicest chat. She was telling me stories about running the hotel for more than fifty summers."

"She's seen it all, that's for sure."

"She seems like a really great person."

"She's the best. We never would've survived without her and my gramps growing up."

"Is that right?"

"Uh-huh."

He waited, hoping she'd say more, but she didn't. After a short walk that took them past the ferry landing, they arrived at the public safety dock where the police, fire and harbor master boats were docked. Deacon went into the office to check in with the officer on duty. "Hey, I'm Deacon Taylor, the new harbor master."

"Oh, hi, I'm Colby, one of the assistants this summer."

Deacon shook his hand. "Great to meet you. I was hoping to take one of the boats out to get the lay of the land, if that's all right."

"Of course. I'll get you set up."

"Awesome. I assume it's okay if I bring someone with me?"

"As long as you have a life jacket for any passengers, you're good to go, and there're a dozen life jackets in each boat."

"Perfect."

Colby walked him through what he needed to know about the oversize inflatable boat with the center console and twin hundred-horsepower outboard engines. The words GANSETT ISLAND POLICE DEPARTMENT were printed on each side of the boat, and a police light was mounted on top of the wheelhouse. The boat was similar to the one he'd used in his last job, so it didn't take long for Deacon to feel comfortable with the setup. "We monitor Channel 16 on the radio," Colby said. "There's a handheld unit in the console."

"This is great. Thank you so much."

Colby shook Deacon's outstretched hand. "No problem. Looking forward to working with you."

"Likewise." Deacon helped Julia onto the boat.

Colby got off the boat and helped with the lines as Deacon stood at the helm to back the boat out of the slip.

Growing up on Gansett, he'd spent most of his childhood on boats of one kind or another, and the routine was second nature to him. As they were exiting the South Harbor breakwater, one of the high-speed ferries approached. Deacon gave the much larger vessel a wide berth and told Julia to hold on as they rode the waves kicked up by the ferry's wake.

"Whoa," Julia said. "That was wild."

"I love this shit. The wilder the better." With Julia seated next to him, he pushed the throttle forward and opened it up for the ride around the island's northern coast on the way to the much larger and busier New Harbor, also known as the Great Salt Pond. Among other things, the harbor master was in charge of collecting fees for transient boaters who picked up the town's moorings and for ensuring safe boating practices in the waterways around Gansett Island.

After a brief, swift ride, Deacon made the turn that would take them through the narrow channel that led into the Salt Pond, passing the Coast Guard station to the right as they went by. The pond was full of boats on moorings and at the docks at McCarthy's and the other marinas.

"So many boats," Julia said.

"It's a fraction of what'll be here by Fourth of July weekend."

"I remember how crowded it would get in the summer."

"The town manages five hundred moorings that turn over on a regular basis."

"Holy crap. That's a lot."

"It's a busy job. Luckily, I'll have help. We have at least three people on duty on the weekends and two on weekdays after this week."

"Is it more than what you managed in your last job?"

"Way more. Like, five times more."

"I can see why you might've been hesitant to take that on."

"It wasn't the job that gave me pause. It was working for my brother and giving him control over me." He shuddered dramatically. "The idea of that is enough to make me puke."

"People speak very highly of him."

"Believe me, I know."

"You might find he's not what you think when you get to know him as he is now, as opposed to who he was when you were growing up. And he might discover the same is true about you."

"Maybe. Who knows?" He didn't hold out much hope for a mid-thirties change in course for brothers who'd been at odds most of their lives. "I don't ever remember a time when we weren't annoyed with each other about something. Just this morning, for instance, he accused me of being inappropriate with his wife because I went over to ask if I could borrow her iron."

"Why would he do that?"

"Because he came home to find me holding his daughter—which is apparently another crime against humanity—and talking to his wife while she ironed my shirt after offering to do it for me. I was actually enjoying the time with my niece and sister-in-law, both of whom I only just met the other day."

"I'm sorry he accused you of that."

"It's par for the course with him. At least his wife, Tiffany, was pissed at him over it, so that's something anyway."

"She should be pissed. Does he think his wife is going to take one look at his younger, handsome brother and think, 'Oh damn, I chose the wrong one'?"

Deacon laughed. "Well, she did pick the wrong one, but it's too late now. She's stuck with the jackass."

Julia laughed. "Yes, she is. But maybe it was just a momentary lapse in judgment on his part. He has to know you'd never go near his wife."

"Of course I wouldn't." He raised his sunglasses and gave her his best sultry stare. "So you think I'm handsome, huh?"

"Oh, shut up."

"Too late. You can't take it back now."

Julia groaned. "Me and my big mouth."

During an hour-long ride through the pond, Deacon took note of the various mooring numbers and observed the boats, people and activity without seeing anything of concern. People were having fun and doing so safely. That was all that mattered. As he directed the boat toward the channel to leave the pond, another harbor master boat was coming in.

Deacon took his boat out of gear so he could stop and talk to the other officer, a young blonde woman. "How's it going? I'm Deacon Taylor."

"Jillian Stark. Good to meet you." Like Colby, Jillian appeared to be in her early twenties and was probably a college student on summer break.

"You, too. Everything's looking good at the moment, but I'll leave you to it. See you soon."

"Have a good one." Jillian waved as she headed into the pond as they made for the exit.

Once clear of the channel, Deacon pushed the throttle forward and headed to the left to make a full circuit around the island. They were nearing the southernmost part of the island when Julia placed her hand on his arm.

"What's that?" She pointed to something in the distance.

"Where?"

"Over there." She stood and leaned forward for a better look. "Is it a seal?"

When Deacon finally saw what she was referring to, he shook his head. "I don't think so." He steered the boat closer and realized at the same instant that Julia did that they were looking at a dog swimming frantically.

He cut the engines down to idle when they were close to the animal.

"Oh my God! We have to get him!" Julia went to the side of the boat and called out to the dog. "Come here, baby. We'll save you."

The dog panicked and swam away from them.

Before Deacon could react, she had stripped down to her bathing suit, dived off the side of the boat and was swimming toward the dog. "Jesus," he muttered. He wasn't sure if he was more afraid of her catching hypothermia in the cold water or being scratched to pieces by the struggling dog. Apparently, she didn't care about either of those things as she swam closer to the dog and spoke softly to him, eventually convincing him to let her help.

Julia wrapped her arm around the dog, who climbed her frantically and nearly dragged her under as a wave broke over them. The small dog was black with a white spot on the top of his head.

Deacon threw her a life ring, hoping she could wrap one arm around that while she held on to the dog. He had to get her out of the water because her lips were already turning blue. Thankfully, she was able to grab hold of the life ring without losing her grip on the dog.

Deacon carefully pulled them closer until he had them within reach. Bending over the side, he tried to take the black dog from Julia.

The dog wasn't having it, snapping at him and biting his arm. "Fuck!"

"Don't bite him," Julia said. "He's trying to help you."

Between the two of them, they wrestled the dog—who was actually a puppy—into submission and got it into the boat. Then Deacon reached for Julia, and that was when he saw blood running down his arm. Crap. He pulled her out of the water and into the boat, where the dog shook frantically from the cold and trying to get the water off his coat. Deacon noted the animal had no collar and wondered how they'd go about finding his owner.

Julia shivered uncontrollably.

"We gotta get you warm."

"There's a s-sweatshirt in my b-bag," she managed to say over the violent trembling of her chin. In a few seconds, he realized she was much thinner than she'd appeared in clothes, but that wasn't his primary concern at the moment.

He found the sweatshirt and a towel in her bag and helped her into the sweatshirt, rubbing her arms and wishing he had another towel or a jacket or anything else he could use to warm her. The sun was covered by a thick layer of clouds, so it was of no help. "I can't believe you just jumped in like that."

"I h-had to. He was s-swimming away from us."

Deacon pressed the throttle forward, anxious to get them back to town as quickly as possible. "You risked your life to save a dog, Julia."

"And I'd do it again in a h-hot second. Are you all right?" She gestured toward his arm, which was bleeding profusely.

"I'm fine."

"Th-that doesn't look fine. Is there a first aid k-kit on board?"

She was on the verge of hypothermia but worried about him? "Check the cabinet." He focused on driving the boat while she got out the first aid kit and began cleaning the wound on his left arm. As her cold fingers moved over his skin, Deacon tried not to react to her touch. The only reason she was touching him was because he was bleeding. Otherwise, she'd be nowhere near him.

Keep telling yourself that. She'd stuck him firmly in the friend zone, and he needed to remember that. But the way she'd rescued the dog without a thought to herself or her own safety had stirred something elemental in him. She was someone he wanted to be around, someone he wanted to get to know, someone who'd be worth the trouble and the risk of getting involved.

After she had tended to his wound, she wrapped the towel she'd brought around the shivering dog, holding the little guy in her arms until he settled. He was clearly exhausted and quickly fell asleep even as he continued to shiver.

Deacon pushed the boat to its limits to get back to South Harbor as fast as possible, and when they approached the harbor entrance, he had to stop and idle while one ferry went into port and another came out. "You okay?" he asked Julia.

"J-just cold."

"You're going to need medical attention."

"No, you are."

"Both of us will." He'd been bitten by dogs three times while on the job and wasn't looking forward to having the wound cleaned or the wait to find out if the dog was rabid. The cute little guy looked wet and cold but perfectly healthy otherwise. However, that didn't mean anything. He'd once had the extremely unpleasant round of rabies vaccines, so his immunity was probably better than most. He sure hoped so. The last thing he wanted was to have to go through that treatment again.

Finally, the ferries were out of the way, and Deacon directed the boat to the police department dock, where, to his dismay, he saw his brother waiting to greet him, hands on hips and visibly angry. "Fucking hell."

"What?"

Deacon nodded toward Blaine. "I apologize in advance for whatever is about to happen."

CHAPTER 10

*D*eacon's brother was fuming. "What the hell are you doing?" He grabbed one of the lines and tied up the boat.

"I was getting to know the area I'm going to be responsible for."

"Who said you could take one of the boats?"

"I asked the assistant on duty, and he said it was fine. My friend rescued a dog and is on the verge of hypothermia. I need to get her to the clinic."

"And he's bleeding because the dog bit him," Julia added.

Only then did Blaine seem to notice the dog on the boat. "Where'd he come from?"

"Julia spotted him swimming offshore. She saved his life. He needs to be seen by the vet." Deacon helped Julia, who was still holding the dog, off the boat and brushed by Blaine. "We'll drop him at the vet and then hit the clinic."

"I'll take you," Blaine said.

Julia could tell that Deacon didn't want the favor from his brother, but he agreed to the ride out of concern for her. He held the back door to Blaine's SUV for her and waited until she and the dog were settled before closing the door and getting in the front.

When they were on their way to the vet, Blaine glanced at his brother. "You shouldn't have taken the boat out before your official first day. You're not on the department insurance yet."

"I have my own insurance that covers any boat I use."

"Still… you should've asked me."

"Well, I didn't, and what's done is done. You don't need to talk to me in front of my friend like I'm twelve."

"Who also shouldn't have been on the boat."

"I asked Colby, and he said it was fine as long as there was a life jacket for her. I know you've gotten comfortable with that police chief stick up your ass, but if you ever talk to me like that again, you'll be finding yourself a new harbor master."

Julia waited breathlessly to see what Blaine would have to say to that. He didn't respond, but she noticed he tightened his grip on the wheel.

"Has anyone reported a dog missing?" Julia asked Blaine as her teeth continued to chatter from the cold.

"Not that I'm aware of, but I'll check with dispatch."

A short time later, they pulled up to the veterinary clinic. Deacon helped her out and held the main door to the clinic for her. A familiar blonde woman wearing scrubs was seated at the reception desk. Julia recognized her from the family weddings. "Hi there. May I help you?"

"We found this guy swimming off the coast," Julia said.

The woman jumped up. "Oh my goodness. Do you have any idea how long he was in the water?"

"No, we don't, but it was probably quite some time."

She gestured for them to follow her to an exam room. "I'm Janey Cantrell. You're Owen's sister, right?"

"Yes, I'm Julia, and this is Deacon Taylor."

"Blaine's brother."

"Unfortunately," Deacon said under his breath.

"I was a McCarthy. My brother is married to Tiffany's sister, Maddie."

"Ah, got it. Everyone is related around here. Would it be possible for us to leave him with you?" Deacon showed her the ugly gash on his arm. "He bit me, and Julia might be hypothermic after jumping in after him. We need to hit the clinic."

"Of course. We'll take good care of him."

"You haven't had anyone report a dog missing, have you?" Julia asked.

"Nope."

"Hmm, I wonder where he came from."

"He might've fallen off a boat."

"And no one noticed?"

"It happens." Janey kissed the top of the dog's head. "Poor baby."

"Would it be possible to get him tested for rabies?" Julia asked. "He bit Deacon, so we'll need to know."

"We can't actually test him for rabies. All we can do is observe him for the next ten days, either here or in quarantine at home, where he would have to be kept away from other animals and people."

Deacon glanced at Julia. "We can keep him isolated at the hotel or at my place."

She nodded in agreement.

"We should get you to the clinic," he said. "Your lips are blue."

Julia didn't want to leave the dog, who gazed at her soulfully even as he tried to keep his eyes open. The poor guy was completely exhausted. "I'll be back to check on him as soon as I can."

"We'll be here all day."

"Thank you." Julia worried about how she'd pay for whatever the vet had to do for the dog, but somehow she'd find a way to get him what he needed.

Deacon ushered her out the door and back into Blaine's SUV for the short ride to the clinic. When Deacon told the woman at reception that he suspected Julia might have hypothermia, she was taken right back to a cubicle, where she was told to change out of her wet bathing suit and damp sweatshirt into a gown. The nurse helped her into bed, took her temperature and blood pressure and then put her under a delightful warming blanket.

"You can go on in," the nurse said to Deacon when Julia was settled.

He came in through the closed curtain and took a close look at her. "Feel better?"

"This blanket is the best thing since ice cream. You need to let them tend to you, too." Blood had soaked through the blue dress shirt he'd worn to brunch. It had touched her to hear that he went to the trouble of making sure his shirt was pressed before joining her family's get-together. She'd also appreciated the way he'd tended to her and indulged her need to rescue the dog—even after the little guy had bitten him. "I'm sorry about all this." She gestured to his bloody arm.

"It's no biggie."

"I wouldn't have been able to live with myself if we'd left him."

"I still say you shouldn't have risked yourself the way you did." She shrugged. "It's fine."

Deacon stepped closer to her bed, took hold of her hand and linked their fingers. "It's not fine. You matter to a lot of people, Julia. I saw that this morning with your family. And you matter to me."

Even though her heart was doing back flips, she tried to keep her voice from giving away her emotional response to his heartfelt words. "You just met me."

He kissed the back of her hand and then released it to tuck her arm under the warm blanket. "You matter to me."

"Why?"

"Do I have to have a reason? Can't it just be because I like you? That I like spending time with you, that I like what you did for that dog even if I don't like that you risked your own safety to do it?"

The intense moment between them was interrupted when a nurse came in to check on Julia. She took her temperature and blood pressure again. "Your temp is up a little, which is good. Do you feel warmer?"

"Getting there." Julia wondered if she'd ever feel warm again. Since she had hardly any body fat, she was almost always cold to begin with. A dip in the still-frigid Atlantic had been about the last thing she'd needed, but she had no regrets. Deacon's sweet words had given her a warm fuzzy feeling on the inside that made the rescue mission doubly worth it.

"Let's get you cleaned up, young man," the older woman said as she approached Deacon.

"Can we do it here so I can stay with Julia?"

She looked at each of them and smiled. "It's like that, is it? Of course. I understand you want to be with your girlfriend. I'll go get what I need to clean that wound."

After she left the room, Julia looked up at him, amused by the nurse's misunderstanding. "So now I'm your girlfriend?"

"If you'd like to be."

"I told you I'm done with all that."

"Ah yes, the dick diet. How could I forget?"

Julia's face burned with embarrassment. What had she been thinking telling him that? "I probably should think before I speak so bluntly."

"Please don't." His gorgeous golden eyes became even more so when he smiled like he was now. "I think it's awesome. If I'd been through what you have, I'd be on a dick diet, too." He paused, seemed to realize what he'd said and then laughed. "Not that I'm a fan of dick other than my own, mind you. I'm a *big* fan of his. Underline the word *big*."

By then, Julia was laughing helplessly. "Stop. I can't."

"You're even more beautiful when you laugh."

Before she could formulate a response to that, the nurse came bustling in with a tray of supplies. "All right, young man, let's see what you've got going on."

He grimaced at Julia and offered his arm to the nurse.

Julia couldn't look away from him. Just when she was sure there wasn't one good man left in the world, she'd met Deacon Taylor. He was giving her reason to question everything, especially her dick diet.

Maybe if she took a spin with him, she'd begin to feel better about what'd happened with Mike.

No. No, no, no. This was what she always did. Swore off men until the next charmer came along and made her willpower disappear in a cloud of smoke. Just because Deacon seemed better than most didn't mean anything. She'd found out the hard way that they always seemed better than most until they showed her who they really were.

She refused to be swayed by another handsome face and more sweet words, even if they seemed sincere.

He winced when the nurse squeezed the wound to produce more blood that she wiped away before thoroughly cleaning it and covering it with gauze. "You're going to want to stay on top of it by regularly applying antibiotic ointment and keeping the wound clean and dry. Do we know the animal's vaccination history?"

"We don't," Deacon said, "and we won't know if he's positive for rabies until he's observed for the next ten days."

"If he's positive, we'll need you back for treatment."

"I already had rabies treatment when I was bitten five years ago."

"Then you might still be covered, but we'll need blood work to confirm."

"Got it."

A couple of hours later, after Julia's grandmother delivered dry clothes for her, they were both discharged when Julia's body temperature returned to normal, even if she still felt chilled to the bone. They were surprised to find Blaine in the waiting room.

"Have you been here all this time?" Deacon asked.

"I left for a while and came back to give you a ride home."

"Oh, thanks." Deacon sounded surprised.

"Where to?" Blaine asked when they were in his SUV.

"The vet, please," Julia said, trying not to shiver from the chilly spring air coming in through Blaine's open window.

"Put the window up, will ya?" Deacon asked. "Julia needs to stay warm."

"Oh, sorry."

With everything Deacon said and did, Julia had to fight harder to remind herself that he was off-limits to her as anything other than a friend. The one thing she couldn't deny, however, was her growing attraction to him. Man diet or not, this man had the potential to be big trouble, and she needed to keep herself in check or run the risk of diving into something new before she'd fully dealt with her last disaster.

That could not happen.

Keep reminding yourself of that.

Deacon turned from his spot in the passenger seat to check on her. "You doing okay?"

"I'm fine. How's your arm?"

"It's good. Nothing to worry about."

"You look like you got shot," Blaine said, referring to the blood all over Deacon's formerly pristine shirt and shorts.

Deacon glanced down at his clothing, seeming surprised to realize it was covered in blood. "I hope it comes out. This is the only good shirt I brought with me."

"I know how to get it out. I'll do it for you." Julia spoke before she took a second to consider the implications of getting in deeper by the second with him. It was just friendship. As long as she remembered that, it would be fine.

"Hey, um," Blaine said to Deacon, "so I wanted to say I'm sorry for what happened at my house earlier. I never should've said what I did. Of course you're welcome in my home and with my family."

Deacon stared at his brother. "Have you had a stroke or something equally mind-altering?"

"Shut up and accept my apology, will you please?"

"Why?"

"Because! I mean it. I'm sorry I said what I did. You weren't doing anything wrong, and I totally overreacted to you being in my house with my wife and daughter. I was out of line, and I'm admitting it."

Deacon continued to stare at his brother for a long moment, and then he smiled. "Tiffany's pissed at you, right?"

"No."

"Yes, she is, and she made you apologize to me. Did she shut you off until you did?" He busted up laughing. "Oh my God! She did! She's closed for business until you fix this with me, right? I *love* her."

"Shut up," Blaine said on a low growl.

"Do I have to tell her you apologized to me before the red light

93

turns green again? Oh damn, I'm gonna be *really* busy over the next week or two with my new job and everything. I might not get a chance to talk to her."

"You'd better tell her *today* that I apologized to you—and that I meant it, which I did."

Deacon hooted with laughter.

Julia put her hand over her mouth so she wouldn't be tempted to join him. She had a feeling Blaine wouldn't appreciate that.

"You really met your match with her, didn't you, bro?" Deacon said when his laughter subsided.

"Something like that." Blaine sounded like he was speaking through gritted teeth.

"I love it. I already knew I liked her, but this takes it to a whole other level. And guess what? Your precious Addie loves me, too. She and I are gonna be best friends."

Blaine seethed silently, his entire body stiff with tension.

"Still want me here for the summer?"

"Fuck no, but you're staying, and that's the end of it."

"This is gonna be an awesome summer. I got my new best friend Julia to entertain me. I've got my nieces to hang out with and my other new best friend Tiffany to get to know. Gansett Island is looking so much better to me this time around. I really have to give you credit, Blaine. You knew just what I needed."

"I'm gonna fucking shoot you before this summer is over."

"If you want to get laid, I'd recommend against that. Tiffany digs me."

"She does not."

"Oh, yes, she does, and that just chaps your ass, doesn't it?"

"You want to know what *really* chaps my ass?"

"I bet I can guess." Deacon lost it laughing. "Having to apologize to me so your wife will reopen for business?"

Blaine pulled up to the vet clinic and brought the SUV to an abrupt halt. "Get out."

Rather than open the door, Deacon seemed to make himself more comfortable in Blaine's passenger seat. "So you're counting on me to report in that you apologized, am I right?"

Julia had to bite her lip to keep from laughing out loud. Deacon was enjoying this way too much.

"Do you mind getting out of my truck so I can get back to work?"

"Of course," Deacon said. "Thanks for the ride. I'll try to schedule some time to have a chat with Tiffany to get you back in the saddle. Not sure I'll be able to fit it in today since I have to make sure Julia's all warmed up and our little puppy is okay. Might be a while before I can get with Tiffany, but I'll be sure to clear things up for you just as soon as I can."

"You do that."

Deacon got out of the passenger seat, opened the back door for Julia and held out a hand to help her out.

She didn't need help, but she took his hand anyway and was surprised when he held on to it after she was out of the car.

Blaine sped off, leaving a cloud of dust in his wake.

Deacon lost it laughing.

CHAPTER 11

"That was the most fun I've had in decades," Deacon said, eyeing the taillights of his brother's vehicle.

"That was mean."

"Oh, come on. Give me a break. He's been busting my balls since I was old enough to walk. This is the first time I've ever had a leg up on him, and you'd better believe I'm going to enjoy it."

"I said it was mean. I never said it wasn't funny as hell."

Laughing, Deacon held the door to the vet clinic for her and ushered her in with a hand on the small of her back.

The proprietary way he touched her gave Julia mixed feelings. On the one hand, she wanted to tell him to knock it off. They were just friends, and there was no need to touch her the way he would a lover. But on the other hand, he'd been nothing but kind and helpful to her, and she didn't want to be a shrew about some harmless touching.

And then there was the fact that she kind of liked it when he touched her.

Dear God, she was hopeless. Her man diet hadn't lasted four full months, and she was already having all the feels for a new guy. But this guy… He seemed different. And yes, at first, Mike had, too. But that hadn't lasted long. There'd been signs he wasn't all he'd pretended to be long before he asked her to help with his mother's medical expenses.

She was so tired of being such a fool when it came to men, and even though she wanted Deacon to be different, she was still wary.

Janey was at the front desk again when they entered the vet clinic. "Hey, guys, you're both looking a little better. Are you all warmed up?"

"Yes, thank goodness," Julia said. "How's my little buddy?"

"He's doing great. We've got him on some fluids, and he's mostly been sleeping. The poor guy is exhausted."

"Can we take him home?"

"Doc Potter wants to keep him here for observation possibly overnight. We can let you know in a couple of hours."

"Um, how much will all that cost?"

"Don't worry about it," Deacon said. "I'll cover it."

Julia wanted to protest, but how could she? There was no way she could cover a hefty vet bill. Not right now, anyway. "Thanks."

"Let me get your number so I can call you when he's set to be released," Janey said.

Julia recited her phone number.

"Great. I'll call you."

"Thanks again, Janey."

"No problem. I'm so glad you guys found him in time."

"That was all Julia," Deacon said. "She's the one who saved him."

Most of the men Julia had met would've taken credit for the rescue. They would've said it was their boat, and they were the one who'd been bitten during the rescue. But not Deacon. He gave her all the credit, despite having been more seriously injured.

They said their goodbyes to Janey and left the clinic, beginning the short walk back to the Sand & Surf Hotel.

"What're you up to for the rest of the day?" Deacon asked.

"I don't have any plans."

"You ought to take it easy and stay warm. Get in bed and watch a movie."

"That actually sounds perfect." She glanced at him. "You want to watch it with me?"

Her invitation surprised him, but he made a poor effort to hide that. "What kind of movie are we talking about?"

"Something like *Sex and the City* or *Dirty Dancing*."

"Hmmm, as appealing as that sounds…"

Julia cracked up laughing. "Just kidding."

"Oh, thank God. I thought you were so cool until you went and ruined it with *Dirty Dancing*."

"That movie is a classic. Everyone loves it."

"No, not everyone."

"This might be a deal breaker."

He cast her a comically puzzled look. "Do we have a deal? I'm still not sure."

"We have a deal to be friends, and friends watch TV together."

"Ah, got it. So you'll be the only one *in* the bed. I see how it is."

"Exactly." He was endlessly amusing. She had to give him that.

"Well, that's not as much fun as it could be, but I'll take what I can get."

Julia couldn't allow herself to think about the many other kinds of fun she might have with him in a bed.

They entered the lobby of the Surf, where a woman Julia didn't know was working at the desk. She nodded to them as they went up the stairs. Julia was thankful that she'd gotten in without anyone from her family seeing her with Deacon. She hadn't considered the potential for gossip when she'd casually invited him to join her in her room.

Why had she done that, exactly? Because she enjoyed his company and wanted more of it. That was the simple explanation. The other, far more complex explanation wasn't something she cared to think about right then, not when she needed all the fortitude she could muster to remember that she wasn't in any condition to get involved with yet another man.

JULIA'S INVITATION HAD SURPRISED HIM. DEACON HAD EXPECTED TO walk her back to the hotel and tell her he'd see her tomorrow, when they would figure out what to do about the dog they now apparently owned together.

They had a baby! And he hadn't even kissed her yet. Deacon wisely chose to keep that thought to himself as he followed her up to the hotel's third floor.

He really wanted to kiss her. She had the sweetest, sexiest lips, and the expressive eyes that gave away her every thought, every fear and every wish had him all twisted up inside, wanting to soothe and comfort and provide whatever she wanted or needed.

Blaine would say he was doing his hero act again, but it wasn't that. Exactly. It was something else with her, something deeper and more compelling than anything he'd experienced before. It should've scared him to be so drawn to a woman who wasn't in the market for the sort of things he wanted from her, but it didn't.

He could be patient when he needed to be, and he had a feeling she'd be worth the effort. More than anything, he wanted to show her that not all men were jerks, that some could be trusted to be honest and straightforward.

When they were in her room, she gestured for him to take the second bed while she got comfortable in the one she'd left unmade. The room was so small, it might've been mistaken for a closet. Other than the twin beds separated by a tiny bedside table, there was only a dresser with a flat-screen TV and an equally tiny adjoining bathroom.

"This was my summer home when I was a kid."

Before he sat on his assigned bed, Deacon went to the one window to check out the view of endless ocean. He could picture Julia curled up on the window seat as a girl, looking out at the water and dreaming of a different life than the one she'd had waiting for her at home. It must've been torture for her and her siblings to leave this place at the end of every summer. He wished he could ask her about that, but he never would. He could only hope that someday she'd share that part of her story with him.

"I can see why you loved it," he said, turning away from the window to kick off his shoes and sit on the other bed.

Julia had curled up on her bed and wrapped a blanket around her shoulders. She looked much better than she had earlier, but a tinge of blue remained in her lips. "Do you want me to get you some tea or soup or something warm?"

"You don't have to."

"I know I don't have to, but I'm offering anyway."

"Maybe some soup from Stephanie's?"

He stood, shoved his feet back into his Sperrys and headed for the door. "Coming right up."

"Let me give you some money."

"I've got it. Be right back." He went downstairs to the restaurant and ordered the ultimate comfort food—takeout bowls of tomato soup and grilled cheese sandwiches for both of them. While he waited, he checked out the dinner menu and decided he'd like to take Julia to Stephanie's Bistro if she ever agreed to a real date with him. The more time he spent with her, the more he hoped she'd agree to that real date.

Despite what she said about wanting to keep her distance, he'd caught her looking at him a few times, as if she was seeing something she wanted but couldn't allow herself to have. He totally got why she'd erected walls around her heart after the nightmare with her ex.

Speaking of that, when he got back upstairs, they were going to make a plan for how they were going to handle him. He wasn't going to get away with stealing from her. Not if Deacon had anything to say about it.

When their order was ready, he took it back upstairs and encountered Julia's mother and her new husband coming down the stairs as he went up.

"Hi, Deacon. How was your boat ride?"

"Eventful." He told them about rescuing the puppy and their trip to the clinic.

Sarah did a double take when she noticed the blood on his shirt that'd been partially hidden by the takeout bag. "Are you all right? Is Julia?"

"We're both fine, and so is the puppy. Your daughter was amazing. She dove right off the boat to get to him."

"That sounds like her. She always wanted a pet growing up, but her father said we had enough mouths to feed. I thought she'd get a dog or a cat as soon as she had her own place, but Katie has allergies, so she never did."

"I hope she gets to keep this one."

"I do, too."

"I'd better get this soup to her. We're still trying to get her warmed up."

"Thank you for taking care of her, Deacon."

"It's my pleasure. Thank you again for inviting me to your wedding brunch. I enjoyed it very much."

"We're glad you could join us."

"Enjoy your first day as Mr. and Mrs."

The two of them beamed with happiness. "That's the plan," Sarah said. "We'll see you later."

When they parted company, Deacon continued to the third floor. He walked into Julia's room, where she was still where he'd left her. The one thing he immediately noticed was that her lips had lost the luster of blue, which was a welcome development.

He served up the soup and sandwich for her and sat on the other bed to eat his.

Julia took tentative sips of the soup and a few bites of the sandwich at first, as if she wasn't sure the food would be welcome by her stomach.

"Taste okay?"

"It's really good. Thank you."

After they ate in silence for a few more minutes, Deacon said, "Let's talk about the guy that stole from you and how we're going to get your money back."

"I LIKE HIM FOR JULIA," SARAH SAID AS SHE AND CHARLIE EMERGED INTO warm sunshine on the hotel's front porch. They'd spent time with each of her children before they were due to take the ferry back to their real lives and had the rest of the day free to spend together.

"He seems like a very nice young man."

"If he's anything like his brother, she'd be very lucky to have him in her life."

Charlie put his arm around her and brought her in close to him, where she fit perfectly in the shelter of his muscular body. "Do I need to be concerned about this crush you seem to have on Blaine Taylor?"

Sarah giggled like a girl. She did that a lot around him. "Don't be silly. I'm old enough to be his mother."

"That doesn't mean anything in this day and age."

"Blaine was a very good friend to me when I desperately needed one, and he'll always have a special place in my heart. But as you know, most of my heart belongs only to you."

"I know, babe."

"Today was so great, wasn't it?"

"One of the best days of my life. If you'd asked me a couple years ago if I'd ever get married again, I would've said no freaking way."

"Me, too. Last thing I thought I'd ever want to do again." Her first marriage had been a complete nightmare from start to finish, except for the seven beautiful children who had come from it. Thank God for them.

"But along came my sweet, sexy Sarah, and suddenly, the only thing I wanted was a ring on my finger and promises of forever with you."

He made her feel things she never had before. "I want everyone we love to be as happy as we are."

"I do, too, but today, on our day, I think we need to focus on *our* happiness." As he spoke, he directed them toward his truck, which was parked in the lot behind the hotel.

"And how would you like to do that?"

He held the passenger door for her and waited for her to get settled. "First of all, I'd like to go home for a while to be alone with my wife."

"Your wife would like that very much."

"After that? We can do whatever we want. Anything at all. Every day. Forever."

"I can't think of anything better than that."

He leaned in to kiss her. "Neither can I."

KEVIN HAD FORGOTTEN HOW ALL-CONSUMING CARING FOR A NEW infant could be. In truth, he'd never really known how all-consuming it was the first time around because his wife had done most of the heavy lifting. Everything was different now. He was older, wiser and well aware of how precious this time was with his baby daughter.

He had a *daughter*.

The thrill of saying that word continued the day after Summer's early arrival. Chelsea had wanted to come home as soon as possible, and when David declared mother and daughter good to go, Kevin had brought them home first thing that morning. Victoria would be by to check on them later, but otherwise, they were on their own with their little bundle of joy.

Chelsea was still wiped out from the delivery, and other than waking up to breastfeed the baby, she'd been sleeping a lot. Which meant Kevin was on duty with his little angel, and he wouldn't have it any other way. His brothers had been by the clinic to visit earlier and had promised to check on them later.

Kevin had received a text from Katie asking him to please fit her sister Julia into his schedule as soon as possible. He planned to reach out to Julia when Chelsea was awake again. There was no way Katie would've asked for his assistance right now unless it was badly needed.

The screen door opened with a telltale squeak that had Kevin turning to see who was there. He smiled at Finn and Chloe as they tiptoed into the house.

"We weren't sure if it was okay to come by," Finn whispered, gazing at the baby sleeping in his father's arms.

"Of course it is." Kevin carefully transferred the baby to her brother, who took her into his arms with a look of pure awe.

"Are you sure I should be holding her?" Finn asked. "She's so little. I'm afraid I'll break her."

"She won't break," Kevin assured him, amused by Finn's reaction to her.

Finn sat on the sofa, and Chloe perched next to him, both of them completely focused on the baby.

"How's Chelsea?" Chloe asked.

"Tired, but she's doing great."

"And you?" Finn glanced at Kevin. "How're you holding up?"

"I'm tired, too, but it's the best kind of tired. She's a doll."

"I can't believe I have a sister. It's so cool."

"I'm glad you think so."

"Of course I do. She's awesome. Riley and I are going to spoil her rotten. We've already got a puppy picked out for her."

"No puppies until she's at least three, you hear me?"

"We'll see about that."

"What're you two up to today?"

"Going to the official grand opening of the Wayfarer," Finn said. "From what Riley told me, things are crazy over there. Nikki worked all night to get ready."

"I'm sure she'll be glad to get the grand opening behind them," Kevin said.

Finn nodded in agreement. "They both will. She's been so insanely busy that poor Riley is feeling neglected."

Chloe rolled her eyes. "Poor Riley. Whatever. Nikki is a master multitasker. I'm sure he's not suffering too badly."

"Do you guys mind if I grab a quick shower while you're here?" Kevin asked.

Finn's eyes bugged. "You mean leave her *alone* with us?"

Kevin laughed. "Just for a minute. I promise."

"We got it," Chloe said. "Go ahead, Kev."

"I ain't got it," Finn said. "Not even kinda."

"You will," Kevin assured his son. "Before long, it'll be routine to have a little one around. It'll be good training for when you have kids of your own." With both his "boys" settling into committed relationships in recent months, Kevin knew it probably wouldn't be long before he added *grandfather* to his list of titles.

As he took a quick shower and shaved the scruff off his face, he marveled at how his whole life had changed in the last couple of years. Had he expected to be newly married with a new baby at nearly fifty-three? Hell no, but the joy Chelsea and now Summer brought to his life was immeasurable.

After he was dressed, he took a minute to text Katie's sister Julia, asking when she might be available to get together. He'd planned to take a few weeks off from work to be with Chelsea and the baby, but he would squeeze Julia in, even if she had to come to the house.

When he rejoined Finn and Chloe in the living room, he found that Chloe was holding the baby while Finn watched over them. Finn was madly in love with Chloe and had recently moved into her place. He expected to hear they were engaged any time now.

Riley and Nikki were already engaged and planning a fall wedding at the Chesterfield.

Things had fallen into place for all of them since he and his sons came to Gansett Island for Kevin's niece Laura's wedding two summers ago and decided to stay for a while. Spending time on the island had helped to heal the wounds from the unexpected end of Kevin's marriage and had led him to a new, unexpected love with Chelsea.

And now they had a *daughter*, and his sons had a *sister*.

If a heart could overflow with love, Kevin's was at the tipping point.

"Why's he looking at us like that?" Finn asked Chloe.

"I suspect he's overwhelmed by everything that's happened in the last few days."

"You suspect correctly," Kevin said, sitting across from them.

"She sure is beautiful," Chloe said.

Kevin thought Summer was the most beautiful baby girl he'd ever seen. "Thank you. We think so, too."

Chloe got up and carefully transferred the sleeping baby back to Kevin's arms. "I'm going to need to see her again very soon."

"Any time you want. We're here, and the company is always welcome."

Chloe kissed his cheek. "Congrats again, Kev. She's a stunner."

"Thankfully, she looks just like her mother."

Finn smiled as he bent to kiss the baby's forehead. "I see you in her, too, Dad. We'll be back soon."

"Tell Nikki that Chelsea and I said good luck today."

"We will."

After they left, Kevin went into the bedroom to check on Chelsea, who was just stirring from a long nap. She opened her eyes and looked at him, her smile lighting up her face.

"There're my two favorite people. How is she?"

"She's delightful. She just had a nice visit with her brother Finn and Chloe. They're absolutely smitten."

"Of course they are. Who wouldn't be?" She sat up and grimaced as she tried to find a comfortable position. Then she reached for the baby.

Seeing the two of them together, Kevin realized that even though he was sleep-deprived and loopy, he was also happier than he'd been in a very long time. Since meeting Chelsea, he'd come to realize how much he'd missed out on by staying in a bad marriage for far too long. Now he understood there was a huge difference between existing and truly living.

"Can I get you anything?" he asked Chelsea.

She looked up at him, eyes brimming with emotion and unshed tears. "You've already given me everything I ever wanted and then some."

Kevin leaned in to kiss her and then leaned his forehead against hers as they gazed down at the wonder they'd created together.

CHAPTER 12

"Start from the beginning." Deacon opened a notebook he'd found on Julia's desk and used a Sand & Surf Hotel pen to take notes. "I need his full name, address, date of birth and anything else you can give me that'll help the local police track him down."

Julia had bought the notebook to start a new journal, but hadn't written anything in it yet, so it was safe for him to use. While he was stretched out on the other bed, she lay on her side so she could see him, still bundled under the blanket.

She recited the man's full name, address and date of birth from memory. "I met Michael, who goes by Mike, through a friend from work. He saw my picture on one of her Facebook posts and asked her about me. She fixed us up."

"How did she know him?"

"He was in a softball league with her husband."

"How long have they known him?"

"A couple of years, but only through softball. They didn't hang out with him other than that."

"So they fixed you up with someone they don't really know all that well."

"They were upfront with me about that. They said they knew him through softball, but not too much beyond that."

"How did you connect with him?"

"At first, we messaged through Facebook, which evolved into talking on the phone and then FaceTime. We had great conversations about our families, our work and lives. He told me about how his mom battled cancer on and off since he was a kid and how that affected him. I shared some things about my life that I rarely talk about. I felt like we'd made a real connection before we ever met in person."

"How long had you known him before you met in person?"

"About four weeks. I took it slowly because I have a bad habit of jumping into things with men and getting in too deep before I realize they're no good. I wanted to do better."

"Where and when did you meet him?"

"We went to a Tex-Mex restaurant because we'd learned that we both loved that kind of food best. It was a Saturday night about five months ago. I can look up the exact date."

"That'd be good to have."

Julia consulted the calendar on her cell phone and gave him the date from late December.

"Did he pick you up, or did you meet him there?"

"I met him."

"What happened that night?" Deacon asked without looking up from the notebook where he was recording the details.

"We had a really good time. The conversation flowed easily with no awkward silences, and I thought he was even more attractive in person." Julia could still remember the hopeful feeling that'd come from meeting someone special, or so she'd thought.

"Do you have photos?"

Julia shook her head. "Not anymore. I deleted them all."

"Does your phone back up to the cloud?"

"Yes..."

"Then you still have them. I need them to show that you thought you were in a genuine relationship with him."

"I'll get them." The thought of seeing his face again made her stomach turn, but she'd do whatever she had to if there was a chance of making him pay for what he'd done to her.

"What happened after dinner?"

"We went to the bar in the restaurant where they had live music and had a drink."

"How did the evening end?"

"He walked me to my car and kissed me good night. I liked that he didn't get aggressive with me the way so many guys tend to do. He was a perfect gentleman." Talking about something she'd much rather forget was beyond painful, but Deacon had convinced her it was worth the effort. If they could recoup the money she'd given Mike, that would mean everything to her.

"When did you see him again?"

"Two days later. He texted me the next day to say what a great time he'd had and how he couldn't wait to see me again. We met for dinner after work that Tuesday night and then again on Thursday. On Saturday, he took me on a picnic by a lake, and when we came back to my place that night, I asked him if he wanted to come in."

Julia swallowed hard as emotion threatened to get the better of her. She'd been so certain that she'd finally found a good man who wanted her for the right reasons.

"I know it's hard to talk about, darlin', but every detail you can give me will help to build the case against him."

What did it say about her and her dick diet that her heart skipped a beat when he called her that? "It is hard to talk about. How do I ever trust my own instincts again after this?"

"You will. When the time and the situation are right, you'll know."

She shook her head. "I'll never know for certain."

"Yes, you will." The fierce look he gave her did weird things to her insides, making her feel safe and protected and—

Stop.

You don't need him or any man to make you feel safe or protected. He's doing you a favor. That's all this is.

"He spent the night, and it was great. After that, we were pretty much together all the time. My friend who fixed us up was so excited that she'd introduced me to someone I really liked. I'd had a rough year after Katie moved here when she met Shane at Owen's wedding. After I met Mike, I felt like things were finally getting back on track."

"The thing I don't get is how did he have someone else on the side if you guys were together most of the time?"

"I wondered that, too, after it all came to light. I figured out that she worked nights as a nurse, so she had no idea he was with me when she was at work."

"Does she know now?"

"I don't think she has any idea that I ever existed."

"That'll change as soon as there're charges filed against him."

"You really think they'll charge him?"

"They'll have no choice but to charge him if we hand them an airtight case." He shifted to find a more comfortable position, the movement stretching the fabric of his shirt over well-defined muscles.

Julia didn't want to notice his well-defined muscles, but she couldn't help but stare anyway. Deacon was a finely built man and had turned into a rather good friend over the last two days.

"Tell me about how he ended up asking you for the money."

"We'd been together a few weeks, and it was still really good between us. He was always bringing me little presents and buying me dinner. Once, he sent flowers to me at work, just because he was thinking of me." After receiving those flowers, she'd told the coworker who introduced them that she was falling in love with him. Julia blinked back tears when she thought of that day and how excited she'd been.

"Are you okay?" Deacon asked.

"I will be." She felt like she'd torn the scab off a healing wound. "One night, he came over with pizza for dinner, and from the moment he arrived, he was different. I asked him what was wrong, and he said nothing I needed to worry about. But as the night went on, he was more and more distracted. We were watching a movie when I looked over and saw tears running down his face. I pleaded with him to talk to me, and that's when he said his mom's cancer had come back. She needed experimental treatment that wasn't covered by insurance. He apologized profusely for dumping his troubles on me. He said he would just go and that he was sorry. I asked how much they needed, and he said twenty-five thousand. I said I could give him fifteen."

"What did he say?"

"He said he could never take money from me but that he loved me for caring—and for many other reasons. That was the first time he'd said anything about love, and with hindsight, I can see that was all part of the plan. He played me from the beginning, and that was his kill shot."

"You said earlier that you sent him the money through Venmo."

"Right."

"And he just took it?"

"No, at first he said he couldn't take it, but he appreciated so much that I cared enough to offer it. I said this was no time to be worried about anything other than whatever his mother needed. I convinced him to give me his Venmo address, and I sent him the money in two transactions. He cried some more and hugged me and told me how much I meant to him before we ended up in my bed having sex. By the time he left the next morning, I was emotionally whipped and totally in love with him. All I could think about was how I could help him get the rest of the money he needed for her treatment."

"What happened then?"

"Nothing," Julia said softly. "I never heard from him again. The first couple of days, I figured he was dealing with his mom and trying to get the rest of the money. After five days of silence, I broached the subject with my work friend, who suddenly didn't want to talk about him or my burgeoning relationship with him. One night after work, I confronted her in the parking lot, and she started crying right away. I couldn't figure out what the hell was wrong with her until she told me he had someone else, that they were expecting a baby. Apparently, she'd only just found this out a few days earlier and had no idea how to tell me. She kept apologizing over and over again for introducing me to someone who'd do this to me. Of course, she had no idea that I'd given him the money."

"You didn't tell her?"

Julia shook her head. "I could barely breathe after hearing what she had to say. It was all I could do to drive myself home. I have to admit that I didn't believe her until I dug a little deeper on his social media and learned it was true. I called out of work the next two days, and that's when I lost my job. The new boss had been looking for a reason to get rid of me, and I handed it to him. I didn't even care that I'd been fired. Fortunately, I'd already bought a plane ticket to my sister's wedding, or I wouldn't have been able to get here. Within a few weeks, I had to give up my apartment because I couldn't find a new roommate, and I couldn't afford the lease renewal after I lost my job. I put my stuff in storage, which was a lot cheaper than the rent, and camped out on my friend's sofa. I couldn't believe how fast everything went to total shit."

"You're the victim of a crime, Julia. It's not your fault that things went to shit."

"I trusted him, believed him, had feelings for him. Surely some of it is my fault."

"None of it is. You were conned by someone who's probably done this before."

"What happens now?" Julia asked, drained after reliving the nightmare.

"Now I type this up and provide photos, texts, the Venmo transaction log and anything else you can give me to back up your story, and send it off to the local police. Which town did you live in at the time he took the money?"

"Plano."

He made a note of that. "I expect they'll take it very seriously, and I'll venture to guess we're going to find out this isn't the first time he's done this."

"How do people get away with doing stuff like this?"

"Primarily because victims don't report it to the authorities. They think the money is gone, so what's the point? The point is stopping them from doing it again and possibly getting restitution."

"Do you really think I'll ever see the money again?"

"I think you have a good chance. He bought a house, so there's equity there. The court could order him to take a line of credit on the house to pay back your money, if it actually goes to court. The cops will probably give him the option of making restitution to avoid charges."

For the first time, Julia felt a tiny glimmer of hope that she might get back the nest egg she'd willingly given to Mike.

Deacon got up and came to sit on the edge of her bed. He took hold of her hand and linked their fingers.

Julia's mouth went dry from his nearness and the wildfire of need that his touch set off inside her. Her first impulse was to pull back from him, to tell him to get away from her, to leave her alone. But she couldn't get the words out.

"I'm so sorry this happened to you," he said, speaking softly, his eyes conveying sympathy and rage at the same time. "The only thing you did wrong here, Julia, was care about someone who didn't deserve it. You're a good person who tried to help someone. If there were more good people like you in this world, it would be a much better place."

"Do you really think so?"

"I know so. When you're a cop, you see the best and the worst of what people are capable of. He took your money. Don't give him your kindness, too."

"Thank you." She squeezed his hand. "For believing me and trying to help. Even if nothing comes of it, I appreciate you trying."

"Something will come of it. I'll make sure of that."

"What's in it for you?"

He gave her a side-eyed look. "What do you mean?"

"Why does it matter if I get my money back?"

"First of all, because you're a good person who tried to help someone and got screwed for your troubles, and second of all, I fucking hate bullies and people who take advantage of the kindness of others. He needs to be brought to justice, and I can't wait for him to get his comeuppance."

His ferocity made her smile. "I wouldn't want to cross you."

"You'd have nothing to fear from me if you crossed me. You know that, don't you?"

Julia was taken aback by the statement as much as the emotion behind it. "Someone told you."

He acted surprised. "Told me what?"

"About my family." Abuse is like a stain that can't be scrubbed away no matter how hard you try. The shame is always with you, no matter how far removed you are from it.

"Yeah. I heard about your dad, and I'm so sorry you went through everything you did with him."

Julia tried to pull her hand free of his. "Is that why you're being so nice to me? Because you feel sorry for me?"

Rather than release her hand, he brought it to his lips. "That's not why."

Julia could barely breathe as she waited to see what he would do next. "Then why?"

"Because I think you're awesome. The way you rescued that dog without a thought to your own safety was amazing. Not to mention, you gave someone all your money without blinking an eye because he needed it more than you did, or so you thought. Who wouldn't want to be friends with you?"

Julia noticed that he made no reference to her physical appearance. In her experience, that was always the first thing men noticed about her. That he hadn't even listed it gave him even more points than he'd already earned with her.

"I'm not going to lie to you, Julia. I'd like to be more than friends with you, but I understand that I'm going to have to earn your trust after what you've been through. So I'm going to work on earning your trust, starting with nailing the bastard who scammed you and getting your money back. I'm going to my place to type this up on my laptop and do some research on who I need to contact to file the complaint. Send me the pictures and any text history, and I'll add them to the report." He pulled the pages he'd written on out of the notebook, wrote down his email address and phone number and handed her the notebook. "Text me when the vet calls, and I'll go with you to pick up your little boy."

He had her on the verge of abandoning her man moratorium with his softly spoken words and the sincerity behind them, so she chose to focus on the dog as her head spun from the other things he'd said. "Do you think I'll get to keep him?"

"If no one claims him, I'm sure you will. You're the one that saved him."

"We both saved him."

"Does that mean we'll have joint custody?" His eyes twinkled with amusement, which was a good look on him.

He was so damned cute all the time, but when he smiled, it was all Julia could do to remember her dick diet. "I'd be very happy to share him with you."

"Get some rest. I'll be back." He stood, seeming reluctant to leave her. At the door, he turned back to her. "I'm sorry about the men who hurt you, Julia. I promise I won't be one of them."

Julia fell back on the pillow, blown away by him, the things he'd said and the sincerity with which he'd said them. Yes, other men had seemed sincere in the moment, but Deacon was different. How she knew that she couldn't say for certain, but everything about him and the time she'd spent with him was different than it had ever been before. Maybe she would end up being wrong about him, too, but what if he was exactly as great as he seemed?

Wouldn't that be something?

Despite her best efforts to stay removed from him and the attraction she felt toward him, a tiny glimmer of hope blossomed inside her that couldn't be ignored.

If she got her money back, she'd be free to leave and go back to Texas to pick up the pieces of her life there. Or, she could stay on Gansett Island for the summer and get to know Deacon better while spending time with her family.

Getting to know Deacon better was becoming a more appealing option with every minute she spent in his presence. He was proving to be a rather good friend in addition to being devastatingly handsome and sexy.

She spent thirty minutes getting him the photos and screenshots of the text messages that he'd requested. Seeing Mike's face again brought back all the hopes she'd pinned on him. Bitterness churned in her stomach when she recalled how effortlessly he'd earned her trust and then stolen from her.

She emailed the photos and screenshots to Deacon and hoped that would be the last time she'd ever have to look at the face of the handsome charmer who'd played her for a fool.

Spent after the unpleasant trip down memory lane, Julia dozed off for a while, coming to when someone knocked at her door. She got up to open the door and was surprised to find her mother there. "What're you doing here? I thought you were off on your honeymoon." She stepped aside to admit Sarah.

"The rest of our life is going to be a honeymoon," Sarah said, blushing. "Charlie and I got home, but I couldn't stop thinking about you, so I asked if he minded if I came back over for a few minutes to check on you."

Julia sat on her bed and pulled the blanket back over her. How could she *still* be cold? "I'm fine, Mom. Go back to your husband."

Sarah sat on the other bed. "You're not fine, Julia, and that's obvious to all of us. Tell me what's going on."

"Just another relationship that ended in dramatic fashion. Nothing to be concerned about. I'm handling it."

"Are you? You left your sister's wedding yesterday without a word to anyone. You took off today in the midst of my wedding. You didn't eat anything yesterday or this morning."

Julia wanted to remind her mother that she was far too old to have to explain herself to anyone, least of all her mother, but she held back words that would make this situation worse. "I've had a rough couple of months. All the wedding joy has been difficult for me to handle in light of the breakup. I'm sorry for making you worry. That wasn't my intention."

"I'm sorry you're hurting, sweetheart."

Julia shrugged. "Seems to be all I know how to do."

Sarah moved to Julia's bed and put her arm around her daughter. "There was a time, not that long ago, when I would've said the same thing. I didn't know anything but how to hurt. And now… everything is different, and I so want you to have that, too."

"Not everyone is meant to find their Charlie, Mom. I don't even want that anymore. Men have caused me nothing but heartache my entire life. I'm over it."

"Don't say that. If you close your heart off to the possibility of love, you could miss out on the greatest thing to ever happen to you. I'm thankful all the time that I had the courage to try again with Charlie. At first, I was resistant because I expected him to be just like your father, but he's nothing like him. He's your father's polar opposite. Since I've been here on Gansett, I've met so many good men. They've restored my faith in humanity." She smoothed Julia's hair back from her face, the gesture so familiar and so comforting, it brought tears to Julia's eyes. "One of the best men I've met is your friend Deacon's brother Blaine. He was so very good to me when I arrived here fresh off being beaten by your father. Without him, I don't think your father would be in prison today."

"He seems a little intense. He and Deacon don't get along very well."

"He may be intense, but he's very good at his job and is madly in love with his wife and daughters. He's a good man, and I get the feeling Deacon is, too."

"He's been a good friend to me when I needed one."

"Will you do something for me? Something big and important and probably something you don't want to do?"

"What?"

"Give Deacon a chance to show you what it's like to be with a good man."

"I don't want any man, good or bad. I've had enough. If I don't put myself out there, I can't get hurt again."

"Can I tell you something my Charlie has taught me?"

"I guess."

117

"When we let the past define our present and future, we prove that we haven't learned anything from what we've been through. What happened with your father and the other men who've disappointed you is in the past. If you let them hold you back from the chance to be truly happy, then what have you learned?"

"I hear what you're saying, and I appreciate the wisdom—yours and Charlie's. The two of you certainly deserve the happiness you've found together. But just because you and Owen and Katie have found your happily ever afters doesn't mean I will. It's just not in the cards for me."

"I can't bear to hear you say that, Julia. Of course it's in the cards for you. You're a smart, talented, beautiful woman with so much love to give. Please don't miss out on what could be the greatest thing to ever happen to you by allowing bitterness to cloud your judgment."

"My judgment clearly sucks when it comes to men."

"Maybe it has in the past, but every day is a new chance to start fresh. Do you like Deacon? Are you attracted to him?"

"Yes, I like him, and I'd have to be dead not to be attracted to him."

"He is rather handsome, like his brother. Charlie teases me about having a crush on Blaine. Of course I don't, but I do have a very special place in my heart for him."

"Why did you invite Deacon to your wedding?"

"Because I saw the way he was looking at you yesterday. I want you and everyone I love to be as happy as I am."

"How was he looking at me?"

"The way my Charlie looks at me, as if he's seen something rare and precious and is wise enough to know it."

"He doesn't look at me like that. We just met!"

"Yes, he does, Julia. The question you have to ask yourself is if you're willing to risk your heart to find out what it's like to have a good man love you."

"What if I'm not meant for that? What if I'm supposed to be single for the rest of my life?"

"If that's the case, then so be it. You're a strong, capable woman who's more than able to take care of herself. But I've always suspected you were hoping to find true love someday."

"I was, and I've found that 'true love' isn't all it's cracked up to be."

"Because you haven't found the real thing yet. Trust me, when you do, you'll know what I mean when I say everything is different. I'm living proof of that."

"I'm happy for you. I truly am. Charlie seems like a great guy."

"Other than you kids, he's the best thing to ever happen to me. I want all of you to find what I have with him."

"That might be a lofty goal."

"Maybe so, but it's still my goal."

"Thus your matchmaking with Deacon."

"I like him, and I've learned to trust my instincts now that your father is no longer in my life to cloud my judgment. I have a very good feeling about Deacon, and I suspect you do, too. Otherwise, you wouldn't be spending time with him."

"I don't want to make another mistake."

"I understand that better than most people would, but if you don't stick your neck out there a little, you'll never know what might be possible."

Her mother made good points. What was it that their grandmother had always told them when they were kids? Nothing ventured, nothing gained.

"I'll think about what you said. I promise."

"That's all I can ask. Now tell me what you're doing about your health."

"Katie is all over it. She's got me appointments with Victoria at the clinic and Kevin McCarthy. She wouldn't leave on her trip until I agreed to both."

Sarah smiled at that. "Good for her. I love the way you kids look out for each other."

"I wish everyone paid a little less attention to me."

"We worry."

"I know, and I realize it's because I've given you reason to in the past. But it's under control. I promise." She'd been doing really well in maintaining her health until everything with Mike happened. That was another reason to treat the risk of another relationship like the potential grenade that it was. When things went sideways emotionally, her physical health suffered, too.

"I'm always here if you need me. I hope you know that."

"I do. Thank you. Now get out of here and go be with your husband." Julia hugged her mom. "Thanks for coming to check on me."

"I love you, and all I want is your health and happiness."

"I'm working on both."

Sarah kissed her cheek and got up to leave. "I'll check in tomorrow."

"You're on your honeymoon."

"I'll still check in."

"If you must."

Sarah left with a wave. Long after her mother was gone, Julia thought about the things she'd said and tried to decide if she had the fortitude to risk her heart one more time.

CHAPTER 13

*D*eacon spent two hours digging into the past of the man who'd scammed Julia and learned this wasn't the first time he'd been accused of stealing from a romantic partner. But it would be the last time.

He wanted to reach out to "Mike" directly and tell him what he thought of scumbags who preyed on women. But that would tip their hand, and he wanted to nail him. So he put through a call to the Plano Police Department and asked to speak to someone in charge of detectives.

"Lieutenant Webb."

"Hi, my name is Deacon Taylor. I was formerly on the job in Boston. I'm calling about a situation in your area that I wanted to make you aware of." He spent the next fifteen minutes detailing the specifics of Julia's case and answering the lieutenant's questions. "I did a basic search and found that this isn't his first rodeo."

"Why am I not surprised?"

"My friend has provided photos, text messages and a detailed summary of what transpired that I've put together into a report that I'd like to send to you. She's interested in filing formal charges and seeking restitution for the fifteen thousand dollars she gave him."

Webb rattled off his email address, and Deacon sent the email he had ready to go.

"Got it. I'm going to need to hear from your friend directly that she's interested in pressing charges."

"I'll have her call you today. Could I give you my number in case you have any questions?"

"Sure."

Deacon gave him his cell number.

"I took a quick look at the report. Thanks for the legwork you did. That'll make things easier for us."

"I want him nailed. My friend gave him money she didn't have to lose, and the whole time he was romancing her, he was planning to con her. That's not okay."

"Agreed. I'll have our officers pick him up and bring him in for a chat."

"Excellent. Keep us posted?"

"Will do."

Elated after the conversation with the detective, Deacon showered, soaked his bloody dress shirt in the bathroom sink the way Julia had told him to and changed into clean clothes before leaving to return to the hotel to update her. Yes, he could've called her, but he wanted to see her and be there when she heard the news that the police had taken the complaint seriously and would be bringing her ex in for a formal conversation. He hoped that scared the living shit out of the son of a bitch.

He walked through town, noting the sun heading for the horizon, promising a spectacular sunset. Deacon went up the stairs to the Sand & Surf Hotel, Julia's mom was coming out the main door. She smiled when she saw him. "Were your ears ringing? I was just talking about you."

"All good, I hope."

"Of course. I was telling Julia what a nice young man you seem to be and how she'd be silly to write you off because of what others have done."

Deacon laughed at her moxie. "How much do I owe you for pleading my case?"

"My services are free of charge to anyone with the last name of Taylor."

"I appreciate the family discount."

"Don't disappoint me, Deacon. My little girl has been through so much. More than you can imagine. I'm not sure she could withstand another big hurt."

He looked her dead in the eye, because he knew it would matter to her. "You have my word that I'll never hurt her intentionally."

Sarah surprised him when she went up on tiptoes to kiss his cheek. "Thank you."

As Deacon approached the front door to the hotel, he put his hand on the doorknob and stopped for a second, realizing that if he walked through that door, went up the stairs to her room and allowed this, whatever it was, to continue, he would be committing to something far bigger than anything he'd been involved in before.

He'd gone out of his way, his entire adult life, to avoid the kind of entanglements this thing with Julia promised to be. He'd never wanted to be tied down or committed or obligated to someone else.

The day after meeting Julia Lawry, he already knew she was special. Everything about this with her was unlike anything he'd experienced with a woman before. And he wanted more. Much, much more.

That final thought had him opening the door, nodding to the young woman working at the desk and charging up the stairs to the third floor. Feeling breathless, and not just from climbing the stairs, he knocked on her door and waited like a teenager about to see his first real girlfriend.

When she opened the door with towels wrapped around her body and hair, his mouth went dry and every word in his vocabulary seemed to desert him, except for one.

Want.

. . .

JULIA FELT HER FACE FLUSH—HELL, HER WHOLE BODY FLUSHED—WITH embarrassment when she found Deacon standing outside her door. She'd expected to find one of her family members when she'd opened the door in a towel.

The way he looked at her...

Her heart pounded and her blood felt warmer as it coursed through her veins. He'd showered and changed and looked gorgeous with his messy damp hair, as if he'd used his fingers to comb it.

Julia had no idea how long they stood there staring at each other, but in those charged moments, everything changed for her. Her man diet might never have happened for the way she wanted this man. "I, um, give me a minute to get dressed."

"Don't get dressed on my account."

She released a nervous laugh. "Well, the vet called. Puppy is doing so well that I can pick him up any time, but I probably shouldn't go there dressed in a towel."

"Probably not, but let me just say for the record, you're rocking that towel."

With other guys, Julia would've chalked the comment up to predictable male bullshit. With Deacon, she felt complimented rather than objectified. She wasn't sure how he managed to pull that off.

"I've got big news."

She went into the bathroom where she'd put her clothes and left the door ajar while she quickly got dressed. "What kind of big news?"

"The kind where your local cops are bringing in your buddy Mike for a chat."

Julia pulled a T-shirt over her head and went to the door, not caring that her hair was a wet mess around her head. "Seriously?"

"Dead serious. I talked to one of the detective lieutenants, and he said they'd get right on it. I also found that Mike has done this before, so the pattern helped to convince the police that they need to act sooner rather than later."

"He's done it before." Hearing that, Julia felt numb. Of course he had. "How do you know?"

"I did a search for him and found a previous complaint had been lodged against him."

"What kind of search? Like a police thing?"

"No, I found it through a basic online search."

"So that info would've been available to me if I'd taken the time to look for it."

He came over to her, put his hands on her shoulders and gazed at her with golden-brown eyes gone warm with compassion. "It's a lesson learned, Julia. There's no sense beating yourself up for what you should've done. You cared about the guy. You thought he cared about you. I hope you never lose the impulse to help others, no matter what it might cost you personally. That's a very rare thing. Don't let him take it away from you."

"I feel so stupid."

He drew her into his embrace and wrapped his arms around her. "Don't feel stupid. You're a kind, generous person who encountered an asshole. That's not your fault."

Julia burrowed into him, breathing in the rich, clean scent of him and absorbing the warmth that came off him in waves.

"You're a good person who had the misfortune of caring for someone who didn't deserve you. That's the only so-called mistake you made. He's the one who did this, not you. And hopefully, he's going to pay for it in more ways than one."

"Is it petty to wish I could see his face when they arrest him?"

"Not petty at all. I don't know him at all, but I'd like to see it, too."

Julia pulled back from him, just enough so she could look up at him. "Thank you. I never would've gone after him or the money if you hadn't helped me."

"It was my pleasure. One of my favorite things is seeing bullies get what's coming to them."

The fierce expression that accompanied his fierce words had her disregarding her plans to keep her distance from all men. She couldn't keep her distance from this man, and if she was wrong about him... Well, she'd have to deal with that when it happened. Right now, with the encouragement of her mother, grandmother and sister, she felt confident stepping off a cliff into the unknown. She flattened her hands on his chest and slid them up around his neck, burying her fingers in his hair as she licked her lips.

"Um, Julia…"

"Yes, Deacon?"

"I… uh…"

She moved her hands to frame his face and bring him down so she could place a soft, sweet, chaste kiss on his very kissable lips. "Thank you."

His hands found her hips in a light but possessive grip. "I'm happy to help you."

"I'm happy to have met you."

"You… You're on a man diet. We shouldn't…"

"I think we should."

"You do? Really?"

"Uh-huh." Hearing that he'd succeeded in getting the cops to go after Mike on her behalf had replaced the vat of bitterness inside her with something new and fragile and hopeful. It'd been a very long time since someone had stepped up for her the way he had, and she'd known him for only two days. She gazed up at him, hoping he would take the hint that she wanted him to kiss her.

He took the hint, shifting his hands from her hips to her face, cradling it like he was holding something special. Then he tipped his head, and keeping his eyes open and fixed on hers, he kissed her with a tenderness that made her knees go weak. She, who had been kissing boys since she was fourteen, had never been kissed quite like this, as if she was precious to him. She'd never been precious to anyone.

But how was it possible that she could be precious to Deacon? They barely knew each other. No, that wasn't true. He'd shown her who he really was from the first minute they met, and nothing she'd seen since then had changed that first impression. And now that she knew how it felt to be kissed by him, she couldn't wait to do it again.

Deacon cleared his throat. "We, uh, we need to go get the pup."

"I know."

Standing there in her tiny room, with their arms wrapped around each other, neither of them was in any rush to end this hypercharged moment in which everything between them had changed.

Deacon's phone chimed with a text that had him reluctantly pulling back from her. "I should check that in case it's the police in Texas. And they want you to call to give the go-ahead to press charges."

"That'll be my pleasure."

Trying not to notice the obvious—and sizable—bulge in the front of his shorts, Julia took a step back from him and went looking for her hairbrush and her equilibrium. She was pulling the brush through her wet hair when she heard Deacon laugh. "What's so funny?"

"This text from Blaine: 'Will you PLEASE'—all capital letters—'tell my wife that I apologized to you?'" He cracked up laughing, which was a very good look on him. "This is so awesome."

"Are you going to tell her?"

"Eventually. When I get around to it."

"That's evil."

"I know, and it's the least of what he deserves for busting my balls my entire life. I need to make him suffer a little bit."

"Sounds like he's already done some suffering."

"Please. One night without won't kill him."

"But two might."

His evil grin made him even sexier, if that was possible. "Let's go get your pooch."

"He's *our* pooch. You're his daddy, whether you want to be or not."

He took hold of her hand as they went down the stairs. "He bit me."

"Because he was scared. You can't hold that against him."

"If he has rabies, I'm definitely going to hold it against him."

"He doesn't have rabies."

"And you know this how?"

"A mother knows these things."

He laughed—hard—and Julia took great pleasure in having made him laugh. They turned the corner on the landing and nearly ran into

Owen, who was on his way up. He immediately zeroed in on Deacon holding her hand.

Julia's first impulse was to pull back her hand, but she didn't. Rather, she gave his hand a squeeze. "What's up?" she asked her brother.

"Going up to help Laura put the wild ones down for a nap."

"Could I come by to see them later?"

"Of course you can. You don't have to ask first."

"With three kids under the age of two, I do have to ask first. I'll text you to see if it's a good time."

"We'll be around. Where are you guys off to?"

"Just a quick errand. We'll be back soon. Did the boys get off okay on the ferry?" Their brothers Jeff, Josh and John had planned to take the three o'clock boat to the mainland.

"Yep. It was great to have everyone here. You're still hanging out for a while?"

"That's the plan. All depends on whether I can find a job and a place to live."

"Cindy went ahead and leased the house where Kevin McCarthy and his sons were living until Finn moved in with Chloe. I'm sure she'd appreciate the help with the rent."

"If I get the job I'm applying for tomorrow."

"Where?"

"Running Mac McCarthy's construction office."

"I can put in a word for you. He's Laura's cousin and a good friend."

"That'd be great, O. Thank you."

"Sure. I'm thrilled you might be staying. We need to hang out. Catch up."

"I'd love that."

He glanced at Deacon and then back at Julia, but thankfully held back the questions he clearly wanted to ask.

Julia had no doubt he'd ask his questions the next time they were alone.

"I'll give Mac a call."

"Thanks again. I'll see you in a little while."

"Sounds good."

They parted company, with Julia and Deacon continuing down while Owen went up.

"Hey, Deacon?"

They turned back to Owen, who looked down at them from the next set of stairs.

"You're holding hands with my sister."

Julia held back a groan as she glared at Owen.

"Yes, I am." Deacon glanced at Julia and smiled, revealing the sexy dimple. "I like her a lot."

"She's a big girl who can take care of herself, but she's got a lot of people around here who love her."

"I hear you."

"As long as we understand each other."

"We do."

"Good." Whistling a jaunty tune, Owen continued up the stairs as if he didn't have a care in the world. These days, he probably didn't. He had his whole life figured out and was happily married with three kids.

"I'm going to smack him," Julia said as they took the last set of stairs to the lobby.

Deacon laughed. "Nah, it's fine. I know how he feels. I have a younger sister, too. I've given my share of thinly veiled threats to guys she dated back in the day. It's always good to let them know that people are watching."

"I'm still going to smack him."

Deacon chuckled and held the main door for her, releasing her hand so she could walk out ahead of him. The second they were both outside, he took hold of her hand again, smoothly, as if he'd been holding her hand for years rather than minutes. The feel of his hand wrapped around hers made her feel giddy and silly.

She was doing it again. Getting all nutty over a man she'd only just met. The pattern was so familiar to her as to be laughable. Julia pulled her hand free.

"What's wrong?"

She crossed her arms so he couldn't take her hand again. "Nothing."

He stopped walking and faced her. "Why do women do that?"

"Do what?"

"Say it's nothing when it's clearly something." He found her hand and gave it a gentle tug. "Why'd you let go?"

"Because I'm doing it again."

"Doing what?"

"Getting giddy and silly and hopeful about a man after I told myself I wasn't going to do that anymore."

"Ah, I see."

"No, you don't. You have no idea what it's like to never be sure who you can trust."

"Does that go back to the fact that you couldn't trust your own father?"

"Of course it does, but just about every guy I've ever dated has been like him in one way or another. Maybe they weren't physically abusive, but they lied and cheated and stole and deceived."

"I can only stand here, look you in the eye and swear on the lives of everyone I love that I'll never do any of those things to you. I can't promise I'll never hurt you or disappoint you, because I'm only human, but I'll never lie to you or cheat on you or steal from you or otherwise deceive you."

He brought her hand to his lips and set her on fire when he sprinkled soft kisses over her skin. "I understand that you have no way to know for sure that I mean what I say, so all I ask is that you let me show you. Give me a chance to show you that not all men are untrustworthy dicks." Deacon tucked her hand into the crook of his arm and continued toward the vet clinic. "Hang on to me. I won't let you down."

Deeply moved by what he'd said, Julia wanted so badly to believe him, badly enough that she did as he asked and held on to him even when her better judgment was telling her to let go and stick to the man diet despite the significant temptation he represented.

CHAPTER 14

*a*t the vet clinic, a tech named Lisa was working the desk and brought the puppy out to them. "I found an extra collar and leash. And because we aren't sure if he's already been vaccinated, Doc Potter wants to get him back for shots as soon as he feels a little stronger."

"What if he's already been vaccinated?" Julia asked. "Will it hurt him to have them again?"

"It's safer than risking diseases by not being vaccinated."

"Is there any way to know if anyone reported him missing?" Julia feared getting attached and then having to give him up.

"He's not microchipped, and we haven't received any reports of missing puppies, but you could check with the police. Usually, they notify us, but they've been busy this weekend with the season starting and the Wayfarer opening. They might not have gotten around to it."

"We'll check with them," Deacon said.

"We've identified him as a lab mix and figure he's about three or four months old."

"That's good to know," Julia said.

"I just need you to sign the credit card receipt." Lisa pushed it across the counter.

Julia glanced at it and swallowed hard at the two-hundred-and-eighty-eight-dollar charge to warm and rehydrate the dog. Thank God Deacon was able to pay it, because she certainly couldn't. Not now, anyway.

He signed the receipt like it was no big deal.

When they were outside on the sidewalk, she looked up at him. "I'll pay you back as soon as I can."

"Don't worry about it."

"I will worry about it."

"He's my puppy, too, so I can pay for him if I want to. Put him down to walk. He might need to pee."

Julia no sooner put the puppy on the sidewalk than he squatted to pee a river. "Are you a puppy whisperer?"

"Nah, I'm just a guy looking out for another guy."

They walked to the grocery store, where Deacon bought food and treats, and then to the pet shop to buy toys, bowls and a bed. Deacon carried their purchases while she held the puppy. They started back toward the hotel, passing the Naughty & Nice boutique as they went.

Deacon glanced at the store. "That's my sister-in-law's store. Do you mind if I pop in for a minute to see if she's there?"

"Not at all."

They stepped into the store, and Deacon put down the dog bed and other items inside the door. He walked past racks of frilly lingerie on his way to the front desk. He looked so comically out of place in the store that it was all Julia could do not to crack up laughing.

"Is Tiffany here?" he asked the clerk.

"She's in the back. I'll grab her for you. Who should I say is looking for her?"

"Deacon."

"Be right back."

While he waited, he turned to Julia and waggled his brows. "Need anything for yourself, babe?"

"I'm good, thanks."

His smile was positively wolfish. "Good to know this is here. Just in case."

"In case of what?"

"In case I need anything."

"That bustier would do amazing things for your pecs."

"I think it would look better on you." He stepped forward to take a closer look at it. "In fact, that might be my first purchase." Gesturing to a second room with rows of beads separating it from the rest of the store, Deacon said, "What do you suppose they've got back there?"

"Sex toys," Tiffany said when she came out from the back of the store.

"No kidding?" Deacon asked her.

"No kidding. Want to see?"

Julia laughed at the way his face flushed with embarrassment.

"Um, not now, but maybe some other time. Quite a place you've got here."

"So I've been told."

"How'd you get this past the oh-so-proper Gansett citizens?"

"You should ask your brother about that sometime. He was instrumental."

"Stick-up-his-ass Blaine was instrumental in getting a sex-toy shop approved in Gansett?"

"Yep. And PS, he doesn't have a stick up his ass. But I do have some other things he likes back there."

"Stop it. I cannot hear that."

Julia giggled helplessly.

Deacon turned to her, his face flushed and his eyes big. "Stop laughing at me."

"Can't help it."

"Do you know Julia Lawry?" Deacon asked Tiffany.

"We haven't formally met, but I know Sarah, Owen and Katie, and of course I've seen you at the weddings."

Julia stepped forward to shake Tiffany's outstretched hand. "Great to finally meet you."

"You, too. I'm a big fan of your family members."

"I like them."

"So I stopped by to tell you the jackass apologized to me. I understand he's been getting the deep freeze at home due to his epically bad behavior."

"I'm glad to hear he apologized. Was it sincere?"

"As sincere as it gets from him."

"I'm sorry that happened, and I hope you know you're welcome to stop by any time to see me and the girls. They'd love to get to know their uncle Deacon."

"I'd like that. I'll definitely come by."

"You can take Puppy to see them when he's out of quarantine," Julia said.

"He's a cutie," Tiffany said. "Where'd you get him?"

Deacon told her about finding the puppy swimming off the coast of Gansett.

"Oh my goodness! Thank God you saw him!"

"Julia was amazing. She dove right in and went after him."

"And then he bit Deacon."

He extended his arm to show Tiffany the bandage on his arm. "That shirt you were good enough to iron for me is a bloody disaster."

"Oh crap. Are you okay?"

"I'll be better in ten days when I know for sure he's negative for rabies."

"Oh jeez." Tiffany strained for a better look at the puppy, who was snuggled into Julia's arms. "What's his name?"

Julia glanced at Deacon. "We haven't come up with one yet."

"So he belongs to both of you?" Tiffany asked, clearly intrigued.

"Yes, he does," Julia said. "Deacon is his daddy."

"Is that right?"

Deacon groaned. "Don't tell Blaine that. He'll bust my balls until they bleed."

Tiffany grinned. "Your secret is safe with me. Are you guys, you know... seeing each other?"

"We are," Deacon said with no hesitation. "And we've already had a baby together."

Tiffany laughed. "Come by when you have more time to shop. I'll give you the family discount."

"I'll do that."

Julia couldn't let her mind wander to Deacon shopping for her at Naughty & Nice. She'd spontaneously combust right on the spot.

"Thanks for stopping by. Your brother will be thrilled to know he's been exonerated."

"You should make him suffer for a few more days."

"When he suffers, I suffer." Tiffany's dirty grin had Deacon groaning again.

"Disgusting."

"Nothing disgusting about it. In fact—"

Deacon held up his hand. "Do not go there, or we can't be friends, and I'd very much like us to be friends."

Tiffany laughed. "I'd like that, too. Nice to meet you, Julia."

"You, too."

"Bring the puppy by to see the girls. They'll go crazy over him, and they'll start begging Blaine for one of their own."

"In that case, I'll be by with him as soon as his ten-day rabies quarantine is over."

Deacon picked up the dog bed and other items and followed Julia out the door.

"She seems rather awesome," Julia said.

"She is. I have no idea what she sees in my brother."

"You don't? Really?"

"Shut up. You can't think he's hot if you're gonna hang with me."

"I hate to be the bearer of bad news, but you rather look like him."

"Ew, I do not!"

"Do, too."

"I used to like you."

"You still like me."

"No, I don't."

"Yes, you do."

"We're in the biggest fight ever right now."

"No fighting in front of the baby."

As they walked and bickered, it occurred to Julia that not only was Deacon sweet and kind and sexy, but he was also fun. She'd never had so much fun with a man, and the more time she spent with him, the harder it was to remember why she'd needed that dick diet in the first place.

IT TOOK ALMOST AN HOUR FOR OWEN AND LAURA TO GET ALL THREE kids settled for naps. "Why does that get harder all the time?" he asked when they had stretched out on their bed to relax while they had a minute to breathe. Three little ones was an ass-kicker, but he wouldn't trade them for anything.

"It's because they're getting older and wiser. I dread the day that Holden stops napping. It's the only break we get."

"How old will they be before we're not constantly tired anymore?"

"Teenagers?"

Owen groaned and then turned on his side so he could feast his eyes on his beautiful, exhausted wife. "We haven't had sex in a week, thanks to those little cock blockers."

"Did you just refer to our children as cock blockers?"

"Can you think of a better way to describe them?"

"Not lately." She turned on her side, too, and moved closer to him. "Is my big baby feeling neglected?"

"Very."

"Awww, we can't have that."

When she pressed her body against his, he groaned from the rush of desire that had him hard and ready within seconds. "I'm afraid to get my hopes up."

She placed her hand over his erection and squeezed, drawing another low groan from him. "It's not your hopes that need to be up. Looks like we're good to go."

Owen laughed, but made sure to be quiet. God forbid he should wake the sleeping babies when things were looking *up* for him and Laura for the first time in days. He wanted to give her finesse and tenderness, but they didn't have time for those things these days. They pulled at clothes until the important parts were revealed, and when he sank into her tight, wet heat, Owen nearly lost control before he'd had a chance to enjoy it.

Laura's hands were all over him, sliding down his back to grip his ass and pull him deeper into her. "Always so much more than your share."

He faltered when he laughed at her regular comment. "Are you complaining?"

"Never." She squirmed under him, looking for more, which he was happy to give her.

Owen gazed at her lovely face, the loveliest face he'd ever seen, even when there were dark circles under her eyes, a knot of what might've been oatmeal in her hair and a stain of unknown origin on her shirt.

"I used to think you were the most beautiful girl I'd ever met," he said softly, holding still to drive her crazy.

"And now I look like a red-hot mess with three babies who puke and pee on me and wear me out."

He brushed the hair back from her face and caressed her cheek. "And now, you're even more beautiful than you used to be. Motherhood is a very good look on you."

She snorted with laughter. "That can't possibly be true. There's a very good possibility that I have BO at the moment because I don't remember the last time I showered and—"

He kissed her. "More beautiful than ever. And for the record, you always smell good."

"Love has made you smell-blind."

"No, it hasn't."

"Yes, it has."

He shook his head, propped himself up on his arms and began to move, slowly at first, intent on making it good for her before it was good for him. By now, he knew just how to get her to the finish line, which he did far more quickly than he'd have preferred, but they were on borrowed time lately.

Afterward, he held her in his arms, running his fingers through her hair until he encountered a knot. "Is this oatmeal?"

"I think it might be from yesterday."

Owen laughed. "They're kicking our asses."

"We're outnumbered. That's the problem."

"We can still hire help."

"We don't need that. We've got your mom and Charlie, my dad and Betsy and lots of other people who pitch in when needed."

"Except you rarely ask for help, even when you're on your last leg. We're going into our busy season at the hotel, and I worry about it being too much for you."

"I'm fine, as long as I have you to help me with everything."

"I'm not going anywhere."

"Do you ever long for your previous life as an unencumbered traveling musician?"

The question, which she hadn't asked in a while, startled him. "Never."

"Oh come on! You must yearn for it sometimes."

Owen propped himself up on an elbow and gazed down at her. "I never, ever, *ever* yearn for anything other than what I have right here with you and our kids and our family."

"Even when all three of them are screaming at the same time?"

He cupped her face and ran his thumb over her sexy bottom lip. "Even then." Her smile lit up her face and his life. As long as she was smiling, he was content. "So I saw Julia holding hands with Deacon Taylor."

"Is that right?"

"Uh-huh."

"You don't like him?"

"I don't know him at all."

"You know Blaine."

"Yeah." He dropped down to his pillow and looked up at the ceiling fan, which was off. Soon, they would need it, but not yet.

"What's on your mind, love?"

"I worry about her."

"How come?"

"She's had some health issues over the years... Eating disorders.

That kind of thing. She looks particularly thin to me, and I'm worried she's back to that again."

"Did you talk to Katie about it?"

"I did, and she's had the same thought. She asked me to keep an eye on Julia while she's away. She hinted that something's up with Julia but didn't give me details. I just wonder if this is the right time for her to be getting involved with Deacon."

"I understand why you're concerned about her, but don't forget how we got involved with each other at the worst possible time. I was pregnant with my ex-husband's child and going through an acrimonious divorce. We proved that sometimes the worst time is actually the best time."

"That's true."

"If Deacon is anything like Blaine, your sister is very lucky to have him in her life."

"I should talk to Blaine about him."

"You absolutely should not do that."

"Why not? If he's going to be dating my sister—"

"Julia is old enough and smart enough to decide for herself if he's worthy of her time and attention." She snuggled up to him, her head on his chest. "I know it's hard to break the old habit of feeling like you have to protect everyone you love from impending doom."

"It's impossible to break that habit. I'm constantly waiting for disaster to strike."

"I think it might be okay to relax a little, O. Everyone is good. Your mom is so happy with Charlie. Katie is happily married to Shane and off on her honeymoon. Julia and Cindy are sticking around for the summer, which is awesome. Your brothers are doing great. Our family is perfect. It's okay to stand down."

"I don't know how to do that." His hypervigilance when it came to the ones he loved was the legacy he'd been left with after a chaotic, violent childhood.

"Let me help. When you want to interrogate Blaine about his brother, come talk to me instead. When you want to interrogate Julia about her health, come talk to me."

"What if I see her heading for trouble?"

"Then you talk to her and express your concerns without telling her how to run her own life." She caressed his chest and belly, which made him hard all over again.

Laura laughed. "Put that thing away. I need to shower and get some work done while the monkeys are napping."

"That *thing* doesn't like being talked to that way."

Grinning, she kissed him. "I love you, and I love the way you love all of us. I'm here for you whenever you need me. Even when I have three kids hanging off me. You know that, don't you?"

"Yeah, baby, I know."

"Take a deep breath, O. Everything is okay. I promise." She kissed him and got out of bed to go shower.

For a long time, he lay there staring up at the ceiling, trying to find it in him to leave his sister alone to run her own life. But old habits were hard to break. If he saw her heading for trouble, he wouldn't hesitate to intervene.

CHAPTER 15

*T*iffany was late getting home from the shop, which had left Blaine in charge of dinner. She never knew what he'd come up with when he made dinner. It could be anything from spaghetti with French fries to grilled cheese sandwiches with pickles. Whatever. It was food that she didn't have to cook, which made it fine with her.

From the driveway, she could hear Addie crying and Blaine talking to her and Ashleigh in the low, patient tone he always used around them. Tiffany had once told him how Jim had often scared her and Ashleigh when he would yell at them. As a result, Blaine went out of his way to never raise his voice with her or the girls.

"She wants her pacifier," Ashleigh told Blaine.

"How do you know?"

"Whenever she cries like that, that's what she wants."

Tiffany held a hand over her heart as she listened outside the screen door.

"Do you know where it is?"

"Of course I do." She scampered off to get it.

"What would we do without your big sister around here?" Blaine asked Addie, who continued to howl with outrage.

"Here it is," Ashleigh said.

"Thanks."

Addie went silent as soon as she had the pacifier.

"You're a magician," he said to Ashleigh.

"You're silly, Blaine." She adored her stepfather, and he loved her madly. "I know what all her cries mean. Whenever you don't know, just ask me."

"I'll do that."

When Tiffany walked through the door, Ashleigh came running to greet her. Tiffany picked her up and hugged her. With the way Ashleigh was growing, she wouldn't be able to do that for much longer.

"Blaine is a silly," Ashleigh reported.

"What'd he do now?"

"He didn't know that Addie wanted her paci. I had to tell him."

"It's a good thing you were here to set him straight."

"I know!"

"I'm right here, ladies," Blaine said. "I can hear you talking about me."

Ashleigh lost it laughing.

Tiffany whispered in her ear, "Thank you for being the best big sister ever." When she put her down, Ashleigh ran off to play while Tiffany went to Blaine to give him a kiss. "Rough night at the ranch?"

"Not bad until about five minutes ago, when Miss Addie became cranky after her bath."

Now that she had what she wanted, Addie was snuggled into her daddy's chest. The sight of him holding their baby made Tiffany love him even more than she already did. "She's not long for this world."

"Your mom said she didn't nap much today."

"It'll be an early night for her." Tiffany held out her arms to take the baby from him, eager to see her after too many hours apart.

The late spring and summer season was tough for all of them, with longer hours at work for Blaine and Tiffany. Thankfully, her mom and Ned loved being with the girls and pitched in whenever they needed help. With Addie snuggled into her arms now, Tiffany sat at the kitchen table. "What's for dinner?"

"Spaghetti and broccoli."

"Yummy." As always, she tried not to giggle at the food combinations he came up with. God forbid he should quit cooking on the nights she worked late. "I'm starving."

He served her a plate and then took the sleeping baby from her to put her down upstairs, returning a few minutes later. "You'll never believe it. Ashleigh is out cold on the sofa."

"Kindergarten is exhausting."

"I guess so. I covered her up." He brought a bottle of wine and two glasses to the table and then went back to make himself a plate.

Tiffany poured wine for both of them.

"Did you get any special visitors to the shop today?"

She knew exactly what he was asking and decided to have some fun with him. "Just the usual. Nothing special."

He scowled. "Did you or did you not see my brother today?"

"Your brother Deacon?"

"I know what you're doing, and he probably put you up to it."

"I have no idea what you're talking about."

"Sure you don't." Blaine ate in silence for several minutes, his focus entirely on his plate.

Tiffany began to feel bad about torturing him, but he'd brought it on himself by making outrageous accusations. "What do you have against Deacon anyway?"

Pausing midbite, he looked at her with fire in his eyes. "Nothing."

"Now you're going to add lying to your list of crimes?"

"I'm not lying. I have nothing against him. He just gets on my nerves."

"Why?"

"Because! He goes through life acting as if he doesn't have a care in the world and gets himself into situations that require me to bail him out."

"Before this latest thing, when was the last time you had to bail him out of something?"

"Long time, but still…"

"So it's not remotely possible that he's changed in all the years since you last had to deal with one of his scrapes?"

"Recent evidence would suggest otherwise."

"I want you to talk to him about what happened the night he got arrested."

"I'm not doing that."

"Yes, you are."

He put down his fork and wiped his mouth with a napkin, keeping his gaze fixed on her. "Says who?"

"Says your wife who thinks you're being a hard-ass for no good reason. Deacon seems like a really nice guy, and you need to get to know who he is right now. Not who he was as a teenager stuck on a remote island with too much time on his hands. You need to know the man he became when you weren't around to see it."

"He got arrested last week for being in a bar fight. What else do I need to know?"

"You need to know *why* he was fighting in that bar."

"He said it was about a woman."

"Get the details before you pass judgment. I like him, Blaine. He's a sweet, funny guy, and I fear that you might be missing out on a closer relationship with your brother because you can't get over the crap he did when he was a kid."

"Half of what he did then was because he wanted to piss me off."

"He was a *kid*. Didn't you ever do anything you shouldn't have done when you were a kid?"

"Yeah, but—"

"No buts. You need to ask him more about the fight."

"Or else what?"

"No 'or else.' I'm asking you to do it for me."

"You had to put it that way, didn't you?"

She smiled widely at him, fully aware that there was nothing he wouldn't do for her.

His deep sigh had her getting up from her seat to stand behind his, rubbing shoulders gone tight with tension that was ever-present this time of year. October had become her favorite month. The weather was still nice, the tourists were gone, and she got her husband back.

"Did he tell you I apologized to him? Yes or no?"

"Yes."

He stood so abruptly, his chair fell over sideways, crashing to the kitchen floor. Wrapping an arm around her waist, he lifted her off her feet and headed for the stairs.

"What're you doing? We need to clean up from dinner and get Ashleigh into bed—"

He silenced her with a kiss that blew the top off her head. Mmm, pent-up Blaine was even wilder than regular Blaine, and regular Blaine was pretty wild. The kiss went on for what felt like hours as he lowered her to their bed, pushed up her skirt, pulled her panties aside, freed his cock from his uniform pants and sank into her. He broke the kiss to release a long sigh that sounded like relief. "Missed you."

"You went without for one whole day."

He gazed down at her, fierce and sexy and all hers. "I missed you and the scent of strawberries that tells me I'm home."

"When I punish you, I punish myself, too, so here's a big idea— don't be a jerk so I won't have to punish both of us."

Filling her to capacity, he stopped moving and looked into her eyes. Sometimes she swore he could see straight through to her very soul when he looked at her in that particular way. "I'm sorry, baby. I never for one second thought you'd be anything other than true to me. I shouldn't have suggested otherwise."

"No, you shouldn't have. Thank you for apologizing to me and to Deacon."

He scowled. "Don't say his name when I'm inside you."

"Stop being a jackass, and make love to your wife."

"Yes, ma'am."

"And you *will* ask him about the bar fight."

"Shut up and make love to your husband."

. . .

THE PUPPY HAD JULIA UP MOST OF THE NIGHT, WHINING, CRYING, shaking and peeing. Even though she'd taken him out almost hourly before bedtime, he'd peed on her three times before he finally settled into sleep around five o'clock in the morning.

With her meeting with Mac McCarthy scheduled for nine, she felt frazzled and sleep deprived. Leaving the little guy to sleep in her bed, she went into the shower and stood for a long time under the hot water, trying to wake up and function.

As she'd never had a pet before, she'd had no idea what to expect. She hoped he wouldn't be up all night, every night. Maybe just the first night when he was scared and uncertain of where he was or whether the person he was with would be kind and take good care of him. The poor little thing had been through so much. He probably had no idea if he was safe.

She knew what that was like and was determined to make sure he knew he could count on her to take good care of him, even if she could barely take care of herself sometimes.

Deacon had stayed with them until ten the night before. He'd left to go home so she could get some sleep. What did it say about her and her dick diet that she hadn't wanted him to go? Today, he had training at the police station ahead of starting his job the next day. She hoped that he and Blaine could find a way to peacefully coexist, or Deacon would be in for a long summer.

Julia emerged from the shower, checked to ensure the puppy was still sleeping and took the time to blow-dry and straighten her hair as well as apply some concealer to cover the circles under her eyes.

She found a clean top and matching skirt that she quickly ironed on the bed as her stomach twisted with nerves that would make it impossible to eat breakfast before her meeting. She'd get something after.

Hopefully, Mac wouldn't have a problem with her bringing the puppy to the interview. Even though he was supposed to be at home, she couldn't bear to leave him alone. She'd read online that as long as she kept him away from other animals and people, it would be fine to have him with her. She could only pray that he wouldn't pee on her before she got to her interview. After picking him up from the bed, she cuddled him into her shoulder, grabbed his leash and her purse and headed out.

She encountered Owen in the hallway. "Morning."

"How's it going?"

"Rough night with the baby. He was up all night."

"Ouch."

"Not sure how you handle three of them."

"Now you know why Laura and I walk around like zombies. You've got your interview, right?"

"Yep."

"I talked to Mac last night. He said he's looking forward to meeting you."

"Thanks for putting in a word for me."

"Happy to do it. I'm so glad you're staying awhile."

"Me, too. It's been too long since I spent a summer on Gansett."

Owen reached out to gently scratch between the puppy's ears. "You want me to keep him for you while you do the interview?"

Julia thought about that for a second. As much as she'd love to leave him with Owen, she didn't want him to be scared when he woke up with a stranger. "I'd better keep him with me. I don't want him to freak out if he can't find me."

"He sure is cute. What's his name?"

She bit her lip. "I'm kinda afraid to give him one."

"How come?"

"What if his owners show up and want him back?"

"If they do, they ought to be told that allowing a puppy to fall off a boat means they shouldn't get to have him."

"True, but we don't know what happened. It could've been an accident. They're probably heartbroken. I know I would be." She already knew she'd be heartbroken if she had to give him up.

"Still, they should've been more careful with him. He's just a baby."

"I know. Well, I'd better go."

"How're you getting to the marina?"

"I figured I'd walk."

"That's a long walk. I'll take you."

"I'm sure you have other things you need to do."

"Nothing that won't keep for a few minutes. Let me grab my keys, and I'll meet you out back."

"Thanks, O." As she continued downstairs, she whispered to the puppy, "That's your uncle Owen. He's one of the good guys." The puppy never stirred. Figured he was going to sleep all day after keeping her up most of the night.

Julia hoped there would be coffee at this interview.

Owen parked one of the Sand & Surf trucks at the marina ten minutes later. "Come on, I'll introduce you."

She wanted to tell him he didn't have to do that, but he was already out of the truck. Still carrying the puppy, she got out of the truck and followed her brother to a group of picnic tables outside a restaurant on the pier. Four men were seated at one of the tables, and she recognized all of them from the wedding.

"Julia, this is Big Mac McCarthy, his brother Frank, his best friend Ned Saunders and his son Mac."

"Nice to meet you all again."

"You, too, Julia," Big Mac said. "Is that the puppy you rescued from the ocean yesterday?"

"It is."

"My daughter Janey told me about that last night."

"She was such a big help to us."

"How's he doing?"

"Other than being up all night crying, he's doing great."

"Awww, poor guy. He sure got lucky that you found him and saved him. Heard you dove right in after him."

"I did, but Deacon was the one who got bitten when we tried to haul him out."

"It was good of both of you to rescue him," Mac said. "Deacon was just here with Blaine."

Just hearing his name had Julia's spine tingling as she thought of him kissing her good night and telling her he'd be by after work. She'd wanted to beg him to stay, but wary of repeating past mistakes, she'd let him go, telling herself to take it slow, don't jump in with both feet, etc. Regardless of the warning alarms sounding in her own mind, she couldn't wait to see him later.

CHAPTER 16

Mac stood and grabbed his coffee. "Let's go inside where we can talk without these clowns disturbing us."

"Who ya calling clowns, boy?" Ned asked with pretend indignance.

"You know exactly who." Mac gestured for Julia to lead the way toward a table inside the large building where the marina's restaurant was housed. "Can I get you a coffee?"

"That'd be great. Thanks."

"Cream and sugar?"

"Just cream, please."

"Coming right up."

He was a handsome guy with dark hair and his father's blue eyes.

Mac returned with a coffee and a plate with three sugar doughnuts.

The smell of the doughnuts made Julia's mouth water.

She took a sip of coffee as he nudged the plate toward her and tossed some napkins on the table.

"You have to try one of my mom's famous doughnuts."

Julia chose the smallest of the three and took a delicate bite. The sweet, greasy flavor exploded on her tongue. "Dear God, that's good."

"Right? Our whole family is addicted to them."

"I can see why."

"So let me tell you about the job. A couple of years ago, when I moved back to the island, I started a small construction company that's grown to the point that I just can't manage it all on my own, especially in the summer when I'm helping to run this place, too. My wife, Maddie, is expecting twin girls in September, and they'll be our fourth and fifth children. The oldest is in kindergarten."

"Holy cow."

"Right? I need help, and I need it now."

"I need a job, and I need it now."

Mac laughed. "I'd say that makes us a perfect match. Owen says you've been an office manager for years in Texas?"

"Yes, I worked for a manufacturing company most recently. I loved the job until we got a new boss. We weren't a good fit."

Mac winced. "I hate when that happens."

"Me, too."

"Well, I'm the only boss you'd ever have on this job, and I'd like to think I'm pretty easy to work for. We have a lot going on all the time, so it's really busy."

"I like to be busy, and I'd do anything I could to make life easier for you. I'm not the kind of employee who can't be asked to do anything outside of her job description. If something needs to be done, tell me, and I'll do it."

"That'd be so awesome, and there's no job description. We'd be making it up as we go."

"I'm fine with that."

"Are you here only for the summer?"

"For right now, but I'm open to staying if the job is working out for both of us. I'm a little worried about being here in the winter. I've never done a winter on Gansett."

"I was the same way when I first moved back here, but I've come to really appreciate the slower pace of winter after the insanity of summer."

"Running two businesses that're booming in the summer, I can see why you love winter." The puppy chose that moment to wake up, whining and growling. "Stop it. Be nice. We're at an interview, and we want Mac to hire us."

"You're already hired, and so is he. Our office needs a dog to keep an eye on things."

"Really? You won't mind if I bring him?"

"Absolutely not. You'll be there by yourself a lot, so it'd be good for you to have the company."

"That would be great." And then she caught herself. "If I get to keep him, that is."

"Why wouldn't you?"

"I'm sure someone must be looking for him. If they come back and want him…" She shrugged.

"Finders keepers."

"Owen said they shouldn't get him back because they let him fall off a boat."

"I agree with Owen."

"I'm hoping they're far away from here by now and that I get to keep him."

"I hope so, too." He detailed a generous salary and benefit package that included vacation and sick time. "Will that work for you?"

"Um, yes, that would be great." She wanted to weep from the relief of knowing she would soon have a decent paycheck to help her dig out of the financial hole she'd fallen into.

"I can help you find housing if you need it."

"My sister Cindy rented your cousin Finn's place. I'm hoping she wants a roommate."

"That'd be perfect. It's within walking distance of my office in town. When can you start?"

"Is tomorrow too soon?"

"Absolutely not. I'll warn you that everything is a bit of a mess, so you'll have a heck of a job at first."

"That's totally fine. I'll get you whipped into shape in no time."

He gave her the address of the office in town. "I'll meet you there tomorrow at nine?"

"I'll be there."

"Tonight, we're having a gathering at the Wayfarer to thank all the people who helped us renovate and get ready for the season. I'd love if you could stop by to meet my team and see some of our work."

"Sure, I can do that."

"Any time after six. And feel free to bring a friend. There'll be dinner and entertainment from your brother and mine."

"Sounds good. I'll be there."

Mac reached across the table to shake her hand. "Thank you so much, Julia. I'm looking forward to working with you."

"Me, too. Thank *you*." He would never know how desperately she'd needed the job or the relief she felt at having landed it, in no small part, she was certain, because Owen had put in a good word for her. Whatever it took.

They walked out to rejoin the others, and Julia was surprised to see that Owen had waited for her.

"Say hello to my new office manager," Mac said.

The others responded with applause that made Julia feel thankful for the series of unfortunate events that had brought her home to Gansett.

Owen stood and gave Julia a hug. "Congrats."

"Thank you for helping to make it happen."

"Anything for you, kid."

The expression brought back a lifetime of memories. She and Katie and Owen had done whatever it took to survive their upbringing.

Anything for you had become their motto. Knowing they had each other had kept them going during the worst of times, and it had fortified them between crises. To know that bond remained in place, unshakable by time or distance or marriage or anything else, was the reminder Julia needed that she was never alone in this world as long as she had Owen and Katie to prop her up the way they always had.

Overcome by emotion, she squeezed her brother's arm. "Back atcha."

"I know."

They shared a look that contained a lifetime of devotion. There was literally nothing they wouldn't do for each other or their siblings, a fact that had been tried and tested more times than either of them cared to remember.

"I need to get to the clinic to meet Maddie," Mac said.

"Is everything okay?" Big Mac asked.

"Yep. Just a routine check. Vic wants to see her weekly since she's expecting twins this time around."

"Let us know how she is," Big Mac said.

"Will do. See you tonight, Julia."

"See you then."

"You're going to the party at the Wayfarer tonight?" Owen asked.

"Yes, he invited me to come to meet everyone."

"Awesome. I'm playing, and Laura is going. Mom and Charlie are watching the kids."

"Sounds like a fun night out." Julia wondered if Deacon might want to go with her. She said goodbye to the other men and walked to Owen's truck with him. "He seems really great," she said of Mac when they were on their way back to town.

"He is. Everyone likes him. He's fun and funny and hardworking and desperately in love with his wife and kids. Their family is a lot like ours, without the horror-show father, of course. His dad is one of the best men I've ever met."

"He was so nice."

"He always is. Not only did he raise his own five kids, but he was like a father to Joe Cantrell, who's now married to his daughter Janey, and Luke Harris, who lost his dad really young and ended up working at the marina. And when he found out about Mallory, the daughter he never knew he had from a previous relationship, he welcomed her into the family with open arms."

"What it must've been like to grow up with a dad like him rather than what we got."

"No kidding." Owen glanced over at her. "John told me he got a letter from Dad."

"What? When?"

"A couple of months ago. He wrote to John because he's a cop, thinking John might be able to help him get special favors in prison."

Julia stared at Owen, shocked to the core. "Tell me John ignored him."

"He did, but he said getting the letter screwed him up for a few weeks."

"Of course it did. Just when we think that son of a bitch is out of our lives, he pops back in, acting as if he has a right to anything from us."

"I'm going to call him and tell him if he ever contacts any of us again, I'll report him to the prosecutors. He'll get time tacked onto his sentence if they tell the judge he's harassing us."

"You shouldn't do that, O. You don't need to hear his voice and fall into that rabbit hole again."

"I'll gladly do it if it means keeping him away from us."

"Have the prosecutor do it. Call him and not Dad."

"I suppose I could do that."

"Please do that. I don't want you talking to him ever again."

"Trust me, that'd be fine with me. I'll call the prosecutor."

"Good," Julia said, releasing a deep breath. Just thinking about her father triggered massive anxiety for her, Owen and the rest of their family. "I hate him so much for what he did to all of us."

"I do, too. And oddly enough, I hate that I hate him. I hate having that in me for anyone."

"I know what you mean. I feel the same. It's like we were assigned this burden as kids that we can never escape no matter how far we run or how much time goes by."

"Finding out that he was abused as a kid helped to explain some of the *why* of it," Owen said, "but you know what? I was abused as a kid, and it never occurs to me to take out my frustrations about that on my own children."

"You could never do what he did. He wanted us to forgive him because of how he was raised, but I don't know if I ever can. He had a choice about how he wanted to live his life, and he chose wrong."

"Yes, he did."

Owen drove the truck into the back lot at the Sand & Surf and parked in an empty space. After killing the engine, he turned to look at her. "I've mostly escaped from it, Jule. Having Laura and the kids has been the best thing to ever happen to me. I'm so busy being happy with them that I have very little time to think about shit from the past. I think Katie would say the same thing since she's been with Shane and got the job at the clinic."

"I can only take your word for it. I've never been busy enough or distracted enough for it to totally disappear for me."

"It doesn't ever totally disappear, but it becomes more manageable when you replace the hate with love."

"I'm so happy for you. After all the battles you fought for the rest of us, you deserve all the good things more than anyone I know."

"You deserve it, too, Julia. You fought most of the battles right along with me."

"Not like you did." She would never forget the night their father had broken Owen's arm and then passed it off as an accident at the hospital. Or when he'd had Owen charged with assault for daring to defend himself. Those were some of many times she'd wished she had the courage to commit murder.

"Still," Owen said. "I want you to be happy. I want you to have more love than you do hate."

"I'm working on that. The job will help me to stay busy. It'll be good to throw myself into a new challenge. Mac said he needs everything."

"You'll love working for him."

"I think so, too. Well, I'd better take Mr. Pupwell for a walk before my appointment at the clinic. And yes, I'm going to the clinic, so you can text Katie and tell her you did your job as my keeper while she's gone."

Owen grinned. "I'll let her know."

"You do that. I'll see you later. And thanks again for the ride, the recommendation and everything else."

"You got it."

He went inside while she took the puppy for a walk through the parking lot, hoping he would quickly learn that peeing was meant to be done outside, not on the shirt of one's mother.

Stop. Don't do that. Don't get attached. Protect yourself from getting hurt.

She'd spent a lifetime trying to avoid getting hurt, for all the good that had done her. Hurt was almost all she'd ever known. Puppy looked up at her, making sure she was still there before continuing to sniff around the bushes.

"Go pee, buddy."

Magically, he lifted his little leg and peed. "What the hell? I have to *tell* you to pee?" She couldn't wait to tell Deacon that. He'd crack up.

Deacon.

Just that quickly, she was back to thinking about kissing him the night before and wondering how long she had to wait before she could do it again.

CHAPTER 17

*M*ac drove faster than he should have, eager to get to the clinic in time so he wouldn't miss the weekly appointment. He'd wanted to pick up Maddie at home and drive her there, but she'd insisted on driving herself. His mother-in-law, Francine, would be at the house with Hailey and baby Mac while Thomas was at school.

Three kids five and under was too much for Maddie, even when she wasn't carrying twins, but this pregnancy was kicking her ass. Not that she'd ever say so.

They'd been arguing lately about hiring help. She wanted to wait until the twins arrived. He wanted help now, as his busiest time of year began, giving him much less time to spend at home helping her. Between the construction company that went full tilt all summer while they had good weather and the marina he ran with his father and their partner, Luke Harris, Mac had way too much on his plate. And his plate was about to get that much heavier when the twins arrived in September.

Sometimes he would swear that he could actually feel his blood pressure rising. His chest ached almost all the time, and his jaw was killing him from clenching his teeth while he slept. Something had to give, for sure, and it wouldn't be his wife and kids. They would always come first with him. Hiring Julia would help. Hiring a nanny would also help, and they were going to talk about that after this appointment.

In the meantime, thank God for his parents, Francine and Ned, all of whom pitched in to help out whenever they were needed. Mac's parents wanted to travel now that they were semiretired, and he didn't want to be the cause of them staying on the island when they wanted to go see the world.

He also planned to have a talk with Luke about taking on more at the marina to free Mac up to focus on the construction business in the summer. He'd been juggling too many balls for a couple of years now, and he was getting tired. As he was soon to be the father of *five* children, he needed to get his shit together so he could be there for them rather than running himself ragged trying to be all things to all people.

His jaw was throbbing by the time he got to the clinic, which meant he was grinding his teeth again. He tried to remember not to do that, but he had so much to remember that he forgot not to clench.

After parking, he jogged into the clinic and stopped short at the sight of his gorgeous wife being supported by Victoria and another woman he didn't recognize. For a brief second, Mac's heart stopped when he wondered what could be wrong. He drove himself mad thinking of the many ways her delivery could turn into yet another disaster. The possibility of anything happening to her or their babies was more than he could handle.

His chest started to seriously hurt, and his jaw... Wow, that hurt, too. He took a step forward, and then he was falling, hitting the floor hard, but he didn't feel anything other than the searing pain in his chest.

Maddie...

She needed him. He had to get up and go to her.

Then he was surrounded by people, and in the background, he could hear Maddie screaming his name. Was she crying?

He hated when she cried. She knew that. Why were they holding him down? Where were they taking him? He needed to get to her. Something was wrong with *her*, not him. The ceiling above him flew by. David was there. Mac used to hate him for cheating on Janey, but he saved Hailey's life and Janey's. They owed David so much.

"Mac. You need to calm down." David's shouted words permeated the fog in Mac's brain.

"Maddie."

"She's fine."

"Mac, I'm here." She was crying. That wouldn't do.

He tried to sit up.

Stronger hands pushed him back down. "I don't want to restrain you, but I will if you don't relax," David said. "Let us figure out what's going on."

"His BP is sky-high," Victoria reported.

Where had she come from? She'd been with Maddie. The babies. Something was wrong. He knew it. He had to get to her.

A pinprick in his hand and then… nothing.

"WHAT'S WRONG WITH HIM?" MADDIE WAS TRYING NOT TO GET hysterical, but when your perfectly healthy husband collapses right in front of you when you're six months pregnant with twins, staying calm was easier said than done.

David had a stethoscope pressed to Mac's chest, which was now covered with patches attached to wires.

Was he having a heart attack?

Dear God, please. It couldn't be that.

"Has he ever had any sort of heart issues before?" David asked Maddie.

"No, nothing." And then she recalled when they first met. He'd come home to Gansett after a health incident in Miami where he'd had a high-pressure job in the construction industry. "There was one thing." She frantically tried to recall the details. "I think it was an anxiety attack. He ended up in the ER because they thought it was a heart attack. Could that be what happened?"

"I like that a whole lot better than a heart attack," David said, "but we'll need to do a complete workup before we can say for certain what happened."

"He'll be okay, though, right?" She simply couldn't fathom what she would ever do without the man who'd stormed into her life and made himself essential to her and her son.

"We'll know more after we get some labs back. Try not to worry."

"Maddie," Vic said. "Let's get you off your feet."

Her ankles had swollen to the point that she feared they might explode at any moment.

Victoria settled her in a chair next to Mac's bed, raised her feet onto another chair with a pillow under them and then put another pillow behind Maddie's aching back.

"Thank you."

"No problem. Try not to worry. He was in the right place when this happened."

Maddie took hold of his hand, noting the roughness that came from hard work. "He's got to be okay. He just has to be."

"Can I call someone to come sit with you?"

Maddie thought about that. She had so many people she could and should call, but she asked for only one person. "Call his dad for me, will you?"

"Of course."

Big Mac would know what to do for Mac, and having him there would calm Maddie as well.

Watching over her normally unstoppable husband, seeing him so still and attached to beeping machines, Maddie experienced a wave of fear unlike anything she'd ever known, even when they'd lost their unborn son, Connor. That had been the worst loss of her life. But if she lost Mac, she'd never survive it.

THE FIRST DAY OF WORK WAS BUSY FOR DEACON. HE HAD A HALF DAY OF training with one of the Gansett Island Police Department officers, who walked him through the system for filing reports and other department policy. None of it was all that different from what he'd seen before, so he absorbed the information quickly and was able to get out on the water right after lunch.

It was a relief to be on the boat after a morning in a stuffy conference room dealing with administrative bullshit. That was always the part of the job he'd hated the most and knew many other officers felt the same way. He liked to be out on the street—or on the water—doing the actual job, not dealing with the paperwork that was a necessary evil.

He wore the uniform of the Gansett Island Police Department, carried a badge and weapon as well as handcuffs and had all the rights and privileges other members of the department enjoyed. But he got to do the best job, if you asked him.

He'd met the other young men and women who would be working with him on harbor patrol this summer, most of them college students on summer break, and had exchanged contact info with them.

All morning throughout the training and now that he was on the boat, his thoughts kept returning to Julia, to the day they'd spent together, the sexy kisses they'd shared and her delight in the puppy. He wanted to know how her interview went and whether she'd gotten the job. Sure, he could text her to check in, but he was afraid of being too much too soon for her. He didn't want to overwhelm her, but keeping his distance from her would take effort. She was just so damned sweet and sexy and wounded. That last part had touched him more than anything.

He wanted to fix everything for her, right all the wrongs and make her whole again. Which was utter insanity and played right into the hero-complex bullshit that Blaine liked to spew at him. Deacon Taylor didn't do commitment or serious relationships or anything that smacked of love or forever. But the second he laid eyes on Julia, first at the clinic and then at the wedding, all bets had been off where she was concerned. He'd been drawn to her like the proverbial moth to a flame, as much by the wounded look in her eyes as her beautiful face and sexy body. And when he'd heard that her ex had stolen money

from her, he'd burned with the desire to get retribution and restitution for her.

That reminded him he'd missed a call during his training. As he
directed the boat around the island toward New Harbor, he checked
his voicemail and found a message from Lieutenant Webb. "This is
Lieutenant Carl Webb calling from the Plano Police Department in
Texas. We've arrested the subject and brought him in for questioning.
Of course he insists it was all a big misunderstanding. We've given
him forty-eight hours to reimburse Ms. Lawry, or he'll be charged
with fraud. She should be seeing an electronic transfer of funds, and
we'd appreciate a heads-up when the money arrives. Thanks again for
bringing this to our attention. We're taking a closer look at him and
other questionable activities that may lead to charges. I'll look
forward to hearing that the money has arrived."

Deacon let out a whoop when he heard that news and immediately
put through a call to Julia. To hell with restraint. He wanted to talk to
her right now.

"Hey." She sounded breathless, probably from chasing the puppy. "I
thought you were at work."

"I am. I'm out on the boat, but I just heard from Lieutenant Webb
that they brought your friend Mike in for a chat, and after he claimed
the whole thing was a big misunderstanding, he was given forty-eight
hours to make restitution or face fraud charges."

"Oh my God! Are you kidding me? They're making him pay me
back?"

"Yep. You built an airtight case that they were able to turn into
immediate results."

"*You* built the case, Deacon."

"Couldn't have done it without your input." She made a sniffling
sound that made him wish he'd waited to tell her in person. "Are you
okay?"

"I'm overwhelmed. Getting the money back will mean so much
to me."

"It hasn't happened yet, but I'm optimistic that it will if he wants to
avoid being charged. What he doesn't know is that they're taking a

closer look at him in light of the info you provided to see who else he's done this to."

"Thank you so much for pushing me to pursue this. I wouldn't have done it without your encouragement."

"I was happy to help. I just hope he comes through with the money."

"Me, too. If so, I'm buying you dinner to celebrate."

"That sounds good. Let me know if it shows up."

"You'll be the first to know."

"How'd the interview go?"

"Great. I got the job."

"That's awesome, Julia. I'm so happy for you."

"I'm happy for me, too. Mac invited me to a party at the Wayfarer tonight, a thank-you for everyone who worked on it. He said it would be a good chance for me to meet his team, and he said I could bring a guest. You want to go?"

"I'd love to. I'll check in after I get out of work."

"Sounds good."

"Hey, Julia?"

"Yes?"

"Last night was awesome. I bet tonight will be even better."

Her entire body reacted to his gruffly spoken words. "Can't wait."

"Me either. See you soon."

Deacon pushed the boat's throttle forward, eager to get his work done for the day so he could leave on time. He had a big date to look forward to.

JULIA ENDED THE CALL WITH DEACON AND LET OUT A SHOUT THAT startled the puppy. "Daddy is the best. The absolute *best*." Tears ran down her face, an unstoppable river of pain over what Mike had done to her as well as relief and gratitude for the new friend who'd already made such a huge difference in her life.

She had to be at the clinic in fifteen minutes for her appointment with Victoria, so she pulled herself together, washed her face, brushed her teeth and headed out with Puppy on a leash. If her money came through, she'd go back to the pet store to buy a crate that she could leave him in when she had to go out.

As she walked, she put through a call to her sister Cindy.

"Hey, what's up?" Cindy asked when she answered.

"I heard you're sticking around on Gansett for the summer."

"You heard right."

"What about your job at home?" Cindy lived an hour north of the Dallas area and had worked for the same hair salon for years.

"I took a leave of absence. When I got here for the wedding, I knew I wouldn't want to leave in three days. Then I heard at the wedding that Chloe's summer helper wasn't able to come this year, and I couldn't resist the chance to stay for the summer."

"I'm going to stay, too."

"Really? That's awesome!"

Julia told her about the job she'd landed that morning. "I heard you rented a two-bedroom place. Would you consider a roommate?"

"I'd love that! Absolutely."

"Thank you."

"It'll be like old times, only better."

"Yeah, for sure." Everything was better now that they no longer lived under the merciless reign of General Mark Lawry.

"I've seen Mac's signs all over the island. You'll be busy."

"That's what he tells me."

"If you want to see the house, you can come by tomorrow afternoon. I'm getting the keys from Chloe's boyfriend, Finn, then."

"That'd be perfect."

"I'll text you the address. I'm so excited!"

"Me, too. I'll see you tomorrow, if not before."

"See you then!"

Cindy was the most upbeat and positive of the Lawry siblings, always able to find the silver lining in any situation. Of course, being seven years younger than Julia and Katie, her experience at home had differed quite a bit from what the eldest three had endured.

Not that Julia begrudged the younger ones for having suffered less than they had. Not at all. Cindy grappled with migraines that'd been a challenge for her since childhood. While they had no way to know if the stress of their childhood had caused the headaches, Julia believed it had.

At the clinic, she was taken right back to a cubicle and told to undress completely. As she sat on the end of the exam table, wearing a gown and cradling Puppy, she tried not to think about her desperate dislike of doctors and all things medical. After the time she'd spent in the hospital during the worst of her disorder, the antiseptic smell of the clinic was enough to bring back more memories she'd sooner forget than relive.

Victoria came breezing in a few minutes later. They'd met at Katie's wedding but hadn't gotten a chance to talk. "Hi there!" Her dark hair was in a bun, and her friendly smile put Julia at ease. "I'm so glad we had an opening in the schedule." She washed her hands and then sat on a stool in front of a rolling desk with a laptop. Victoria glanced at Julia and did a double take when she saw the puppy cuddled in her arms.

"Who've you got there?"

"This is Mr. Puppy Pupwell, who was found swimming off the coast of Gansett yesterday when I was out on a boat with a friend."

"Ah, yes, I read you were treated for hypothermia."

"Yes, but I'm fine now. He can't be left alone yet. I hope it's okay that I brought him. He's fairly well behaved." She hoped and prayed that he didn't pee on her while she was extolling his good behavior.

"He seems very sweet. I'm glad you were able to save him."

"So am I. I just hope he doesn't show any sign of rabies after he bit Deacon. He was scared when we rescued him. He's been super docile ever since."

"The poor guy must've been terrified."

"He was."

"He's very lucky to have you. Katie mentioned you've had some chronic conditions that need to be monitored while you're here, but she didn't say what."

Julia hated talking about this, but knew she had to keep her promise to Katie. "I've suffered from anorexia and bulimia since I was a teenager. For the last seven or eight years, it's been mostly under control. But I, um…"

"It's okay. Take your time."

Victoria's kindness went a long way toward making it possible for Julia to share that she'd had a major disappointment that'd stirred up old wounds and caused a setback in her recovery. "When I'm upset or anxious, it's almost impossible to eat. I get a lump in my throat that just feels so big, and I can't even think of eating because my stomach is so agitated."

"That's got to be an awful feeling." Victoria typed notes into the computer as Julia spoke. "Do you recall how old you were when eating and food became a problem?"

"I was fourteen or fifteen. I can't recall exactly."

"Did something particular trigger it, or was it a slower evolution?"

"It'd been an issue for a while but got much worse after my father beat up my brother and broke his arm."

"God, Julia, I'm so sorry."

Julia shrugged, the way she had for years whenever someone expressed sympathy for the way she'd grown up. She rarely talked about it, but whenever she did, the reaction was usually the same— shock, horror, sympathy. "I tell myself it was a long time ago, but…"

"Some things stay with you forever."

Her throat closed around a hot ball of emotion, so she only nodded while trying not to cry.

"Have you lost weight during this most recent episode?"

"About five pounds." She'd been shocked to realize that when the nurse weighed her. It was the most weight she'd lost in years, and it was five pounds she didn't have to lose.

They talked about the medication Julia took to control the anxiety that contributed to the eating disorders, and Victoria suggested a slightly stronger dosage for the next thirty days.

"When was the last time you had a full exam?"

"It's been a few years. After the last hospitalization, I went out of my way to avoid doctors."

"I'd like to do a full exam with a pelvic and pap. Is that all right?"

"I suppose so."

Forty minutes later, Julia had been thoroughly poked and prodded and had a new prescription in hand. She made a follow-up appointment with Victoria in two weeks so they could monitor her weight and make sure she was staying healthy. Victoria had also given her a birth-control shot that would be effective in a few days.

Not that she would need it, or so she told herself.

CHAPTER 18

*J*ulia put Puppy Pupwell down to walk and headed for the pharmacy to fill the script. Hopefully, they wouldn't mind if she brought him inside, because there was no way she was leaving him alone outside.

Gansett Island had always been a dog-friendly place, which was another thing she'd loved about it as a child. Her father wouldn't allow them to have pets, but each summer, she made friends with dogs she encountered on the island and then missed them the rest of the year. The first thing she'd do when she returned was to look for her friends from the summer before.

In Texas, she hadn't been able to get a dog because of Katie's allergies. After Katie decided to stay on Gansett, Julia had held off on getting a dog of her own because she worked too many hours and it wouldn't be fair for the dog to be alone most of the time. It had been a huge relief when Mac said she could bring Puppy to her new job.

At the pharmacy, a woman named Grace waited on her. Julia recognized her from the wedding. "Ah, the maid of honor," she said after reviewing the prescription.

"That's me."

She extended her hand to Julia. "Nice to meet you. I'm married to Evan McCarthy."

Julia shifted the puppy so she could shake Grace's hand. "That makes us practically related."

"I know! Are you hanging out on Gansett for a while?"

"For at least the summer. I just got a job managing Mac McCarthy's construction office."

"Oh, that's awesome. He needs the help. He's my brother-in-law."

"There're so many McCarthys. It'll take me a year to figure out who goes with who."

Grace laughed. "It won't take that long. You should come to the party at the Wayfarer tonight. I'll introduce you to the whole family."

"I'll see you there. Mac invited me so I could meet everyone."

"Perfect. And I'll make sure Laura and Katie invite you to our girls' nights. We have a *lot* of fun."

"That sounds awesome."

"I'll get this taken care of for you right away."

While Grace worked, she kept up a steady conversation with Julia, who told her the story of how she'd come to have the puppy.

"That is so amazing! You jumped right in after him!"

"I never hesitated. The minute I saw him, I had to get him. I've been a dog lover my whole life, but I've never actually had one of my own." Julia glanced down at Puppy Pupwell, sleeping in her arms, and prayed she'd get to keep him. Despite her best efforts, she was already attached.

Grace rang her up and handed over the prescription. Fortunately, she had health insurance from her old job until the end of the month, and her new insurance with Mac would kick in next month. With her ongoing health issues, Julia couldn't afford to let her insurance to lapse.

"Thanks again, Grace. I'll see you tonight."

"Looking forward to it."

As she walked the short distance back to the hotel, her phone chirped with the sound of a cash register. She withdrew it from her back pocket and juggled the phone and the puppy, who'd protested when she tried to put him down. Her eyes nearly bugged out of her head when she saw the message on her screen.

Mike had sent seventy-five hundred dollars.

The phone chimed again with a second alert for the same amount.

Right there on the sidewalk where anyone might see her, Julia broke down into tears of relief and gratitude. And in that moment, the door to her heart swung wide open to let in Deacon Taylor. Even as her better judgment screamed that it was far too soon for doors to be opening, Julia knew it was already too late to stop what had been inevitable from the first time she talked to him at the wedding.

He was going to mean something to her. She'd known it then, and she knew it now for certain. What exactly he would mean to her remained to be seen, but after he'd gone all out to get back the money that'd been stolen from her, she had all the proof she needed that he was someone worth letting into her life—and her heart.

DEACON WAS ON HIS WAY BACK TO SOUTH HARBOR TO END HIS DAY when he received a tearful call from Julia.

"Hey, what's up?"

"He sent me the money."

"Oh my God. That's fantastic news."

"Thank you so much, Deacon," she said, sniffling. "I'll never be able to properly thank you for doing this for me."

Her tears, even happy tears, gutted him. "It was my pleasure to make sure that scumbag paid you back and got what's coming to him."

"I'll never forget this."

"Are you at the hotel?"

"Yes, I just got back."

"I'll be there soon."

"Deacon..."

"I know, honey. I'm on my way."

Elated to hear the news from Julia, he made a quick call to Lieutenant Webb to let him know the transfer had been completed.

"I want to thank you for alerting us to this guy," Webb said. "We've found that he has a long record of scamming people. We have three documented instances so far and expect to find more."

"Wow." He hoped it would help Julia to know she'd helped to put a stop to Mike's criminal activities. "Thanks for letting me know."

"Tell your friend she did the right thing reporting him."

"I'll do that. It'll mean a lot to her. Will you keep me posted on what goes down with him?"

"You got it. Thanks again for the info."

"Thank you for the quick action. You can't begin to know what it means to her to get that money back. She gave the son of a bitch everything she had."

"I'm glad we were able to get restitution for her. I'll be in touch."

Deacon stashed his phone and fist-pumped the sky, thrilled to have helped right a terrible wrong for Julia. That had been his favorite part of being a cop, getting justice for people who deserved it. They didn't always get justice, but when they did... That was a good day. Today had been a good day, and he was determined to help her celebrate.

He pulled into the town dock to secure the boat and was dismayed to find his brother waiting for him with the usual stick up his ass and the pissed-off expression he wore whenever Deacon was nearby.

Deacon expertly docked the boat and began securing the lines before shutting down the engine. "Chief. How lovely to see you."

"How'd it go out there today?"

"Great. I managed to collect on ninety percent of the occupied moorings, and Colby is working on the other ten percent. I wrote one ticket for speeding in the pond and pulled a fishing net out of the water." He gestured toward the mangled net on the deck. "Not good for marine life or propellers."

"Sounds like a good first day."

"It was. Did you need something?"

"Nope. Just checking on you."

Deacon wanted to tell him he didn't need to be supervised, but he bit his tongue. Fighting with Blaine would keep him from Julia that much longer.

"Tiffany wants me to invite you to dinner some night."

"Does it cause you pain to invite me to your house?"

"Yes, it does."

Deacon threw his head back and laughed. "You're such an idiot."

"So you like to tell me. Dinner or not?"

"Sure. I can't tonight, but maybe tomorrow?"

"Fine."

"Can I bring Julia?"

Blaine stared him down for a long moment.

Deacon refused to blink.

"What's going on with her?"

"We're friends."

"That's all?"

"Is that any of your business?"

"It will be if my friend Owen is unhappy because my brother broke his sister's heart. Then it becomes very much my business."

Carrying the net to drop in the dumpster, Deacon got off the boat and brushed by his brother on his way to the ramp that led to the parking lot where he'd left the bike that morning.

Blaine grabbed his arm and spun him around. "Don't walk away from me when I'm talking to you."

Deacon pulled his arm free. "Fuck off. I'm not on duty and don't have to put up with your crap. My off-duty life is none of your business."

"Until you do something to piss off one of my friends, and then it will be."

"I hope you sit around at night holding your breath waiting for that to happen. That'd be a good use of all the extra time you seem to have to waste bothering me."

"If you hurt Julia Lawry, I'll hurt you."

Deacon walked away before he did something stupid like flatten his new "boss." He fumed all the way home, where he showered and quickly changed his clothes before setting out for the hotel on the bike. He absolutely hated the way his older brother thought he was nothing but a fuckup. He drove past Tiffany's shop and decided to stop to get a present for Julia.

He parked, went inside and was happy to see his sister-in-law behind the counter.

"Hey," she said, smiling warmly at him. "How was your first day?"

"Good until the very end."

"What happened?"

"Your husband happened. He's such a pain in my ass."

"Sorry to hear that."

Deacon shrugged. "Whatever. It doesn't matter. He said you want me to come to dinner."

"I do. Maybe tomorrow night?"

"I'd love to. Can I bring a friend?"

"Of course. A friend named Julia maybe?"

"Maybe. I want to get something for her. I want something pretty and sexy but not *too* sexy, you know?"

Tiffany rolled her lips together to keep from laughing.

"What?"

"You're cute."

He rolled his eyes. "Are you going to help me or what?"

"I'll help you." She came around the counter. "What message exactly are you trying to send?"

He had no idea what that meant.

Thankfully, she realized that. "Are you looking for 'I like you a lot' or 'I'd like to get to know you better' or 'I think you're hot, and I want you in my bed'?"

"Um, all of the above?"

Tiffany laughed. "Which one is at the top of the list?"

"I like you. A *lot*."

"Aww, that's so sweet." She sorted through racks of frilly bits and lacy things, her brows furrowed and her lips pursed. Clearly, she took her business seriously. "How about this?" She held up a dark maroon silk robe. "It would be lovely with her dark hair."

Deacon agreed. He could picture her in it, and the thought of that would've made him hard if he'd allowed his brain to wallow in that image. But because now was not the time and certainly not the place, he forced himself to think about what Blaine would say about him sporting wood in front of his wife rather than how Julia would look in that robe.

As always, Blaine was a buzzkill.

"I'll take it." Deacon followed her to the counter. "Can you throw in a bottle of that fancy lotion there, too?" He felt like a total idiot, but then again, he couldn't recall the last time he'd bought a gift for any woman who wasn't related to him. Even his relatives went without more often than not.

He stood at the counter and watched Tiffany go through an obviously well-practiced ritual of wrapping his purchases in fancy paper sealed with a gold-foil Naughty & Nice sticker. "Do you by any chance offer free advice with every purchase of sexy lingerie?"

"Not *every* purchase. But for you? Sure."

He thought for a second about how he wanted to word his question. "When you first met what's his name, was there something different about it or did that take a while?"

Tiffany looked up at him, seeming intrigued by the question. "I knew the first time I saw him that he was different from anyone I'd ever met."

A distinct feeling of panic came over Deacon at learning it could happen that fast. "Were you guys together from then on?" He felt a little ashamed that he couldn't recall the details of how Blaine and his wife had ended up together.

Tiffany laughed. "God, no. I was still married to my first husband and going through a contentious divorce. It wasn't until many months later that Blaine and I were able to act on that initial first impression. And when we did? Phew." She fanned her face dramatically. "Hot."

"Gross."

"Not even kinda." She flashed a dirty grin. "Tell me the truth."

"About?"

"Do you feel something 'different' for Julia?"

"Um, well... Maybe... Yeah, I guess I do."

Tiffany laughed again. "You're a bit of a red-hot mess, aren't you?"

"I know! I can't figure out what's going on. I met her three days ago, and here I am buying her a present and counting the minutes until I can see her again. What the hell *is* that?"

Tiffany pinched her lips together in an obvious attempt to hold back more laughter at his expense. "Do you really want me to tell you, or would you prefer not to know?"

Deacon shifted his weight from one foot to the other as a prickle of elation mixed with panic settled in the vicinity of his heart. "I'm afraid to answer that question."

She met his gaze, her eyes dancing with delight. "Could I give you one piece of advice?"

"Please do. I'm at a total loss here." He gestured to the red-and-white striped bag as he handed over his credit card. "I don't do this shit."

Tiffany ran the card and handed it back to him. "Meeting Blaine, falling in love with him, marrying him… He's the very best thing to ever happen to me, other than my daughters. Don't be a fool and miss out on something that could be the best thing to happen to you just because you 'don't do this shit.'"

Deacon absorbed her words of wisdom, trying to sort out how they applied to his situation with Julia.

"If you feel something different for Julia, Deacon, figure out what it is and be careful with it. She could be one of your best things ever." She handed over the bag to him. He had to give her credit—the bag was a work of art by the time she finished with it. "One other thing I want to say. The Lawrys… They've been through some heavy crap."

"I know. Julia told me."

Tiffany seemed surprised to hear that. "Owen and Katie don't say much about it, so I'd take it as a pretty big deal that Julia actually told you. I would just ask you to be gentle with her. She's been hurt enough. If you aren't serious about her, stay away."

"How can I be serious about someone I met days ago?"

"You're in here buying her gifts and talking to me about her. I hope you and I will be great friends, but we just met, too. I don't know you very well yet, but I think it means something that you talked to me about her."

She was right. It did mean something that he'd unloaded on the sister-in-law he'd only just met. Julia meant something to him. What exactly, he couldn't say. Yet. But Tiffany's warning about hurting Julia resonated with him. The last thing he'd ever want to do was hurt her when she'd already suffered enough hurt in her life. "Thanks for this, Tiffany. The gift and the words of wisdom. For what it's worth, I think my brother is a lucky man."

"You're damned right he is, and he'll be getting even luckier tonight."

Deacon pulled a disgusted face. "You had to go and ruin it, didn't you?"

Tiffany was still laughing when he left the store, eager to get to Julia. He couldn't wait to be with her again, even if he still had no idea what it meant that she seemed to be all he could think about.

CHAPTER 19

*M*ac came to slowly, trying to figure out where he was and why his mouth was so dry, he could barely move his tongue. And why were his parents there, and *why* was Maddie *crying?*

He tried to sit up.

His father's strong hand on his shoulder kept him reclined. "Take it easy, son."

"Maddie." Why did his voice sound so weak and strange? What the hell was going on?

"I'm here, Mac." It took her a second, but she managed to stand, get her bearings and sit on the edge of his bed.

"What's wrong? Why are you crying?"

She wiped her tears and then reached out to fix his hair the way she always did.

"You don't remember collapsing earlier?"

He'd *collapsed?* Mac racked his brain but couldn't remember anything after the meeting with Julia Lawry. She was going to start tomorrow and save his life. He'd been on his way somewhere after meeting Julia, but he couldn't recall where.

"You were coming to meet me for the appointment, and you collapsed inside the clinic door."

Mac couldn't remember any of that. "The babies…"

"They're fine and so am I, as long as you are."

"You had a major anxiety attack, son," Big Mac said. "David checked your heart, and everything is fine, but he said you need to ease up on the stress before anxiety turns into something much more serious."

Mac tried to process what his father was telling him. This was the second time that'd happened. The first time had been in Miami, right before he came home to Gansett and ended up staying after he met Maddie. He rubbed his chest where residual pain confirmed what his father was telling him—just like before.

This was the last freaking thing he needed going into the busiest season of the year at the marina and the construction company. He had no time to be sidelined by fucking anxiety, of all things.

"David says you have to take it easy for the next few weeks."

That wasn't going to happen, but Mac couldn't say so. Not now.

"I'm going back to work full-time at the marina," Big Mac said. "You're relieved of duty for the summer. Luke and I have it covered."

"And until Shane gets back from his honeymoon, Riley is in charge of the construction company," Maddie said. "He was here earlier and said he's happy to help in any way he can."

"We also postponed the family party at the Wayfarer until you're feeling better and Shane is back on the island," Linda said.

"Christ," Mac said. "How long was I out for?"

"Long enough to scare the shit out of everyone who cares about you most. Your sisters and brothers have been here for hours, hoping to see you." Big Mac wore the strain of the last few hours in his face and eyes. "This is nonnegotiable, son, so you'd better just wrap your head around the fact that your days of being Superman are over."

Mac hated to see his parents looking so stressed out, but it was Maddie who truly got to him, with her eyes red and swollen from crying over him. She was under enough pressure carrying their twins without him adding to it. "Fine, whatever you guys want."

"Really?" Maddie asked, her eyes flat with surprise.

"Really. I don't want to cause you any more strain than you're already under. And we're getting that nanny now. I'm not discussing that any further."

"Okay."

Mac crooked his finger at her and then chuckled at how her ungainly belly made it impossible for her to get much closer to him. He sat up so he could kiss her, ignoring the way his head swam from the sudden change in position. "Everything is fine. I promise."

"We'll give you kids a minute alone," Big Mac said as he and Linda stepped out.

"Scared me."

"I'm sorry, baby."

"Please don't leave me, Mac. I'd never survive it."

"You'll have me to kick around for the next fifty years."

"That's not long enough."

He closed his eyes and held her as close to him as he could get her with the belly in the way. "Love you, Madeline."

"Love you more, Malcolm."

Mac cringed at the name he hated. "That's not possible."

"Yes, it really is. Seeing you collapse… I'll be having nightmares about that for the rest of my life."

"I'm right here, and I'm not going anywhere. I promise."

"You're going to do what David tells you and take it easy, do you hear me?"

"Yeah, baby, I hear you." Taking it easy went against everything he believed in, but he'd do it to put her mind at ease.

As Maddie pulled back from him, her eyes went wide and her mouth fell open.

"What?" Mac asked, instantly alarmed.

"A weird pain." She winced when it happened again.

"*Victoria!*"

JULIA SHOWERED AND DRIED HER HAIR UNTIL IT FLOWED IN WAVES DOWN her back. As she applied mascara, she realized she was nervous but excited, too. It had been only a few days since she met Deacon, and she was breathless with anticipation to be with him.

Was she falling into old traps and habits, or was she finally beginning what could be a healthy relationship with a man? She had no idea, and the not knowing was worrisome. However, she'd decided to take the advice of her mother and grandmother and give him a chance.

When her cell phone rang, she left the bathroom to take the call.

"Hi, Julia, this is Kevin McCarthy. I got Katie's message. I'm sorry it took me so long to get back to you."

"No problem. I understand you just had a baby. Congratulations."

"Thank you. She's a doll. I'm taking a few weeks off, but I'd be happy to find an hour for you if you wouldn't mind coming to my house."

"That's all right. I don't want to intrude."

"It's no problem at all. I promised Katie we'd get together soon. Can you come by at some point?"

Julia realized there was no point in trying to put him off. "Sure, when are you thinking?"

"Late afternoon seems to be the quietest time around here. Would five o'clock tomorrow work for you?"

"I can do that. Do you mind if I have a sleepy puppy with me?"

"Not at all. I'll have a sleepy baby with me." He gave her his address. "I'll see you then."

"Thank you."

Julia hated that Katie had forced him to see her during his time off and would tell him so when she saw him. He sounded like a nice guy, though, although there was no way Katie would send her to someone who wasn't great at what he did.

Her phone chimed with a text from Luke Harris, who said he worked with Mac and wanted to let her know that the get-together at the Wayfarer had been postponed because Mac wasn't feeling well. Luke said he'd meet her in the morning at nine to let her into the construction office and get her started.

Julia wondered what was wrong with Mac and hoped it was nothing serious. She typed in a response to Luke, while wondering what could've happened to Mac in the short time since she'd seen him.

Thanks for the update. Hope Mac is okay. See you in the morning.

She settled the puppy in the crate her grandmother had unearthed from the hotel basement, took her phone so she wouldn't miss a text from Deacon and went down the hall to Owen and Laura's suite. From outside the door, she heard babies crying and Laura's low, calm voice. How her sister-in-law managed to remain calm in the midst of never-ending chaos was amazing to Julia. She knocked on the door, hoping Laura could hear her over the din.

When Laura opened the door, she had baby Jonathan in her arms while his twin, Joanna, cried on a playmat on the floor. Holden was toddling around his sister until he tripped, fell and bumped his head on the floor.

"I'll get him," Julia said when Laura stepped aside to let her in.

"Welcome to Bedlam, where the inmates have taken over the asylum."

Over the next half hour, the two of them worked together to settle and then play with the three children.

"This moment calls for some 'Baby Shark,'" Laura announced as she turned on the TV. "It makes them into zombies, so we don't let them watch the video very often. And I apologize in advance for the earworm."

Sure enough, one minute after the TV was on, all three kids were captivated, and Julia understood the warning about the earworm. "That song is awful."

"I know! We hate it, but they love it, as you can see. Come." She grabbed Julia's arm. "Let's have a drink and some adult conversation while we can." In the kitchen, Laura pulled a corked bottle of white wine from the door of the fridge. "Wine?"

"Yes, please."

Laura poured healthy glasses for each of them. "They've driven me to drink today."

"I don't know how you do it."

"I love every second of it. Don't get me wrong. But three is a lot. I blame your brother for everything. He's the one who knocked me up with twins." She followed the words with a smile and a wink. "It's a good thing I love him so much."

"I'm so glad you do. No one deserves to be loved like that more than Owen."

"He's the best, and he has been from the very start, when I was suffering morning sickness. It never once occurred to him to be bothered by the fact that I was pregnant with another man's child. At my lowest moment, he just saw *me*." Laura blinked when tears flooded her eyes. "I can't even think about that time in my life without getting emotional."

"I couldn't believe it when he told me he was spending the winter on Gansett because he'd met someone."

"I couldn't believe when he stayed for me. That was such a special time for us."

"I'm so happy it all worked out for you guys."

"Me, too. Owen tells me you've been seeing Deacon Taylor."

"We've been hanging out since the wedding."

"He's *gorgeous*."

"Is he? I hadn't noticed."

Laura laughed. "Sure you haven't."

"He did the hugest thing for me."

"Is that right?" Laura topped off their glasses. "Do tell."

Julia spilled the story about Mike, the money, the police and the shocking development earlier when he'd actually returned the money to her.

"Holy shit. That's amazing! Not the part about Mike stealing from you, but Deacon..."

"I know. He was incensed and immediately formed a plan to get it back. I still can't believe it actually worked." Julia took a healthy sip of wine, enjoying the heat that spread through her when it settled in her belly. "I have the worst judgment when it comes to men, but Deacon..."

"He's proven he's legit."

"Yes! And now, I just want..."

"What?"

"*Everything.* I want to dive into this thing with him headfirst, which is what I always do, and it's how I end up screwed in the end. I leap before I think, and I always regret it. Every single time."

"Has it occurred to you that this time might be different?"

"Yes! But I always think that. 'This one, he's special. He's different.' But they aren't. None of them are special."

"I think it's pretty damned special that Deacon used his professional skills to make your case to the cops at home and got back your money."

"It's incredibly special."

"Don't you think it's also an indication of who he really is?"

"I want to believe that so badly. You have no idea how badly I want to believe that."

Laura placed her hand on top of Julia's. "I think it might be safe to believe in him, Julia."

"I think so, too, but I'm not sure I could take it if he turned out to be like the rest of them."

"I was once right where you are—coming off a heartbreaking disappointment after I found out my new husband was still dating."

"I've heard this story, and I still can't believe it."

"I know. Me either, but it happened, and at the worst possible time, there was Owen to show me that not all men are scum, despite my recent experience."

"At least you had your father and uncles to show you how it's supposed to be."

"That's true. I certainly did, and even having their outstanding examples to follow, I still chose wrong the first time. It's proof, I think, that no matter how we were raised, sometimes it's hard to tell the difference between the frogs and the princes, especially when they only show you what they want you to see."

"Yes, exactly. Mike was so charming and attentive and romantic. I thought he was everything I'd ever wanted. If only that was the first time I'd been wrong, but it was, like, the tenth time. I have zero confidence when it comes to men. They've shattered me. All of them."

"I'm sorry you've been through such a nightmare. I hate that people are so awful to each other. Why can't everyone just be kind and loving? Can you imagine what a nicer world this would be?"

"That would be something."

"Well, we both know all too well that the real world is often shitty, but that doesn't mean everyone in it is shitty. Look at what Deacon did for you right after you met. Imagine what he's capable of if that's how he starts."

"I want him to be as great as he seems. I want that so badly. And wanting it that badly pisses me off, because I'm supposed to be on a dick diet—"

Laura sputtered, and wine shot out of her mouth as she coughed and cried with laughter. "A *what?*"

"You heard me. I'm off the dick. And now, all I want is to be back on it. With Deacon."

Laura laughed helplessly. "A dick diet. That's the best thing I've ever heard."

"What's so funny?" Owen asked when he came into the kitchen.

"Your sister is on a dick diet. Maybe that's what I need after having twins."

"Shut your filthy mouth." Owen shot her an appalled look. "That's the last thing you need, and my sister needs to stop filling your head with ridiculous ideas."

Laura rolled her eyes at her husband.

"I can't believe you told him that," Julia said, amused by Laura and Owen and slightly mortified that Owen knew about her dick diet, such as it was.

Her phone lit up with a text from Deacon that made her feel warm all over with anticipation. *On the way over. Can't wait to see you.*

"Hey, O," Laura said. "Check out our girl's face. I think she's about to blow her dick diet."

Owen cracked open a beer. "Don't say *blow* and *dick* in the same sentence unless you're prepared to deliver."

185

"With that," Julia said, standing, "I'm outta here." She gave her brother a quick squeeze on the way by.

"Oh crap," Laura said. "I just got a text from my dad. Mac is in the clinic with a suspected anxiety attack. Apparently, he collapsed as he was coming in to meet Maddie for her appointment."

"Oh my God," Owen said. "If you want to go over there, I'll stay with the kids."

"I think I will."

"I got a text from Luke that Mac wasn't feeling well," Julia said. "I'm so sorry that happened. I hope I can help to alleviate some of his stress."

"Hope so, too," Owen said.

Laura followed her to the door. "Hey, Julia?"

Julia turned to face her sister-in-law. "Give Deacon a chance. I have a feeling he'll be worth it."

Julia hugged Laura. "I have a feeling you might be right, and I hope your cousin is okay. See you tomorrow."

"I'll be here all day, wrangling three kids. Come by to rescue me."

"Will do, and thank you for listening."

"Any time. I've got my fingers crossed for you and Deacon."

Julia gave her another quick hug and then turned to leave in time to see Deacon taking the stairs two at a time to the third floor. In his left hand, he carried a striped gift bag.

He came to a stop when he saw her there, his face lighting up with a big smile. "Hey, beautiful."

From behind her, she heard Laura's sigh and had to suppress one of her own. As far as opening lines went, that was perfection.

CHAPTER 20

"*H*i," Julia said, feeling flustered and overwhelmed by the mere sight of him.

"Where's our little boy?" Deacon asked as he followed her down the hall to her room.

"Napping in his crate."

"He has a crate?"

"My grandmother unearthed one from the hotel basement. She says there's nothing we could need that's not down there somewhere." She opened the door and led him inside, glancing at the sleeping puppy, who didn't stir when they came in. Julia turned to Deacon and couldn't hold back the need to touch him, to hug him, to thank him. Placing her hands on his chest, she gazed up at him. "Thank you so much."

He dropped the bag he'd brought to the floor and wrapped his arms around her, drew her into his embrace and kissed her bare shoulder. "I'm glad it worked out."

"It only worked out because of you. I'll never be able to thank you for what you did."

He pulled back to look down at her. "You got your money back, and your ex is in a world of trouble. That's all the thanks I need."

When his lips came down on hers, Julia welcomed his kiss with her whole heart and soul. She moved her hands up to encircle his neck and opened her mouth to his tongue. Dear God, the man could kiss. Julia had no idea how long they stood there kissing like maniacs before the need for air became more pressing than her need for him. She pulled back, gasping.

He stared down at her, his gaze intense and laser-focused.

"This has been a really, really good day. I got a job, I got my money back, I got to spend all day with my puppy, I got to play with my niece and nephews, and then I got kissed by a very handsome, sexy man."

"A very good day indeed." He skimmed his lips lightly over hers, setting off a new wave of desperate desire she felt everywhere. "I'd planned to take you and Puppy to dinner somewhere, but then I saw you standing in the hallway looking so, so pretty, and all I could think about was kissing you and touching you and holding you and everything else with you."

He set her on fire with his words as well as the movement of his hands, which slid down her back to cup her ass and pull her in tight against the hard ridge of his erection. "I don't get this, Julia. I don't do this stuff. I don't count the minutes until I can see someone again, or think about them all day, or buy them presents, or—"

Ridiculously moved by him, she said, "You bought me a present?" She chose to focus on the simplest of the things he'd said, because the rest had left her breathless.

"I did." He was bashful and shy and adorable as he released her to retrieve the bag he'd brought. "I saw this and thought of you, which is another thing I never do."

She took the bag from him and sat on the bed just as the puppy woke up and realized they were there.

Deacon retrieved him from the crate and joined her on the bed, sitting close enough that his leg brushed up against hers.

How was it that when this man touched her, it felt like she held lightning in her hand? That had certainly never happened to her before—and she'd kissed her share of frogs. Perhaps this was what it felt like to kiss a prince for once.

She pushed aside the tissue paper and withdrew the smaller of the two packages inside. When she unwrapped it, she found lavender-scented lotion. She squirted a bean-sized bit into her palm and rubbed it into her skin before holding her hand up to Deacon to smell. "You like?"

"Mmm, I like."

Then she opened the second, larger package that contained a gorgeous burgundy silk robe. "This is beautiful, Deacon."

"I'm glad you like it."

"I should be getting you gifts, not the other way around. So far, you've gone to bat for me with my ex, gotten my money back, gotten bit by my dog, paid my vet bill—"

He stopped her with another sexy, tongue-twisting kiss. "I've loved every second of it, and hello, it's *our* dog and *our* vet bill."

Her earlier decision to put her faith in him felt even more right to her now that she was with him again. If she was wrong about him, she would deal with that when the time came. For right now, she wanted more with him.

She glanced at him. "Do you want to see it on me?"

He swallowed hard enough that his Adam's apple bobbed. "More than I've ever wanted anything."

His gruffly spoken words fueled her determination to take her mom and Charlie's advice, to not let the past dictate the present or the future. She grabbed the bottle of lotion and the robe and, giving him a saucy look, went past him to the bathroom. With the door closed, she removed her clothes, rubbed the lotion onto her arms, breasts, legs and everywhere else she could reach and then put on the robe.

The silk against her skin made her feel sexy and desirable and worthy of being cared for by a man like Deacon.

She caught a glimpse of her reflection in the mirror and saw that her skin was glowing, her eyes were bright and her lips swollen from his kisses. Julia couldn't recall the last time she'd looked so healthy or felt so alive and wished she could bottle that feeling for the next time she was low. Taking all that confidence with her, she walked into the room, where Deacon waited for her, sitting now on the end of the bed, facing the bathroom, hands clasped between his legs.

When he looked up at her, his eyes heated with blatant desire that he did nothing to try to hide. "You're beautiful, Julia. Inside and out."

Could he ever know what those last three words meant to her? That in just a few days of knowing her, he already understood her better than any of the many men she'd dated ever had, that he'd looked beyond the surface to find the essence of her? She'd been told all her life that she was beautiful, but never once did she truly believe it until Deacon told her.

He held out a hand to her.

She moved toward him, linked her fingers with his and breathed through the tsunami of emotions—desire, fear, need—that threatened to derail this perfect moment.

When she was standing between his legs, he put his hands on her hips and drew her in until his lips were pressed against the silk against her belly.

"I told Tiffany I wanted something pretty and sexy but not *too* sexy. I didn't want to send the wrong message. We totally failed."

"How so?"

Deacon pulled back to look up at her. "I've never seen anything sexier in my entire life than you in this robe."

He moved her as much with his words as he did with how he looked at her, as if she was the most precious thing he'd ever seen. How could that be when three days ago, she'd never seen his face or heard his name?

"About that dick diet you told me you were on..."

"I think it's safe to say my dick diet is blown."

His low chuckle and bright smile made her feel lighter than air as the insistent flutter in the vicinity of her heart had her breathless with anticipation. "It's dangerous to say those words in the same sentence."

Smiling, she looked down at him, taking in every detail of his sinfully handsome face. "It's a big deal for me to trust you this way."

"I know, and I promise to be worthy of your trust. Always."

As promises went, they didn't get much better than that, which was why when he tugged on the knot that held the robe together, she let him. He slid his hands inside the robe and wrapped them around her waist, bringing her even closer to him, close enough that he could press his lips to her belly.

She ran her fingers through soft brown hair streaked with blond, learning the feel and texture of it as she held him to her. Now that she'd decided to give him a chance, she wanted all of him.

He ran his hands from her hips down the backs of her legs and then up again to squeeze her ass before moving up her back, leaving goose bumps in his wake.

Her skin had never felt more alive than it did under his touch.

He handled her carefully, as if she were fragile and might break if he was rough with her. She didn't want him to think of her as fragile but wouldn't object to him being careful with her.

Julia let the robe fall from her shoulders, leaving her bare to his ravenous stare. She was too thin after the strain of the last few months had made it difficult for her to eat. She knew it but hoped he wouldn't notice or care.

He released her only long enough to pull his shirt over his head, revealing a defined chest and abdomen that had her licking her lips in anticipation of touching him there, everywhere. His hands were once again on her, caressing her with a tenderness that made her weak in the knees.

Apparently, he realized that, because he gathered her into him and moved them so they were reclined on the bed. His effortless strength was as attractive as his kind golden-brown eyes, the dimple in his cheek that appeared only when he smiled, the late-day scruff on his jaw and the reverent way he gazed at her.

No one had ever looked at her the way Deacon did. Other men had looked at her with appreciation, but Deacon... He looked at her as if she *mattered* to him. All he did for the longest time was look at her, running his fingertips over her cheek and mouth as if trying to commit her to memory.

"What is this exactly?" Judging by the way he looked at her as he asked that question, she wasn't the only one being powerfully affected by what was happening between them.

"I don't know, but it feels good."

"So good." He tucked a strand of her hair behind her ear. "Does it scare you?"

"It terrifies me."

Cupping her cheek, he kissed her softly. "No, don't be terrified."

"Can't help it. These things never go well for me."

"Maybe this time, it will."

"Maybe."

He continued to run his thumb over her cheek. "I went to Tiffany's store to get you something, and while I was there, I asked her if it was different when she met Blaine. She said it was like nothing that had ever happened to her before. Instantaneous understanding that he was on a whole other level. That's how this is for me with you."

Her eyes filled with tears that she wished away, not wanting to appear weak to him when she'd worked so hard to stay strong through all the storms. But she couldn't help the emotional reaction to what he'd said. "Are you scared?"

"Strangely enough, I'm not, even though I know I probably should be."

"Why?"

"Because these things don't happen to me either. I've made a career out of staying unattached, but all I want now is to be attached. To you." He moved in closer to her for another of the kisses that made her head spin. "I keep telling myself this can't be real, you can't be real, but then I see you again, and I know that nothing has ever been more real than you are."

Julia reached for him, wrapped her arms around him and kissed him with all the emotion he'd stirred in her by sharing his truth. She understood how he felt, because she'd felt the same thing every time she'd been with him.

If this was wrong, she never again wanted to be right.

. . .

DEACON COULDN'T GET ENOUGH OF HER SWEET LIPS, THE SENSUAL torture of her tongue rubbing against his, the silky softness of her skin or the sweet scent that belonged only to her. He wanted to touch her everywhere, to kiss her and love her and show her that she had taken over his world in only a few days' time.

For the rest of his life, a life that he hoped would somehow include her, he would marvel at how she'd stormed into his world and changed everything. He would be lying if he didn't note how painfully thin she was, but he found her unbearably sexy, nonetheless. She'd told him how she struggled to eat during times of stress, and the situation with Mike had clearly taken a toll. Deacon would do whatever it took to make sure her worries were few so she could regain full health. Her worries were now his, and the noncommittal bachelor he'd been only a few days ago was now fully committed.

He kissed from her lips to her neck, moving down to cup full breasts and worship the tight tips of each one, absorbing every gasp and moan and subtle lift of her hips against his straining erection. Determined to make this first time with her memorable, he moved slowly, savoring every taste, every sound, every moment of this life-changing event.

For more than thirty-five years, he'd gone out of his way to ensure that his life belonged to him and only him, and now... She was changing everything one sigh at a time, and he was allowing it to happen. His eyes were wide open to the earthquake he was inviting into his life that would divide his existence into two distinct halves, a fault line down the middle of *before Julia* and *after Julia*.

He settled between her legs and set out to demolish her control with determined strokes of his tongue over her clit and his fingers inside her tight channel. Everything about her turned him on to the point of madness, especially the enthusiastic way she responded to him.

Her fingers tangled into his hair, tugging to the point of pain, but that only added to the desire pounding through him. His entire world was reduced to her pleasure and the sharp cries of fulfillment that fell from lips swollen due to their kisses. Her internal muscles gripped his fingers so tightly that he nearly lost his mind imagining how that would feel around his cock.

In the aftermath of her orgasm, she lay sprawled on the bed, legs spread, chest heaving from deep breaths. When she opened her eyes, he saw everything he'd ever wanted in the way she looked at him.

Deacon left her only long enough to find the strip of condoms he'd stashed in his pants pocket—just in case—tearing one off and rolling it on quickly but carefully before returning to his new favorite place between her legs. "You still with me?" He kissed her and brushed the silky dark hair back from her flushed face.

"I'm here."

"All good?"

"*So* good."

He pressed his cock against her entrance. "I can make it even better."

"Not sure that's possible."

"Oh, I do so love a challenge."

She smiled up at him. "Knock yourself out."

"Don't mind if I do." As he entered her in slow, careful increments, she wrapped her arms around him and drew him into a sweet, soft, achingly sensual kiss that made his heart flutter with awareness of her.

She raised her hips, asking for more, which he gladly gave her, and the feeling that came over him as they joined their bodies couldn't be described in mere words.

Deacon trembled from the effort it took to stay focused on pleasing her again before he took his own pleasure.

Her hands on his back soothed and aroused him. "Julia…"

"Hmm?"

"Feels so good. So, *so* good."

"Yes. So good. Don't stop."

He gasped out a laugh. "Stopping isn't in the plans, sweetheart."

As if she could sense the battle he was waging with himself, she wrapped her legs around his hips and tightened her internal muscles around his cock. That flipped a switch inside him that made him forget all about finesse or tenderness or anything other than the driving need for more of her. He wanted *all* of her. Everything she was willing to give him.

Thankfully, she seemed to be right there with him, giving as good as she got.

"*Deacon.*"

"Tell me, love. What do you need?"

"This. Just you." Her fingers dug into his shoulders, and her legs tightened around his waist until they were both soaring, coming together in the most perfect moment he'd ever known. As he came down from the highest of highs, he had the presence of mind to understand that absolutely everything had changed, and there was no going back to who he'd been a few days ago.

He withdrew from her, disposed of the condom into a tissue and moved so he could see her face. Her stunned expression probably mirrored his as they stared at each other in the aftermath.

Deacon reached for her, needing to kiss her more than he wanted his next breath. She opened her arms to him. They stayed that way for the longest time, making out like teenagers who'd only just discovered the pleasure to be found in kissing. Although it was safe to say he'd never found this kind of pleasure from kissing.

"What're you doing to me?" The room had begun to go dark, and music drifted up from the back deck of the Sand & Surf along with the clatter of dinner service at Stephanie's Bistro.

"The same thing you're doing to me."

He scooped up a handful of her fragrant hair and brought it to his face, breathing in the distinctive scent, committing it to memory so he would never forget this night. As if that was even a remote possibility. Deacon caught a glimpse of something on the back of her neck and lifted himself for a better view of a tattoo of a turtle, looking back over its shoulder as its shell seemed to blow away, leaving the rest of its body unprotected.

He immediately understood the significance of a turtle without its shell, but he wanted to hear it from her. "Tell me about the turtle." With his index finger, he traced the outline of the turtle's fragile body.

"The turtle is me. I walk around without a shell to protect me from the pain of being alive."

Deacon had no idea how to respond to that except to vow, to himself for now, to protect her from ever being hurt again. He wanted to be her shell. Leaning over her, he placed a kiss on the turtle's body, and then, easing her onto her belly, he kissed down her back to the dimpled indents at the base of her spine, to her soft ass cheeks and below. He kissed her until she was squirming beneath him.

He reached for another condom and entered her from behind this time, coming down over her, grasping her hands and raising them above her head. "Let me be your shell." The words were out before he could decide to say them, because the thought of her walking around unprotected was unbearable to him. As he kissed her shoulder, the back of her neck and then her other shoulder, the words poured out of him as he made love to her. "I'll protect you. No one will ever hurt you again."

A sob erupted from her chest that had him holding her closer to him. "I've got you, darlin'. I've got you."

She held on tight to his hands as he moved in her and discovered the fundamental difference between having sex and making love.

Much later, the longest after-sex kiss in history was interrupted by an obnoxiously loud growl from Julia's stomach.

They broke apart laughing.

"That was mortifying."

"Someone is hungry."

"For the first time in months."

When he heard that, his brows furrowed with concern, but he already knew she wouldn't appreciate him picking apart her issues with food and eating. "Let's get you some dinner."

"I need a shower first."

"Mind if I join you?"

She hesitated, but only for a second before she nodded.

He ran a finger over the hint of blush on her cheek. "Still shy after what we just did?"

"A little."

"That's okay. You go, and then I will." He noted a flash of relief in her expression before she quickly corrected herself.

She wrapped the sheet around her body and got up. "I'll be quick."

"Take your time. I'm not the one who's hangry."

"Not hangry yet, but getting there."

She picked up the robe from the floor and went into the bathroom, closing the door behind her.

While he waited for her, Deacon looked up at the ceiling, watching the mesmerizing spin of the fan while trying to process the remarkable events of the last few days. He'd heard Blaine say something about a wedding at the newly reopened Wayfarer and had decided to stop by to see what the McCarthys had done with the old place. If he'd also managed to irritate his annoying brother by crashing the wedding, that would've been a bonus.

He hadn't been there five minutes when he'd noticed the stunning bridesmaid standing on the sidelines, looking lost and alone in a sea of people. He'd watched her for quite some time before he approached her, inexplicably drawn to her.

Only a few days later, he was relaxing in her bed after the best sex of his life. It would probably take until the end of time to reconcile the head-spinning events that had led him to this moment.

The puppy let out a pathetic whimper that had Deacon rising from the bed to retrieve him from the crate. "Hey, buddy. Sorry you had to hear that, but Mommy is just too sexy." He snuggled the puppy into his chest and was rewarded with a warm stream of urine.

Deacon laughed. "I suppose *I* deserved that." He really was too cute.

Julia came out fully dressed and put together, stopping short at the sight of him sitting naked on her bed with the puppy.

He dug the way she looked at him—as if she liked what she was seeing so much, she couldn't look away. "I really need a shower now. He peed on me."

"Pupwell! Don't pee on Daddy!"

Hearing her call him that did strange things to his insides, making him feel elated and slightly freaked out at the same time. It had never occurred to him that he would meet someone who made him want to be a daddy—to a puppy or a child. But now... Jesus. He needed to get his shit together. Deacon took the towel she'd gotten him and handed the puppy to her.

"I'll take him out while you shower. Just in case there's more where that came from."

They shared a smile full of parental pleasure in their little boy. Deacon stole a kiss before heading for the shower. Freak-out aside, he was falling hard for her, and falling had never felt so good.

CHAPTER 21

This cannot happen again. That was the only thought in Mac's head as Victoria and David worked frantically to determine the source of Maddie's pain. They'd assured the panic-stricken parents that the babies were fine, that Maddie was not in labor, even as the pain kept coming in her lower right side.

She couldn't be in labor. Not yet. The babies weren't due until September. It was way too soon.

Mac's chest tightened once again as anxiety gripped him. He stood by Maddie's bed, trying to stay calm for her when he wanted to howl from the fear of something going wrong.

"Mac," Maddie said between pains. "Stop spinning. Everything is fine."

"You don't know that."

"Yes, I do. Please... I can't be worried about you collapsing again. You have to stay calm."

Easier said than done. "I'm trying, honey. Seeing you in pain is making me nuts."

"I know. But the babies are fine, and it's not labor. Isn't that all that matters?"

"No, it isn't. You matter, too."

"I'm fine. It hurts, but it's not unbearable."

Victoria had performed a full internal exam, and David had ordered blood work. Waiting for results was going to make Mac crazier than he already was.

"Have you talked to my mom?" Maddie asked. "Are the kids all right?"

"Everyone is fine. Tiffany is there to help with bedtime. The rest of the family is in the waiting room."

"You should send them home. We're okay, and they have stuff to do."

"They're waiting to hear for sure that you and the girls are okay." Mac brought the hand of hers he was holding to his lips to kiss the back of it.

"Tell them we'll text them. I swear it's not going to be anything big. I know it."

He didn't want to question her certainty or give her more reason for concern, so he agreed to pass along the message. "I'll be right back. Don't go anywhere."

She laughed even as she grimaced from another wave of pain.

Mac tore himself away from her and went to the waiting room to deal with the family members who occupied every available seat.

His dad jumped up when he saw Mac coming. "How is she?"

"Fine, or so she says. She's definitely not in early labor. They're trying to figure out what's causing the pain, but Maddie wants you all to go home and get some rest. She promises it's nothing to worry about, and we'll text when we know what's up."

"What about you, son? You're supposed to be taking it easy."

"I'm doing all right. We're both fine. I promise. It's safe to stand down." He could tell his father didn't want to go, but when his mom put her hand through his arm and gave a gentle tug, Big Mac relented.

"You'll call if anything changes?"

"Absolutely." Mac gave his dad a hug, because he looked like he needed it. "It's all good. I promise."

"Don't let me see you at the marina any time soon, you got me?"

"I got you, but I will be by to do the paperwork. I'm not letting you undo all my hard work to get that place organized."

"Send Julia over to take care of that."

"I didn't hire her to manage the marina."

"Maybe she'd be willing to do both for some extra money."

Mac hadn't thought of that. "I'll ask her."

"Do that. It's time to take some of the load off your shoulders, son. I'm sorry I let it get to the point where you were buckling under it all."

"You didn't let that happen, Dad. I did it. It's been a crazy few months, but now that the Wayfarer is done, things will calm down."

"Until your twins arrive."

"I'm gonna get my shit together and find ways to manage the stress. Today was a wake-up call, and I promise I'm going to take it seriously. My family needs me. I can't let anything happen to me."

Big Mac placed a large hand on Mac's shoulder and looked him dead in the eyes. "You're damned right we need you."

"I'll check in later. Go on home."

"We're going." Linda hugged him and crooked her finger to bring him down for a kiss to the cheek. "Call if you need anything."

"Will do."

He hugged his siblings and their partners. "Thanks for coming, everyone. We appreciate the concern."

Janey gazed at him tearfully. "Don't scare us like that again."

"I won't, brat. I promise."

It took fifteen precious minutes away from Maddie to reassure his family members that it was safe to leave the clinic and go home. When he returned to her, he was relieved to find her dozing. He hoped that meant the pain had let up somewhat.

Mac sat in the chair next to her bed and dropped his head into his hands. He'd meant what he'd said to his dad about the incident serving as a wake-up call. The thought of his children growing up without him there to guide and love them was unimaginable. Though he still couldn't recall what'd happened before, he certainly remembered the first time it'd happened in Miami. That time, he'd been all but certain he was having a heart attack.

Hiring Julia would help, but he needed to go even further by sharing the load with the people he worked with. Shane was more than capable of doing more. Riley and Finn had committed to sticking around long-term now that each of them had found love on the island. Mac wondered if his cousins would be interested in becoming partners in the construction business.

He liked that idea a lot and would bring it up with his cousins the first chance he got. Between the construction business and the marina, he made more than enough money to support his family. There was no need for him to be killing himself making it all work when he had plenty of people who'd be willing and able to help.

Mac took hold of Maddie's hand and was on his way to dozing off in the chair when Victoria came into the room, putting Mac on immediate alert.

Maddie came to with a start, panic etched into her expression.

"You can relax," Vic said. "Everything came back normal, which is a relief. We'd suspected appendicitis at first."

"If everything is normal, then why is she in pain?"

"We suspect one of the babies is sitting on a nerve."

"That can happen?"

Victoria smiled and nodded as she leaned against the counter that housed a sink and medical supplies. "As the babies grow, they'll take up more of the space inside Maddie and are apt to cause other aches and pains."

Mac couldn't believe what he was hearing. "How can childbirth be the most natural thing in the world if it takes such a toll on the mother?"

"Women are built to give birth, as hard to believe as that can be at times like this."

"It is hard to believe. What can we do to make it better for her?"

"I'm going to recommend bed rest for the remainder of her pregnancy."

Maddie's loud groan told them what she thought of that plan. "No way. I have three kids to take care of."

"I know it'll be difficult for you and your family, Maddie, but—"

"We'll do it." Mac said the words to Maddie. "If it's what's best for you and the babies, we'll make it work. We've done it before." She'd been on bed rest for part of her pregnancy with Mac.

Tears filled her gorgeous eyes. "The whole summer in bed?"

"You don't have to be in bed the whole time," David said when he joined them. "You just have to be off your feet, relaxing and taking it easy most of the time. Hopefully, we won't need to go to full bed rest, which would mean getting up only to use the bathroom and shower."

Tears rolled down Maddie's face. "I can't believe this."

"It'll be fine. I'll work less and be home more, and our parents will help with the kids. Everyone will help. You know that."

"There's, ah… one other thing," David said.

His hesitant tone put Mac on high alert.

"I'm also recommending you refrain from any kind of sexual activity until the babies arrive."

Ugh, not again! How could no sex for months be good for anyone's health? "Um, well, okay. If that's what's best for Maddie and the babies."

"She needs rest and relaxation. The babies need a calm, serene environment to continue growing. We want to get them to thirty-five weeks if we can. That's the goal."

Maddie wanted sex all the time when she was pregnant, which he had joked was the best part of keeping her pregnant. She looked as disappointed as he felt. "We can abstain, Mac. It's only a few months."

Only a few months? He wanted her all the time. Like last time they'd been forced to abstain, it would be torture to keep his hands to himself for that long. But of course he'd do whatever he had to in order to protect his wife and daughters, even if that meant going without.

He leaned over to kiss her cheek. "It's all good, baby. Whatever it takes to bring these little girls into the world and to keep you all safe and healthy."

"How's the pain, Maddie?" Vic asked.

"Better than it was."

"It's apt to come and go as the babies move around."

"Oh joy."

Despite her sarcastic reply, Mac knew she felt the same way he did about doing whatever it took to ensure a safe delivery. After the agony of losing Connor, they were painfully aware of worst-case scenarios.

David removed the monitors that had been attached to Maddie. "I'm fine with releasing you both, provided you take it easy and check back with me if you experience any other symptoms or have concerns. Maddie, any other random pain needs to be fully investigated. Please call me if anything comes up—day or night."

"Will do," Mac said.

"There's one other thing I want to say to you guys." David made sure to look at both of them. "In the past couple of months, you've both been here with anxiety-related symptoms, and I don't think that's a coincidence. Losing Connor understandably rocked you, and as hard as it is to go through something like that, there's no reason to believe it'll happen again."

Maddie sniffled and wiped away tears that came any time Connor's name was mentioned.

Mac put his arm around her as he blinked back tears of his own.

"The thing is," David continued, "you can't let the fear of that happening cause secondary health concerns. That kind of anxiety isn't good for either of you. I know it's really hard to believe that everything will be okay with the twins, but there's no reason to believe it won't be. Okay?"

Maddie nodded and wiped away more tears.

Mac shook his hand. "Thanks, David."

"I'd say it was a pleasure, but I hate to see you in here for anything other than routine visits."

"We hate it, too," Mac said as he helped Maddie sit up so she could get dressed. "No more crises. We've had enough of them for one lifetime."

David signed the discharge paperwork, and Victoria promised to check on them the next day.

When they got to the parking lot ten minutes later, Mac realized they had two cars there. "I'll send someone to get the truck tomorrow." He helped Maddie into the passenger seat of her SUV. Fortunately, it had a third row of seats, which they would soon need to transport their *five kids* around.

Breathe, Mac. You've got this.

As they rode through the dark winding roads that led to home, Mac looked over at Maddie. "David's right. We're letting the stress get to us."

"I know."

"We have to try harder to focus on the good things and the three successful pregnancies rather than the one that didn't work out."

"I know that, too."

"Easier said than done, though, right?"

"Yeah."

At home, they found Francine sacked out on the sofa. Rather than disturb her, Mac texted Ned that she was asleep. He covered his mother-in-law with a blanket and shut off the lights before going upstairs to find Maddie already in bed.

He unbuttoned his shirt and took it off. "What a day."

"One I'm not going to want to remember years from now."

"Me either, but we have a lot to be thankful for. I didn't actually have a heart attack, and you didn't go into premature labor."

"True."

"My grandmother used to tell us to see the glass as half full rather than half empty, and it would make anything seem better than it was."

"She had a point."

Mac went into the bathroom to brush his teeth and dropped his work clothes into the hamper. He got into bed next to Maddie and stared up at the ceiling, focusing on breathing the way David had told him to. When he looked over at Maddie, he found her watching him. "What?"

"Just looking."

"Don't look at me. Don't come near me, and for the love of God, do not touch me."

She lost it laughing. "Is that what it's going to take to get through the next few months?"

"Yes."

His gorgeous wife slid across the mile he'd put between them, snuggled up to him and rested her hand on his abdomen. "That's not going to work for me. I can't go months without touching you or kissing you or sleeping in your arms."

"Madeline…"

She slid her hand down to encircle his hard cock. "He said *I* can't have sex. He never said anything about you."

He put his hand on top of hers to stop her from moving it. "That's exactly what it means. If you can't have it, I can't either."

"That's ridiculous, Mac. Why should you suffer just because I'm laid up?"

"You're laid up because you're carrying my babies. What's fair is fair. We're officially on the wagon."

"You can't go two days without sex. How will you stand to wait months?"

"I've done it before when you were expecting Mac, and I went weeks without it after you had Hailey and Mac, and after we lost Connor. Contrary to popular opinion, I'm not a complete horn dog."

"Um, well, you're a pretty horny dog."

He gave her a foul look. "So are you. And by the way, I *can* control myself when I have to, and right now I have to because it's what's best for you and the girls. It's no big deal."

"You say that now…"

"I say that until six weeks after these babies are born."

"Want to make a bet?"

He raised a brow. "What kind of bet?"

"That you can't go that long without taking the edge off."

"Maddie! Are you suggesting that I…"

"Spank the monkey? Well, don't you?"

Hearing the words *spank the monkey* coming from her made him so hard, he saw stars. "My brother Adam says there are guys who do it and guys who lie about it."

Maddie laughed. "So which one are you?"

"I've been known to spank the occasional monkey in my life, but far less often since I've had my beautiful wife to spank it for me. But trust me. My monkey can go without spanking, if need be."

"And that's where the bet comes in. I bet you can't make it to the end of my pregnancy without doing some spanking."

"I can, too!"

"Cannot."

"Fine. I'll take your bet. What's the wager?"

"Hundred bucks?"

He held out his hand.

She shook it.

"How will you know if I fall off the wagon?"

"You have to tell me. You're on the honor system."

"Won't be anything to tell."

"If you say so."

"I do."

"We shall see."

"Yes, we shall." Even as he made the wager and talked a big game, he hoped he could stick to it.

"Mac?"

"Yes?"

"Will you kiss me good night?"

He gave her a chaste peck on the lips.

"I want a real kiss."

"You're not allowed to have real kisses."

"Yes, I am! I'm not allowed to have sex. David said nothing about kissing."

"Kissing leads to sex."

"Not if we don't let it. Please? I can't go months without at least kissing you."

"I can't go that long without kissing you either." He turned on his side to face her. "I hope these girls go easy on us when they're teenagers. They're going to owe us for the *enormous* sacrifices we're making for them."

"Which you will not ever tell them about."

"I love when you're stern with me. It's so hot."

"Put some ice on it. We're on the wagon."

"Don't remind me. Are you going to kiss me or what?"

"I'm going to kiss you."

And when she did, Mac quickly realized that, despite his bravado, abstinence was going to be pure torture, because like always, any time he kissed his sexy wife, he only wanted more of her.

CHAPTER 22

*J*ulia was ravenous. Sitting with Deacon in Stephanie's Bistro, she perused the menu. After weeks in which nothing appealed to her, suddenly everything did.

"What looks good to you?"

"All of it."

Stephanie approached their table. "Hey, sis."

Julia laughed at the face Stephanie made as she tried on the new tag. "Hi there."

"Sorry. I've never had siblings, so getting seven of them all at once has turned me into a bit of a dork."

Julia couldn't imagine life without her six siblings. "You're not a dork, and we're thrilled to have you."

"Really?" The bright, hopeful look on Stephanie's face was nothing short of adorable.

"Really."

Stephanie cleared her throat and made a visible effort to pull herself together. "May I tell you about our specials?"

"Yes, please," Julia said.

After Stephanie went through the list, Deacon gestured for Julia to order first.

"I don't know what I want. It all sounds so good."

"Could I offer you a taster platter? You could have some of everything."

"That'd be awesome."

Deacon nodded in agreement and handed his menu to Steph.

"I love having a sister with a restaurant," Julia said.

"Stop," Stephanie said, taking Julia's menu. "You'll make me cry. I'll send some wine over."

"We take for granted what we've always had," Deacon said after Steph had walked away.

"Right? I was thinking before that I can't imagine life without my siblings."

"Same, even if I sometimes wish I was an only child."

"I've never once wished for that. I wouldn't have survived without Owen and Katie, in particular."

"I'm sorry. I didn't mean to be insensitive."

"Don't be sorry. As Owen likes to say, it was what it was, and we made the best of it."

"Still… It was a nightmare, and I'm sorry you had to grow up that way."

They drank the wine and devoured the appetizers Stephanie sent over. Julia ate it all—the calamari, clams casino and goat cheese spread.

Deacon chuckled at her enthusiasm.

Julia took a sip of wine and ventured a tentative glance at him. "This is what I do."

"What do you mean?"

"When my anxiety is bad like it's been the last few months, it's all I can do to eat enough to stay alive." Embarrassed to be confessing such a thing to him, she looked down at the table.

He put his hand over hers. "It's okay, Julia. I'm not judging you. I swear I'm not."

She turned her hand up so their palms were joined and curled her fingers around his hand. "After the anxiety passes, I eat everything in sight, which makes me sick. It's a rather vicious cycle."

"I imagine so."

"I'm really thin right now. Too thin."

"Maybe so, but I think you're beautiful no matter what." He gave her hand a squeeze. "You'll start to feel better now that you've gotten the money back."

"I already do." She forced herself to look at him, to acknowledge the intensity of their connection. "Thanks to you."

"It gave me great pleasure to help you. Since I left the job, that's the part I've missed the most. Helping people. Righting wrongs like what happened to you. Protecting people who don't have anyone else to look out for them. It was very satisfying work."

"I'll bet you were really good at it."

"I enjoyed it."

"You must've been heartbroken to have to retire early."

"Completely. It was devastating. I didn't know who I was without the job."

"Have you figured that out yet?"

"Nope. Still a work in progress. I've been kind of lost without it, to be honest. I like doing the harbor master job, but it's not the same. People on boats aren't often in crisis except when they party too much or overdo it in the sun." He took a sip of his wine, put his glass down and glanced at her, looking serious. "I should tell you the real reason why I'm here this summer so you don't hear it from someone else."

"Okay..."

"I was in a bar fight and got arrested."

"Were you helping someone?"

He tipped his head, seeming intrigued by the question. "In fact, I was."

"Why am I not surprised?"

"My brother, who bailed me out and made me come to Gansett for the summer, says I have a hero complex."

"There're worse things people could say about you."

"Not according to Blaine."

"Does his opinion matter so much to you?"

"It matters more than it should. Our dad worked on the mainland,

211

so Blaine took it upon himself to supervise me and our other siblings when my dad wasn't around. I guess you could say I gave him a run for his money because I didn't want him telling me what to do. He's never been able to get past that."

Julia propped her chin on her upturned fist. "What kind of stuff did you do?"

"You name it, I did it. Drinking, partying, chasing girls, sneaking out of the house, driving too fast, skipping school."

"You were a bad boy."

He leaned in, lowered his voice. "Still am."

"I never did any of that stuff. I was too afraid of what would happen if I got caught."

"I can teach you how not to get caught."

Julia laughed. "I bet you know all the tricks."

"Stick with me, baby. I'll show you some trouble."

"I've had more than enough trouble, thank you very much."

"My kind is the good kind." He brought her hand to his lips and kissed the back of it, the rough caress of his whiskers against her skin setting off a wildfire of reaction inside her. "You need to cut loose a little, have some fun and take some risks."

"I'm already taking risks. Great big ones."

"I know, and I'm very determined not to disappoint you."

"Why me? I'm sure there're a lot of much less complicated women on this island who'd love to keep you company this summer." Although, the thought of him with anyone else made her seethe after only a few days. This was not good at all.

He grinned widely, revealing that devastating dimple in his cheek. "Are you already trying to get rid of me?"

"Not at all. I'm just pointing out that you could certainly have anyone you wanted."

"Is that right?"

She rolled her eyes. "Don't act like you don't know that. In all seriousness... You should know... I've got, you know, some rather big issues."

"Show me someone who gets to be thirtysomething without a few issues."

"I have kind of a lot of issues."

"Okay."

"Be serious."

"I'm as serious about this—about you—as I've been about anything since I left the job, Julia. I hear what you're saying, and I appreciate that you're saying it, but it doesn't matter to me in any way except I hope maybe someday you might feel better about the things that trouble you."

She leaned into him, close enough to kiss his cheek. "You're very sweet."

"Fuck that. I am not."

Julia laughed, harder than she had in months. "Yes, you are."

"Whatever." Deacon smiled at a man walking by their table and then stood to give him a bro hug. "It's so good to see you, man. Do you know Julia Lawry? Julia, this is Evan McCarthy. We went to high school together."

Julia shook hands with Evan, who was tall and dark-haired and had the distinctive McCarthy blue eyes. "I know Evan. He's Owen's best friend." To Evan, she added, "I love your music."

"Oh, thanks, that's nice to hear. Good to see you again."

"Are you here for the summer?" Deacon asked.

"Until mid-July. I'm recording some new music at the studio, and Grace needed to check in at the pharmacy before we go back out on tour."

"You're a big star these days. I'm surprised you remember us little people."

"Shut up." Evan laughed. "Are you hanging out for a bit? Owen and I are going to play."

"Yeah, we'll be here."

"Great. Let's grab a beer while I'm home."

"I'd love to. Hit me up. Still got the same number."

"Me, too."

Deacon returned to his seat and slid an arm around the back of Julia's chair. "He's a good guy."

"Owen loves him. They've been best friends for years."

Over the next hour, Deacon and Julia ate the delicious food, drank more wine and asked each other silly questions.

"What's your favorite color?" she asked, feeling buzzed and mellow after the food and wine.

"Red. You?"

"Purple."

"Dogs or cats?" he asked.

"Duh. Dogs. Sheep or goats?"

He gave her an adorably perplexed look. "Am I supposed to have a preference?"

Julia laughed. "Yes! Goats are the cutest. Have you ever seen baby goats? I'm going to have baby goats at my house someday, but not until I'm settled somewhere permanently."

"Okay, then, goats it is."

She smiled triumphantly. "City or country?"

"Both? I loved living in Boston, but I can also see the benefit of the country. I was in Harwich before this, and I liked being there, too. That's not really the country, but the pace is nothing like Boston."

"I like both, too, but prefer island life to just about anything."

"Island life used to drive me bonkers when I was a kid. I used to dream of just getting in the water and swimming to the mainland to get out of here."

"You had no idea how lucky you were to be raised here, to never have to leave."

"No, I didn't." He waggled his brows at her suggestively. "But I'm starting to see the benefit to being stuck here."

Julia's face flushed with heat as his gruffly spoken words set off the wildfire inside her once again. Never before had a man been able to turn her on using mere words the way this man could.

"Beach or mountains?" she asked.

"Beach every day and twice on Sunday."

"Me, too. I miss the beach so much when I'm in Texas."

Deacon spread goat cheese on a small piece of bread and fed it to her. "What was your favorite place you ever lived?"

"Right here. Every summer at this hotel with my grandparents was the best time of my entire life. Those months here were the only respite we ever got from the shitshow at home. We used to cry for days when we had to go home."

"None of you ever told them what was going on at home?"

Julia shook her head. "We were too afraid to. He told us what would happen if we 'told tales out of school.' He said what went on in our home was our business and no one else's. We were also fearful of what would happen to our mom, because she didn't get to come with us. She was stuck at home with him. My grandmother was inconsolable when the whole story came out years later."

"I can only imagine. I know he's your dad and everything, but I'm so, so glad he's finally where he's belonged for years."

"I am, too. Sometimes I still can't believe it actually happened, that he pleaded guilty and was thrown in jail. I'll hear someone screaming or shouting, and I tense up. Then I remember. He's not coming for me ever again."

"Did he..." Deacon swallowed hard, his jaw tensing.

"My mom and my brothers were the ones he hit and physically abused. He used his words against me and my sisters. His favorite form of warfare with us was emotional."

"God, Julia. I'm so sorry you had to grow up that way."

"Me, too, but at least you understand why I am the way I am."

"I think the way you are is pretty damned awesome."

"Thank you. That's sweet of you to say."

"I mean it."

Julia had been so caught up in the conversation with Deacon that she'd failed to notice that Owen and Evan had begun their set on the stage located on the far side of the big dining room.

She tuned in to hear Evan sing "My Amazing Grace," his chart-topping hit, with Owen accompanying him on background. "I love this song."

"I do, too. It's so great to see him getting the attention he deserves. He's so crazy-talented."

"He really is."

"So is Owen."

Julia nodded. "The music saved him during the worst of it with our father. He just lost himself in it." She had, too, but she wasn't about to share that part of herself with him or anyone. That had gotten lost along the way, and it'd been years since she'd played or sung.

Almost as if he was reading her mind, Owen stepped up to the microphone and began to speak directly to her. "I'm not the only Lawry who got the music gene."

Julia felt like she'd been struck by someone she trusted and loved more than just about anyone. He was not doing this. No way. She stood, needing to get out of there before he could force her to confront something so painful, the mere thought of it threatened to swallow her whole.

"My sister Julia is a gifted musician and has the most incredible voice I've ever heard. She hasn't performed in public in a while, but I really hope she'll gift us with her talent tonight, because once you've heard her play the piano and sing, you'll never forget it."

CHAPTER 23

*J*ulia wanted to die, to melt into the floor before he could say something that would force her to confront the past once again. She would've fled, but her legs couldn't seem to get the message from her brain that she needed to get the hell out of there right now.

Owen handed his guitar to Evan and brought the microphone with him when he came down off the stage to meet her.

"My beautiful sister Julia is here, and you guys… How about we give her a round of applause and see if we can get her up here to play for us?"

As the rest of people in the room went wild clapping, whistling and stomping their feet, Julia couldn't breathe. How could Owen do this to her?

She shook her head.

Owen came to a stop right in front of her. "Pretty please?" He compelled her with his eyes to be bigger than the fear, bigger than the past.

Maybe it was the wine she'd consumed or the way Deacon smiled so widely at her when she glanced back at him as he clapped and whistled louder than anyone. She summoned the courage from deep inside, took the hand Owen extended to her and held on tight to the brother who'd been her rock. They walked toward the stage and the instrument that'd been such a huge part of her life until that, too, had been lost to the madness.

"I'm gonna kill you for this," she muttered.

His broad smile touched her heart. "Take it back, Jule. It's been waiting a long time for you to come home to it."

She blinked back tears as she nodded and took her strength from him the way she had all her life. Her big brother, her protector, her dearest friend, her fellow survivor. If he could do it, so could she.

Owen and Evan left her alone on the stage, fighting back panic, memories and pervasive sadness to focus on the thing that had kept her alive through some of the darkest days of her life. As long as she could lose herself in the music, she could find her way through to the other side of whatever crisis faced her. Until the monster had taken it from her by forbidding her to play or sing in public or at home.

He'd known how much it meant to her, so he'd taken it, the way he'd taken everything else that mattered to her. The music had lived inside her and given her a purpose. When he'd taken it from her… That'd been the first time her heart had been broken.

Julia sat behind the piano and thought about the recent hit song she'd fallen in love with. She'd never played or sung it before, so it was risky to do it for the first time in front of a packed house, but her fingers found the keys, and the magic came back in a tsunami of emotion that had her throat closing for a full minute until she got herself together and found the words she needed.

From the first time she'd heard Lady Gaga sing "Always Remember Us This Way," Julia had connected to the song like she hadn't connected to anything musical in years. As the song poured from her soul, she forgot about everything and anything that wasn't the music, the way she had when she'd used music to escape the night-mare that'd been her life.

By the time she played the final notes, she was on the way to a crash landing from the emotional high until the room exploded in applause that had her climbing once again. People were standing, cheering, whistling. Owen wiped tears from his eyes as he joined her on the stage. "Am I right?" he said into the mic, setting off another round of wild applause.

Julia stood on trembling legs to accept a hug from her brother. "Most beautiful thing I've heard in forever," he whispered in her ear. "Stunning."

She clung to him the way she had all her life, holding on to one of the six people who had never let her down.

Owen released her, stepped aside and led another round of enthusiastic applause. "One more?"

Julia rolled her eyes at him.

"Pretty please?"

The enthusiastic support of the audience had her playing the opening notes to Kelly Clarkson's song "Because of You." Julia vividly remembered sitting in her car with tears rolling down her face the first time she heard that song and understood that it was about someone like her, who'd been abused and would carry those scars with her forever.

Like then, the song made her cry even as she tried to power through it without becoming overly emotional.

The audience's applause was even louder when she finished the second song. She wiped away her tears and forced a smile for Deacon, who was standing and smiling and clapping with enthusiasm.

"Ladies and gentlemen," Owen said, "one more round for my sister, Julia Lawry."

While the crowd went wild, Deacon came to the steps to offer her a hand.

Owen sat on a stool and strummed his guitar. "I've always hated having to follow Julia, and now you know why. But the show must go on." He played the opening notes to "Yellow" by Coldplay.

Deacon put an arm around Julia and kept her close to him as people praised her performance on the way out of the crowded restaurant. "That was the most incredible thing I've ever heard," he said in the gruff voice that was quickly becoming her favorite sound ever.

"I'm going to lose it any second now," she said so only he could hear her.

He stepped up the pace, steered her toward the porch and held her as the emotion poured from her in a torrent of tears that made her feel weak, but damn if she could contain them.

"Sweet Julia," Deacon whispered. "There's so much more to you than I ever could've imagined."

He held her while she got it all out in a flood of memories and emotion and yearning for more of the thing that had sustained her.

"Excuse me," Evan said from behind them. "I'm so sorry to interrupt."

Julia raised her head from Deacon's chest and wiped her eyes, embarrassed to have been caught having an emotional meltdown by a singer of Evan's caliber.

"I just want to say..." Evan shook his head, seeming flabbergasted. "Your voice is *magical.*"

"Thank you so much. That means a lot coming from you."

"Julia... I'm rarely at a loss for words, but why in the hell are you not a professional singer?"

"I found myself on a different path," she said, simplifying one of the more complicated things she'd ever confronted.

"I'd love to talk to you about it if you have a few minutes." He handed her a business card. "I own Island Breeze Records, and I'll be there every day until mid-July. Feel free to stop by any time."

Julia took the card from him, the whole thing too surreal for words. "Thank you."

"You have a rare and special talent. I really hope you'll come by." He nodded to Deacon. "You guys have a great night."

Evan walked away, leaving Julia stunned and unnerved by what he'd said and offered.

"Holy shit," Deacon whispered. "Julia... Oh my God!"

She couldn't seem to form a rational thought or reaction to what'd just taken place. Just over a week ago, she'd been sleeping on a friend's sofa after losing her job and her apartment. Today, she had Deacon and a puppy and a new job, and now Evan McCarthy wanted her to "come by" his studio to talk about her "rare and special talent."

No, there was no way that last part could be real. No way. She was still having trouble believing Deacon was for real. Evan, well… That was too crazy to be believed.

"What do you need, darlin'?"

"I, uh… I just don't know."

Julia didn't know what she needed, but apparently, Deacon did. He put that strong arm around her again and guided her inside to the stairs that led up to the sanctuary of her room. Tomorrow, she'd meet up with Cindy to see about the house they were thinking of renting. But for now, for tonight, the hotel, her favorite place in the world, was home.

When they reached her door, Deacon found the key in her purse and dealt with the lock, ushering her in ahead of him. He cared for her so naturally, as if he'd been doing it forever rather than only a few days.

Julia turned to him, put her arms around his neck and kissed him. "Thank you."

"For what?"

"For everything. For being you. For being just what I need when I needed you most."

He wrapped his arms around her and buried his face in her hair, his lips finding the sensitive skin on her neck. "You're making a mess of me."

That voice, dear God, she would hear it in her dreams for the rest of her life and shiver at the memory. "Is that a good thing?"

"It's the best fucking thing ever."

MUCH LATER, DEACON LAY ON HIS SIDE IN JULIA'S BED, DRINKING IN THE sight of her in the moonlight pouring in through her window. He'd intended to go home, to get a good night's sleep before work in the morning, but he'd been unable to find the energy to leave her after loving her once again.

From the crate, Puppy's little snores had had them cracking up earlier. He'd crashed hard after Deacon took him out to pee.

In the soft afterglow of wild passion, Deacon ran his hand up and down Julia's arm, delighting in the goose bumps that broke out on her sensitive skin. "Tell me about the music."

Her deep sigh made him wish he hadn't asked, but curiosity had gotten the better of him.

"When we were little, we all had to have an activity. We got to pick what we wanted to do, but we had to do something. My dad wanted us all to do sports, so I played soccer—not well—and took piano lessons. I really loved playing the piano, and my teacher in Virginia told my mother I was a prodigy. My grandparents bought me a gorgeous little baby grand piano that I played for hours every day. I played until my fingers ached and my back hurt, and then I played more. I could hear something once and play it without sheet music. By the time I was eleven, I was playing in church and performing the music for a local dance studio's recitals."

"At eleven? That's incredible."

"I loved it so much. It was the thing that made me special. Owen played the guitar from the time he was twelve, but he didn't get really good until he was older. When I was sixteen, I was invited to play with a local cover band at a festival. It was the greatest day of my life. We killed it. The guys in the band were so happy. My dad, though... He was furious."

"Why?" Deacon wished he could have five minutes alone with the man who'd fathered her.

"He said he didn't like me spending time with men who looked at me like I was their little whore."

"Come on." He ached for her even as he wished he had something he could punch.

"I didn't know what a whore was. I had to look it up."

Deacon put his arm around her and brought her as close to him as he could get her. He wanted to hold her and protect her and keep her from ever being hurt again. And he'd never wanted that with any other woman. Not like this.

"When we moved that summer, he told me we couldn't fit the piano in the move, so he'd sold it. I was hysterical for days. I begged him to reconsider. My mom begged him. But he wasn't having it. The people who bought the piano came to get it and took it away. I hadn't played again until tonight, when Owen basically forced me to."

He couldn't believe she hadn't played since she was sixteen but had sounded like an angel tonight. "I'm so sorry that happened to you, sweetheart."

"It was nothing compared to what happened to Owen."

"It was everything to you." He ran his fingers through her hair, over and over again, trying to contain the rage that boiled in his gut. "Evan's right. You have a rare and special gift. I've never heard anything more beautiful."

"Thank you."

"Why didn't you go back to it when you were free of him?"

"I've spent a lot of time in therapy discussing that. The best explanation I can give is that you end up in survival mode after living the way we did for so long. You're conditioned to avoid the things that caused pain in the past. Music equaled pain for me, so I avoided it."

"I want you to have the music again, this time without the pain. I want that for you so badly. I want it for me, too, and everyone else who'll have the pleasure of hearing you sing and play."

"I don't know if I can."

"You can. You just did. Your dad is never going to be able to hurt you again."

"I know." She looked up at him, her expression so open and trusting. "You should know that I've never talked about this with anyone, not even Owen or Katie. I refused to discuss it after it happened. I just locked it away and tried to move on."

"Thank you for sharing it with me. It means a lot to me that you did."

"I couldn't believe Owen was doing that…"

"He wants you to have it again, too."

"When I got to the stage, he said, 'Take it back, Jule.'"

"That's exactly what you should do. Your father forced you to give it up. Now you can take it back and give him a massive middle finger."

Julia laughed at the ferocious way he said that.

"What's so funny?"

"You are."

"I'm dead serious, Julia."

"I know, and I appreciate it. I really do."

"You're free of him. You're all free of him. Your mom has remarried. Owen and Katie have made beautiful lives for themselves. Your other siblings are doing well. There's no reason whatsoever that you shouldn't have anything and everything you want. If you want to play and perform, then that's what you should do. You should play every single day, if that's what you want to do."

His encouragement meant so much to her. "I used to think Katie was ridiculous for never dating until she met Shane, but as much as I mocked her for it, I understood her reasoning. She'd rather be alone than take a chance that she'd end up with someone like the man who fathered us. I did the same thing, only in a different way. I avoided things I used to love out of fear they'd be taken from me again."

"Is it okay for me to say that I hope he gets the shit beat out of him in prison?"

She snorted with laughter. "It's okay for you to say that, but I don't hope for that, because I'd never want anyone to be hurt the way he hurt us, even him. I just can't carry that kind of anger around, or it'll swallow me whole. That's something I've learned in therapy, too."

"Is it okay for me to say that I've known you... Is it four whole days yet?"

"I think today is day three."

"I've known you three days, and I've never met anyone I admire more than I do you."

"I'm not sure I deserve that."

"You absolutely do. You deserve everything, and you should have anything you want. The sky's the limit." He would move heaven and earth if that was what it took to make sure she got whatever she wanted.

"Right now, I'm thrilled to have a new job to go to in the morning, an adorable puppy to love, my money back in the bank where it belongs and a sexy new guy in my bed. Life is good."

He kissed her neck and made her shiver. "I'm very glad to have made the list of things that're making your life good."

"You're at the top of the list. I should've started with you." Over his shoulder, she watched the digital clock on the bedside table hit two a.m. and groaned. "We need to sleep, or tomorrow will be a nightmare."

"I should go so you can get some rest."

When he would've gotten up, Julia stopped him. "Stay."

"Are you sure?"

"Mmm, I'm very sure."

"Very sure, huh? I like that."

"I like you."

Deacon tipped her chin up to receive his kiss. "I like you, too. A whole lot." He settled her head on his chest and rubbed her back until she fell asleep, but he was awake for a long time thinking about the things she'd told him and aching for her.

CHAPTER 24

*J*ulia's first day of work at McCarthy Construction was chaotic and busy and challenging. She loved every second of it. Luke reported that Mac was resting comfortably at home and was available by phone if she had questions. However, Julia was determined to leave him alone to rest, so she made piles of things she needed to discuss with him and moved forward with organizing the office and triaging the various needs from customers.

Luke had told her that the guys were renovating the Curtis family's Victorian home on Westview Road, a job they expected to take most of the summer. In the off-season, they'd be doing a major renovation to the McCarthys' hotel in North Harbor as well as building the new spa on the property. He had mentioned that Mac's cousin Riley McCarthy would be by at the end of the day to check in with her.

While she waited for Riley, she took Pupwell outside to pee and stretch his legs. He'd been a trouper during the long day at the office, and she was thrilled that she was able to have him with her while she worked.

Throughout the day, she'd found her thoughts frequently returning to Deacon and the night they'd spent together. She had broken all the rules she'd recently set for herself by getting so involved with him so quickly, but she couldn't come up with a single reason to keep him at arm's length. He'd been nothing but a good friend, confidant and advocate for her in the short time she'd known him.

She'd dated other men for months who didn't know her anywhere near the way Deacon already did after only a few days. That was a testament to him. He made it easy for her to share things with him she hardly ever talked about.

Everything about this with him was different than it had been before. He was different. He wasn't like guys who were after one thing only, and once they got that, they lost interest in her. As she waited for Pupwell to find a bush that pleased him, she thought about what Tiffany had said about Blaine, how he'd been unlike any man she'd ever met—and that her reaction to him had been unprecedented from the get-go.

Julia could relate to that. She'd been intrigued by Deacon the first time she saw him in the clinic, the night that Finn and Chloe had been stabbed by his crazy ex. At the wedding, he'd captivated her further with his astute, amusing observations as well as his questions about why she was so miserable at her sister's wedding. Up until then, she'd been doing a pretty good job of keeping her recent disappointment far away from her sister's big day, but watching Katie with Shane, seeing their obvious love for each other, had resurrected all the hopes she'd pinned on Mike and the searing pain of his betrayal.

Deacon, who'd only ever seen her once before, had tuned right in to that while a roomful of people she'd known most of her life hadn't noticed. They would have eventually, but they'd been focused on Katie that day, as they should've been.

She was so excited about her feelings for Deacon that she'd forgotten to be worried about the many ways it could still go badly for her.

Her thoughts were interrupted by Riley's arrival, which was just as well. She'd rather not think about the many ways it could go wrong with Deacon.

Riley hopped out of his truck and came over to her, extending his hand. "Sorry I'm late. I'm Riley." He was a younger version of Mac, with the same dark hair and the trademark McCarthy blue eyes.

Julia shook his hand. "Julia. Nice to see you again."

"Same. Mac asked me to make office keys for you." He handed over a key ring and told her which key was for which door.

"Thank you."

Riley bent to pet the puppy. "What a cutie. What's his name?"

"He doesn't really have one yet. I'm not sure if I'm going to get to keep him, so I'm afraid to name him. We've been calling him Puppy Pupwell."

"That sounds like a name to me."

"I know! I'm trying not to get attached and failing miserably."

"What's the deal with him?"

"Deacon Taylor and I found him swimming off the coast."

Riley looked up at her, shocked. "Say what?"

Julia nodded. "He must've fallen off a boat."

Riley stood and brushed his hands on his dirty jeans. "I hope you get to keep him."

"Me, too." She couldn't bear to think about the possibility of having to give back the puppy. "How're Mac and Maddie?"

"Recovering at home from a day they'll never forget." He filled her in on how both of them had ended up being treated at the clinic. "They've had a lot of stress. A while ago, they had a miscarriage, and I guess the fact that she's expecting twins has them both really worried. Victoria and David put Maddie on bed rest for the remainder of her pregnancy, so they're going to need a lot of help."

"Whatever I can do, just let me know."

"It's a huge deal for Mac to have your help here. He said he'll check in with you tomorrow and sends his apologies for not being here on your first day."

"Tell him it's no problem. I found plenty to do."

"Great, I'll let him know. Let me give you my number in case you need anything while he's not available."

Julia punched his number into her contacts and saved it. "Got it."

"Feel free to head home for the day. We'll pick it up in the morning."

"All right. See you then."

"Have a good night. Bye, Pupwell."

The puppy surprised them both when he yipped in response.

Julia laughed. "That's the first time he's talked."

Smiling, Riley waved as he drove off a few minutes later.

Julia locked up the office and walked the short distance to meet Cindy at the house they planned to rent together.

Cindy was already there when Julia arrived. Her sister had her light brown hair up in a messy bun that managed to somehow look stylish and put together. "Hey, come in. This place is perfect for us." She did a double take when she saw the dog. "Who's this cutie pie?"

"This is Puppy Pupwell." Julia told her sister how she'd come to have him.

"I really hope you get to keep him, Jule. I know how much you've always wanted a dog of your own."

"I hope so, too."

Cindy led Julia through a quick tour of the small two-bedroom house.

Julia was relieved to see that the backyard was fenced, which would be perfect for the puppy. If she got to keep him. *Keep saying that so you won't forget.* It was already far too late to warn herself about getting overly attached. She was completely in love with the little guy and would die if she had to give him up.

She didn't realize she was holding him too tightly until he uttered a little squeak of protest. "Sorry, baby."

"Finn said we can move in whenever we want to—and they're leaving the furniture for us. He has the lease through the thirty-first, and I signed it as of June first. We just have to put down the security deposit and first month's rent."

"Sounds good." A couple of days ago, she wouldn't have been able to pay the deposit or the rent, but thanks to Deacon, she had money in the bank again and a whole new outlook.

"I'm going to move in tomorrow if you want to do the same."

Julia didn't have much to move, just the clothes she'd brought with her. "I will. After work."

"Mom told me you've been hanging out with Deacon Taylor."

"Uh-huh."

"Is it serious?"

"I don't know." *Liar.* "Could be."

"He's a hottie."

"I noticed."

Cindy laughed. "Good for you."

"How're things at the salon?"

"Busy so far. I like it."

"That's good."

"It's so nice to have the whole summer to spend on Gansett. I'm giddy! Reminds me of being a kid and visiting Gram and Gramps."

Julia loved to see Cindy so happy and excited. "I know. Me, too. The best of times." Julia glanced at the clock on the kitchen stove and saw she had fifteen minutes to get to Dr. McCarthy's house for their appointment. "I've got to run, but thanks for doing the legwork to get this place."

Cindy gave her a hug. "No problem. It's going to be fun!"

As Julia walked to the address Dr. McCarthy had given her, Puppy trotted along next to her. She wondered how many more days had to go by before she could consider the dog hers to keep. Thankfully, he'd shown no sign of rabies. Tomorrow, she had an appointment to take him in for his vaccinations.

She arrived at Dr. McCarthy's house right at five o'clock and gave a gentle knock, hoping she wouldn't wake a sleeping baby.

He came to the door with the baby asleep on his shoulder and let her in. His hair was a lighter shade of brown than his son Riley's, but he had the same blue eyes. "Hi, Julia, I'm Kevin. Come in."

"Thanks so much for seeing me when you've certainly got better things to do."

"It's no problem at all."

Julia tipped her head for a better look at the sleeping baby's face. "She's beautiful."

"Thank you. We think so, too."

"What's her name?"

"Summer Rose."

"I love that."

"Thanks. Can I get you some water or something else to drink? I think we have iced tea, too."

"Water would be great, but I can get it myself."

"Glasses are right up there." He waited for her to fill a glass and then led her into a cozy living room.

She gathered Pupwell into her arms and sat in an easy chair while Kevin took the love seat.

"He's a sweet little guy," Kevin said of the dog.

"He's the best. I'm totally in love with him. I just hope I get to keep him."

"Why wouldn't you?"

Julia told him the story of how they found him.

"He's lucky you spotted him. You saved his life."

"I'm so glad we were there when he needed us, but I'm terrified his owners are going to show up and want him back."

"A reasonable concern, I suppose."

"I've always wanted a dog, but I was never allowed to have one growing up. Katie had allergies when we lived together, and later, I worked too much to have one."

"Why weren't you allowed to have one growing up?"

"My dad..."

"Ah, right."

"Of course, you know about the Lawry family and our dramas."

"I do, and I'm sorry you were forced to grow up that way."

She shrugged off his sympathy, the way she had her whole life when people found out the truth about her family. "It's over now."

"Is it?"

For a minute there, she'd forgotten she was talking to a shrink. Until he said that and reminded her of the many therapists she'd seen over the years.

"Things like what happened to you and your family tend to leave rather deep scars behind."

"So I've been told."

"I assume there's a good reason why Katie wanted me to see you and used the word *urgent* to describe the situation."

"That's a little dramatic."

"How so?"

"Well, Katie worries about me more than she should."

"I've gotten to know her pretty well since she moved here, and I don't find her to be an alarmist or overly dramatic."

Julia had to admire the way he'd neatly boxed her into a corner. "She's not." There was no point in dodging him after Katie had flipped the urgent switch. "I suffered from anorexia and bulimia when I was younger. I've been much better until recently."

"What happened to cause the setback?"

Julia didn't want to talk about Mike ever again, but knew she had to one more time so Kevin would have the complete picture. "I'm coming off a rough couple of months. I was in a relationship with a man who misled me and stole from me." She cleared the emotion from her throat and shared the full story of what'd happened with Mike and how Deacon had helped her to make a case against him, leading to the return of her money. "When things happen that stress me out like this did, I have a very hard time forcing myself to eat. It's just physically impossible."

"I can understand how that kind of stress would be debilitating."

"It was terrible. My life just fell apart so suddenly and took my health down with it. When I showed up here looking particularly thin and obviously troubled, Katie homed right in on it, which is why she called my situation urgent."

"I see."

"I've felt so much better since I got the money back and have been eating normally again."

"That's great news."

"I feel good, so it's probably safe to dial down the urgency."

"I don't know if I agree with that. By now, you know the next life crisis is waiting around the corner, right?"

"Yes, I suppose."

"So the goal becomes how to prepare you to handle a crisis without endangering your health."

"That's a lofty goal."

"Most goals worth pursuing tend to be lofty."

"I hear what you're saying, and other therapists have certainly talked to me about coping skills. It's just that when things go sideways for me, as they tend to do far too often, my physical reaction is involuntary. My throat closes, and my stomach is uninterested in food."

"All the systems within the body are designed to work in concert with each other. When your brain sends out alarms, it puts the rest of your body on alert to danger."

"That sounds about right."

"It's not easy to overcome these sorts of reactions, but it can be done. Have you ever tried meditation?"

"No, not really."

"Meditation and yoga can be extremely beneficial in helping to quiet the mind. Many of my patients have found both to be very soothing and helpful in dealing with challenges that cause stress."

"I'm not opposed to trying either or both."

A door opened down the hall, and a tall, pretty blonde woman came into the room. "Sorry to interrupt. I'm Chelsea."

They'd seen each other at the wedding, but hadn't been introduced. "Julia. Nice to see you again."

"You, too." She took the baby from Kevin, who'd lit up at the sight of his wife. "She'll be awake any minute and hungry."

"Sorry to barge into your home when you have a new baby."

"No problem at all," Chelsea said. "We'll leave you to chat." She took the baby with her when she returned to the bedroom.

"Well, she's rather beautiful," Julia said.

Kevin responded with a big, goofy grin. "I know. And she's way out of my league, but for some reason, she loves me anyway." He cleared his throat and refocused on her. "We were talking about yoga and meditation."

"Worth a shot."

He leaned forward, elbows on knees. "Here's my take on it, for what it's worth, knowing your family's background. Katie has told me about how you two and Owen ran interference for your younger siblings and even moved along with your family so you could be close to them. That's a huge thing you did for them. The three of you have been in defensive mode for most of your lives, always on alert for the next disaster. Is that a fair assessment?"

"It's pretty spot-on."

"Your father's in jail, and he's going to be there for a very long time. He can't hurt you or anyone else you love anymore. That threat has been neutralized. Other things have happened and will continue to happen that you'll find upsetting and difficult, but if you focus on taking really good care of yourself all the time, you may find that when the speed bumps come, you'll be better prepared to deal with them."

Julia processed what he'd said, especially the part about taking good care of herself all the time. It was nothing she hadn't heard before, but this time, she was determined to do everything she could to stave off another health crisis. She was so tired of everyone being concerned about her.

"What do you think?" he asked after a long silence.

"I could do better in the area of self-care."

"Most of us could, but when you've battled foes like anorexia and bulimia, it becomes even more important. It should be as important to you on a daily basis as bathing and eating and washing your clothes and cleaning your home and going to work. You have to make it a priority, and if you do, hopefully when the next crisis comes along, you'll have the reserves to battle it more effectively than you have in the past."

"That would be nice."

For the next few minutes, they went through a list of things she could do to help manage her stress and keep her body in balance, such as exercise, yoga, meditation and massage, to name a few.

"These are small things you can do to pamper yourself," he said. "Give yourself the same TLC you'd give that sweet puppy. In my practice, I believe in starting with small changes and building a foundation that can help to hold up the house during the rough times."

Different therapists had different approaches. Some came at the problem by focusing on food and helping her find nutritious meals that appealed to her even when she didn't feel like eating. Others addressed the psychology behind the ailments in an attempt to curb the behaviors. Kevin McCarthy was the first to suggest ideas that had nothing whatsoever to do with food or food-related illnesses to address her challenges. It was a new approach that appealed to her—and made sense, too.

She liked the idea of caring for herself the way she would the puppy. "It's worth a shot, for sure."

"As you certainly know by now, dealing with your illness is not as simple as taking up meditation or yoga. It's a complicated challenge with no simple answers or one-size-fits-all solution, which is why it's important to do the hard work in here and to regularly consult with your doctor."

"I agree, and I admit that I let my health slide after my relationship with Mike ended. I want to do better and stay healthy."

"That's the first step toward making it happen."

Julia bit her lip, trying to decide if she wanted to talk to Kevin about Deacon.

"Something else on your mind?"

"I hate to take any more of your time."

"No worries. I've got all night to spend with my girls."

"I've met someone since I've been here, and it's gotten very intense kind of quickly. That's a pattern for me—one I was trying to break until I met him and all my best intentions disappeared. He's the one who made the case to get back my money, and after that, I was just sunk."

"He sounds like a good guy if he'd go to that kind of trouble for someone he'd only just met."

"He is a good guy. I know that, but still... I can't shake the feeling that I'm setting myself up for another disaster."

"That's your preconditioned point of view. All you've ever known is disaster, so why would you think this situation would be any different from all the others?"

"That's it exactly. I'm not sure how to get past that. Deacon has been so good to me from the first time we met. There's no reason at all to distrust him or question his sincerity, and yet..."

"It's a choice you have to make to either take a chance knowing the risks going in or take the safe route and avoid anything that could ever hurt you."

"That's what Katie did before she met Shane. She never dated at all because she was afraid she'd end up with a man like our father."

"That sounds like a very lonely existence for her and for you."

"Life has been a lot less lonely and unsettled since I met Deacon. He has a way of making everything better just by being in the room."

"I know that feeling." Kevin's gaze shifted toward the hallway. "Loving people, letting them into your life, trusting them not to hurt you... It's always a risk, even for those of us who didn't grow up the way you did. Your upbringing makes it harder for you to trust people, especially men. The most important man in your life disappointed you so profoundly."

"Yes, he did." She thought about the piano and the day he'd sold it without telling her, and then quickly pushed that memory into the past where it belonged.

"I don't know Deacon, but I know his brother. He's a good man. Does that mean Deacon is, too? Certainly not."

"Deacon is a good man. I've seen that with my own eyes."

"Even good men aren't perfect, Julia. He'll let you down and disappoint you, because he's human. Not because he's bad."

"You're very wise."

Kevin laughed. "I don't know about that."

"What you said about him being human is a good reminder that no one is perfect. That helps."

"If something I said helps you, then that makes my day."

"You have helped. Very much. And you've given me a lot to think about."

"Come back next week? Same time."

"I don't want to bother you while you're on leave."

"It's no bother. Please come by. Let's keep doing the work so you're ready for the next storm."

"Okay. Thank you again."

"It was entirely my pleasure to meet you, Julia. Owen and Katie speak so highly of you. I'm glad I got a chance to get to know you." Kevin walked her to the door and handed her a business card. "My cell number is on there. I'm available any time if you need me. Don't hesitate to call."

Julia took the card from him, touched by his compassion. "Thank you so much for taking the time, especially right now."

"No problem at all. I'll see you next week, if not before."

"See you then." Julia walked to the hotel, thinking about the things Kevin had said, especially about Deacon. For her entire life, she'd put people into two categories—good and bad. But what Kevin said about good people doing things that hurt or disappointed others had really resonated with her. No, Deacon wasn't perfect. But maybe, just maybe, he might be perfect for her.

When she returned to the Surf, Julia glanced into the restaurant and saw that it wasn't super busy yet. Bending at the waist, she picked up Puppy and walked in, powerfully drawn to the piano on the stage.

"Hey, Julia," Stephanie said. "Everything okay?"

Julia nodded, her gaze fixed on the instrument that had defined her for so long before it was taken from her. *Take it back*, Owen had said. *Take it back*. She glanced at Stephanie. "Would you mind if I played for a bit?"

"Would I mind?" Stephanie laughed. "No, Julia, I wouldn't mind if you dazzle my customers with your amazing talent."

"Thank you."

"Um, no, thank *you*."

"Is it okay if I keep him on my lap?"

"It's Gansett Island. Everything is okay here."

Truer words had never been spoken. "Thanks, Steph." Julia gave her stepsister a quick hug and then headed for the stage. *Take it back, take it back, take it back.* Owen's words were a chant, guiding her to where she'd longed to be for as long as she'd lived without it. She could admit that to herself now that she had the freedom to take it back. No one would ever take it from her again.

She would make sure of that.

Seated on the bench, with Puppy curled up in her lap, Julia placed her hands on the keys and played the opening notes of Adele's "Someone Like You." Over the years, there'd been so many songs released that she'd loved and wished she could perform, and now she could. As if the floodgates had been thrown open with no limits or restrictions, she lost herself in the music, the lyrics, the exhilaration of playing for an appreciative audience and the sheer joy of doing something she loved.

Kevin had told her to practice self-care. This… For Julia, playing the piano and singing was the very definition of self-care.

CHAPTER 25

*A*fter work, Deacon stopped by the department store to pick up a couple of extra dress shirts, since he'd all but ruined the only one he'd brought with him. While he was at it, he got a couple of new pairs of khaki shorts so he'd have something fairly decent to wear when he saw Julia.

Julia.

Julia.

Julia.

She was all he'd thought about during the endless day at work. If he hadn't already figured out that she was special, he would've known it simply by how much he thought about her when he wasn't with her.

At home, he showered, shaved and put on one of the new shirts and shorts. When he was ready, he went down the stairs to the yard, where Blaine was supervising Ashleigh on the swing set while holding Addie. She let out a squeak when she saw Deacon coming.

He held out his arms to her, and she leaned toward him.

For a long moment, he waited to see what Blaine would do. Finally, his brother handed the baby over to Deacon, albeit begrudgingly. "There's my buddy. How's it going?"

Addie patted his face and tried to pull his hair.

"Watch out. She's grabby."

"That's okay," Deacon said, besotted by the tiny girl who looked up at him with big trusting eyes. She had Blaine's eyes, he realized, which meant she had his eyes, too. Funny how family and genes worked that way. Deacon made the barfing sound that had amused Addie the other day.

Sure enough, she cracked up, so he did it again.

"Where you heading?"

"To Julia's."

"Spending a lot of time with her."

"Yep."

Blaine took a sip from a beer and then glanced at Deacon.

"Something on your mind?" Deacon didn't really want to know, but he was enjoying the minute with Addie as well as watching Ashleigh swinging, so he put it out there.

Blaine hesitated for so long that Deacon figured he wasn't going to say anything.

"Tell me about the fight," Blaine said.

Deacon hadn't expected that. "You really want to know?"

"That's why I'm asking."

"My friend Sherri… Her ex-husband harasses her nonstop, and even though she has a restraining order against him, there's not much she can do about the harassment because they have joint custody of their kids. He came into the bar, drunk and spoiling for a fight. I intervened because I heard him say something awful to her and was legitimately afraid he would kill her with the way he was acting. And in case you're wondering, even after everything that happened, I don't regret it."

"Were you seeing her?"

"Here and there, but it wasn't a big deal. We hung out a few times. After working the domestic unit in Boston, I know trouble when I see it, and he was looking for trouble that night."

"Hmm."

"What does that mean?"

240

"I really hate having to apologize to you—ever—but especially twice in one week."

Deacon laughed, which made Addie laugh. God, he was crazy about her. "Sorry to force you to confront your inner a-hole." He glanced at his brother. "I'm not the stupid kid I was when I lived here and you had to clean up my messes all the time."

"I see that."

"Do you? Do you really?"

"I do."

"Well, that's progress."

"Bring Julia to dinner tomorrow night around seven."

"Okay…"

"Give me my daughter back."

"She likes me better than you."

"Don't push your luck. I can still put you on your ass."

"I'd like to see you try."

Because he had much better things to do than scrap with Blaine, Deacon gave Addie a noisy kiss on the cheek and handed her over to her dad. He took perverse pleasure when Addie immediately leaned toward him, holding out her arms.

"Sorry, sweet girl. I know you like me better than Daddy, but Uncle Deacon has to go. I'll see you tomorrow, though."

"She does not like you better than me."

"Keep telling yourself that. See you, Ashleigh."

"Bye, Uncle Deacon."

"My work here is finished." He flashed a cocky grin at his brother and headed down the driveway, whistling a jaunty tune that was sure to annoy Blaine.

He walked quickly through town, wanting to get to Julia as quickly as he could, but not wanting to get there sweaty and disheveled. As he went past the Beachcomber, Evan McCarthy was coming down the steps.

Deacon stopped to say hello. "How's it going?"

"Great, you?"

"Doing well."

"Heard you're the new harbor master."

"Yep. It's a fun way to spend a summer."

"I'll bet. Hey, listen… About Julia…"

"What about her?"

"I thought I might hear from her after last night. Dude, she is *crazy*-talented. All I can think about is recording that voice of hers."

"She hasn't said anything about it. Not to me, anyway."

"Hmm, well, tell her I'd really love to talk to her."

"I'll do that."

"Let's grab that beer soon."

"Absolutely. See you." Deacon continued on his way, walking a little faster now that the Surf was within sight. The second he walked through the front door, he heard her… That voice sent chills down his spine. My God, she was talented. He followed the music into Stephanie's Bistro and stood in the back, watching her, listening to her, riveted by her.

Evan was right. She was crazy-talented and destined for big things if that was what she wanted. Why did the thought of her chasing big things scare him? Maybe because he'd only just found her and the possibility of her being anywhere but right there with him was something he couldn't bear to consider. Hell, if she ran off to chase the music dream, there was nothing at all to keep him from going with her.

Jeez… Had it really come to that? Would he chase around the world after a woman? If that woman was Julia, hell yes, he'd chase her to the far corners of the globe if it meant he got to be with her.

The realization stunned him, leaving him spinning as he tried to wrap his head around the magnitude of what'd transpired in the days since he first saw her. But as he listened to her pour her heart and soul into "Your Song" by Elton John, all he knew was that he wanted her in his life. He wanted her heart and soul to belong to him, and he wanted to give his to her.

He loved her.

Oh my God. I love her. That's what this was. How else could he explain the overwhelming feelings he'd never had for anyone else?

Indeed... *How wonderful life is while she's in the world.*

When she finished the song, the room exploded into applause that startled Puppy awake. Deacon cheered louder than anyone. He would never forget the exact moment when she saw him there or the flush that overtook her cheeks or the way she shyly acknowledged the audience as she gathered Puppy into her arms and stood to leave the stage.

Everyone wanted to talk to her, but she was laser-focused on him as she came toward him. Deacon held out his arms to her, and she walked into his embrace as if she belonged there, which of course she did. He kept his arm around her as he escorted her from the restaurant and walked her upstairs, noting the way she trembled as he held her.

He managed to get her keys from her bag and get the door open without releasing his tight hold on her. The second the door closed behind her, he put his arms around her and the puppy as she continued to tremble.

"Are you okay?"

She nodded. After a long pause, she took a deep breath and let it out slowly. "I did it."

"You certainly did."

"I didn't think about it or obsess about it. I just went in there and I *played*, Deacon. Do you know how huge this is for me?"

"I think I do. I'm so, so proud of you. Your music is incredibly beautiful."

She pulled back to look up at him, her eyes sparkling with pure joy. "I love it so much. It was my favorite thing ever until..."

He kissed her. "Don't go there, darlin'. It can be your favorite thing again. Just like before."

"It's *one* of my favorite things. I have a couple of new ones, too."

Cocking his head, he studied her intently, wanting to memorize the way she looked as she overflowed with happiness that had been so very hard-won. "Is that right?"

"Uh-huh. Puppy is one of my new favorite things."

"He's one lucky puppy to be among your favorites."

"You are, too."

243

"I'm a lucky puppy?"

Her smile lit up her face and filled him with a ridiculous amount of happiness. "You're one of my new favorite things."

"Am I?"

She nodded and went up on tiptoes to kiss him.

Since Deacon had been dying to kiss her for hours, he fell into the kiss like he'd found gold at the end of a long rainbow.

Puppy let out a squeak of indignation that made them both laugh.

"I guess he doesn't like it when Mommy and Daddy squish him," Julia said. "Hold that thought."

"I'm holding on. Just barely."

She giggled at the face he made and went to put Puppy in his crate, leaving the door open so he could get out if he wanted to.

He curled up in a ball in his bed and sacked out.

Julia returned to Deacon, offering the shy smile that made his heart ache with love for her. He wanted to tell her he loved her, but he feared it was too soon. Rather, he set out to show rather than tell, undressing her, holding her, kissing her, caressing her with tender reverence. He lowered her to the bed and knelt on the floor in front of her, taking in the sight of her open and vulnerable to him.

Knowing how difficult it was for her to be vulnerable, he wanted to be worthy of the amazing gift she'd given him. He kissed the inside of her leg, dragging his lips over her inner thigh and making her tremble again, but for different reasons this time. He slid his hands under her ass and lifted her, giving her his tongue in sweeping strokes that made her gasp and moan and squirm. It thrilled him to give her pleasure, and he wanted her out of her mind with it. He wanted her to forget anything and everything that wasn't him and them and the incredible connection they'd found in each other.

He kept it up until her body went stiff in the second before she came with a sharp cry of completion that thrilled him. Moving quickly, he freed his hard cock from his shorts and drove into her to ride the waves of her orgasm. That sparked a second wave for her that had him fighting to hold on so he could make this even better for her.

"Deacon…"

"What, darlin'?"

"You... That... *Wow.*"

"Mmm, you're so hot, so sexy, so sweet." He bent to kiss her lips, cheeks and throat before he drew the tight tip of her left nipple into his mouth.

Her inner muscles clamped down hard on his cock, making him groan as sensation flooded his entire body. The words he wanted to tell her burned to get out, but he held on to them. He wanted to be sure she was ready to hear them before he told her.

His Julia was so strong in some ways but fragile in others. He loved her fragility as much as her strength. He loved everything about her.

"Fuck," he muttered. "Need a condom."

She kept him from withdrawing. "It's okay. I'm protected."

Hearing that triggered a ferocious wave of need that took him right to the edge of complete madness. When he couldn't hold back any longer, he pushed into her and held still, letting the incredible wave crash over him, taking him up so high, he felt invincible, especially when she came, too, her fingers digging into his back as she held on to him. He wanted her to always hold on to him, to lean on him, to let him be there for her.

As he came down from the highest of highs, he breathed in the scent that belonged only to her. With her arms and legs wrapped around him, Deacon understood so many things that had eluded him up until then. This feeling was why people rearranged their entire lives to be together. It was why they did whatever it took to make it work so they'd never again have to be without the person who made them feel that way.

"Am I crushing you?"

"I love it."

"I do, too." He raised his head so he could see her face and was stunned by what he saw.

She loved him, too. He had no doubt whatsoever.

"Julia..."

"Hmm?" She reached up to fix his hair and then ran her fingers over his face and lips.

That was all it took to make him hard for her again.

She laughed and wiggled under him, letting him know she was fully on board with round two.

"I, um…" He wanted so badly to tell her how he felt, and he'd never wanted that before. If anything, he'd gone to great lengths to avoid feeling things that would change everything. But this…

"Are you okay?"

"I'm so much better than okay. That's what I'm trying to tell you. This… with you… It's just…"

"Amazing."

"Yes," he said, overcome with relief that she felt the same way he did. "It's incredible. *You* are incredible."

"*We* are. We're incredible together."

"I agree. Want to go steady?"

She laughed as hard as he'd ever seen her laugh and loved every second of that joyful sound. "Does that mean we'll be exclusive?"

The question shocked him. "We're not already exclusive?" The thought of her doing *this* with anyone but him made him crazy.

That brought more laughter. "Of course we are, you dope. You didn't really think…"

"No."

"I hope not."

"So yes to being exclusive?"

"Yes to being exclusive. Yes to everything."

CHAPTER 26

Over the next few weeks, Julia settled into her new home, her new job and her new romance. She and Deacon fell into a routine of spending every night together, usually at his place, where they could be completely alone. They had dinner with Deacon's parents, with Blaine, Tiffany and their girls, with her family and by themselves more often than not.

They attended a party Adam McCarthy and his wife, Abby, had to celebrate their son Liam's adoption being final. One night, they babysat for Ashleigh and Addie so Blaine and Tiffany could go out to dinner to celebrate their anniversary. Another night, they babysat for Laura and Owen so she could watch him play at one of his gigs.

If they weren't working, they were together, and with every day that passed, Julia fell more in love with her sweet, sexy harbor master.

Deacon loved his job and sported a dark "farmer's tan" from the long hours on the water that made Julia laugh every time he removed his shirt to reveal a dark V on his chest and tanned forearms. They laughed at everything, especially the antics of Puppy Pupwell, who'd officially become theirs when they registered him in both their names with the town after two weeks in which no one had come forward to claim him.

On a Saturday in late June, they were invited to a wedding at the Southeast Light. Slim Jackson, an old friend of the Taylor family, was marrying his fiancée, Erin Barton, at the place where their romance had begun while she was the lighthouse keeper. From what Julia had heard, the entire town was invited because Slim knew everyone—and somehow he'd gotten the town to approve of them having their wedding there when they'd said no to Jenny and Alex out of fear of drunken guests falling off cliffs.

She and Deacon rode to the lighthouse with Shane and Katie, who were still glowing with newlywed bliss weeks after returning from their honeymoon.

Julia wondered if she, too, glowed with the same happiness she saw in Katie. Probably so, because she'd never before been happy like she was with Deacon. It was a pervasive, bone-deep kind of elation that was all new to her, and she'd become addicted to the feeling.

He gave her hand a squeeze and smiled at her, revealing that dimple she was also addicted to.

At the lighthouse, they joined the crowd that had gathered for the happy occasion. Deacon stood behind Julia, his arms wrapped around her as they watched Slim and Erin exchange vows.

"She lost her twin brother in the 9/11 attack in New York," Deacon whispered in her ear. "He was engaged to Jenny, who's the matron of honor."

Hearing what the two women had endured gave Julia a deeper perspective on what this day must mean to both of them and everyone who loved them. She had tears in her eyes by the time Frank McCarthy declared Slim and Erin husband and wife.

The party that followed could be described only as epic. On a perfect summer day, friends and family of the happy couple enjoyed a traditional New England clambake under a tent that had been erected next to the lighthouse.

Julia went to say hello to Mac and Maddie, who was seated on a padded lounge chair that had been brought in just for her. "How're you feeling?" she asked Maddie.

"Tired, cranky, fat and saggy," Maddie said with a cheerful grin. "Other than that, all is well."

"She's doing great." Mac looked at his wife with such pride. "She's a baby-making goddess."

"Don't you mean elephant?"

"I mean goddess."

Julia had gotten to know them quite well during the weeks she'd been working with him and had become very fond of them and their children. Per Mac's request, she'd agreed to take on some of the management of the marina for additional salary that gave her a financial cushion she'd never had before. "It won't be much longer until the twins arrive."

Maddie moaned. "I can't believe they're not due for another two months."

"The longer they stay in the oven the better," Mac said.

"Easy for you to say."

"Not easy for me, as you well know." He winked to make his point, and his wife's face turned bright red.

"Shut it, Mac."

"Just speaking the truth, my love."

"Sorry, Julia. He's unmanageable."

She'd found the opposite to be true, but she kept that to herself. After all, she wasn't the one married to him.

The other big news at the wedding came from Jenny's husband, Alex Martinez, and his brother, Paul, who'd successfully moved their mother, Marion, back to Gansett Island. She was now living at the elder care facility that Jared and Lizzie James had started, which was run by Dr. Quinn James and his nurse fiancée, Mallory Vaughan. The Martinez brothers and their wives, Jenny and Hope, were thrilled to have Marion close by once again so they could see her more regularly. Her battle with dementia had led them to find alternate care for her on the mainland, but they'd hated having her so far from them.

At the wedding, Julia met Nikki Stokes's famous twin sister, Jordan, who was on the island for the summer after the spectacular public breakup of her high-profile marriage to rocker Zane earlier in the year.

Nikki and her fiancé, Riley McCarthy, were getting married in the fall, as were Dr. David Lawrence and his fiancée, Daisy Babson.

At Slim and Erin's wedding, she also got to meet celebrity lawyer Dan Torrington and his wife, Kara.

Before she'd come back to Gansett for the summer, Julia would've thought life on the small island would be quiet and boring. She'd found the reality to be anything but.

By far the best part of Erin and Slim's wedding day for Julia was when she got to dance with Deacon, who held her the way he always did, as if she was his whole world. She'd never been anyone's whole world before, and she rather liked being his. He'd taught her how to let go and have fun and not worry about what might happen in the future. *Right now is all we have,* he'd say. *Let's enjoy the hell out of it.*

So that was what she'd done. While enjoying the hell out of life with Deacon, she continued to see Kevin each week, and she took care of herself by attending yoga classes, practicing meditation and playing the piano at Stephanie's every chance she got. Her weight had stabilized, and Victoria had cut her back to monthly check-ins rather than weekly.

Life was good, as good as it had ever been, and yet... In the back of her mind remained the nagging worry of how it would blow up in her face. It always did, so why should this time be different? As much as she tried to tell herself that everything was fine, the nagging fear lingered.

She was preconditioned to expect the worst-case scenario. There was no reason to believe she had anything to be concerned about, but still, she worried.

Evan McCarthy had repeatedly asked her to come by the studio, but Julia hadn't taken him up on the offer. She'd thought about it and had decided that as long as she could play at the hotel any time she wanted, that was more than enough for her. She had no desire to pursue a career in music.

Maybe in a previous life that career might've interested her, but now she wanted the easy, stress-free life she'd found on Gansett. She was self-aware enough to know that the fast-paced, high-drama life of a professional musician wouldn't be healthy for her.

After another long day of work at the job she loved, she snuggled on her bed with Puppy while she waited for Deacon to arrive. He'd been working longer hours than usual for reasons he hadn't fully shared with her. Something about a boat he was keeping an eye on and a case he'd been building. Puppy was full of energy, so she decided to take him for a walk to meet Daddy at the dock.

The second Puppy saw her with the leash in her hand, he went bonkers, the way he always did. He'd grown so much in recent weeks and was full of energy.

"You have to hold still for one second." She finally got the leash on, and they headed out toward the town dock. Puppy peed at least four times before they got there, which amused her. Everything he did amused her. They passed Deacon's bike in the parking lot. What did it say about her that seeing his motorcycle was enough to make her body hum with desire for the man who owned it? One of her favorite things to do was ride on the back of his bike, wrapped around his muscular body as the powerful bike hummed beneath them. It was almost as good as foreplay.

She'd have to tell him that when she saw him. He'd like that.

Puppy pulled hard on the leash, leading the way to Daddy's dock. They'd met him at the end of the day before, so Puppy knew where to go. She and Deacon had discussed finding a better name for him than Puppy Pupwell, but that name had stuck, and he answered to Puppy and Pupwell, so it was probably too late now.

Deacon joked that they'd name their future children Baby and Kid.

Whenever he talked about their future children, it was all Julia could do not to tell him she was madly in love with him and couldn't wait to have his children. But she hadn't said that yet. Neither of them had used the L word, but she knew he felt it every bit as much as she did. Maybe tonight, she'd tell him how she felt. Why was she bothering to hold back when she loved him more than anything?

As she went down the ramp, she couldn't think of a single good reason not to tell him. She was on the floating dock where he tied up when she noticed another woman sitting on the equipment box where Julia usually sat to wait for him. Julia didn't recognize her.

"Hey." The woman smiled at Julia. She had long blonde hair and intricate sleeve tattoos. "Adorable dog."

"Thanks."

"What's his name?"

"Puppy Pupwell."

"That's cute. Is he friendly?"

"Very."

She slid off the box and bent to pet Puppy. "What a sweet boy you are."

Since Puppy had never met a stranger, he leaned into her, seeking as much attention as he could get. The woman laughed at his antics.

"Do you live here, or are you visiting?" Julia asked, scanning the horizon for Deacon's boat.

"I wish I lived here. It's so beautiful. But I'm only here for a couple of days to see my boyfriend."

"Oh, are you seeing Colby?" She seemed quite a bit older than the young man who worked with Deacon, but Julia wasn't one to judge.

"No, Deacon. Do you know him?"

Julia was stunned speechless. Deacon had a *girlfriend*? How was that possible when he spent every available second he had with her? She had to force herself to remain calm, not to overreact, to wait and give him a chance to explain. Surely there had to be some explanation.

The woman stood to her full height. "Are you all right?"

"I'm fine. And yes, I know Deacon." *I know him as well as I know myself,* Julia thought, *or at least I thought I did. Stay calm, keep breathing...* Easier said than done when your heart is about to explode in your chest. This could not happen again. It just couldn't.

"He's the best. I've missed him so much since he's been gone, and I couldn't wait another day to see him."

Breathe. Just breathe.

Julia wasn't capable of making conversation while they waited for him, so she focused on the puppy and keeping him entertained so she wouldn't lose her composure and break down in front of this stranger who'd staked a claim on Deacon.

She thought about how Finn McCarthy's ex had shown up on the island a month or so ago, determined to get him back, and how she'd stabbed him and his new girlfriend, Chloe. Maybe this woman was like that one had been—a delusional ex who didn't know how to accept when something was over.

It had to be something like that. There was simply no other explanation. He'd known how big of a deal it'd been for Julia to go all in with him, especially after everything that'd happened with Mike. He wouldn't hurt her this way. Would he?

No. Not Deacon. He wouldn't do that.

Remaining calm and continuing to breathe in the ten minutes it took for his boat to appear at the entrance to South Harbor was one of the more difficult things she'd done in quite some time. But she'd done it, and she credited her new coping skills with getting her through the challenge.

When Deacon got close enough to see her and Puppy waiting for him, his face lit up with the smile that had become so familiar to her, complete with that damned dimple that got to her every time it appeared. She was watching him so closely, she was able to see the exact moment when he saw who else was waiting for him.

He couldn't hide the shock or the nervous reaction he had to seeing both women waiting for him. Time seemed to stand still as he brought the boat into the dock and tied one line at the center of the boat. "Julia," he said, looking at her with fierce determination. "Do not move. Stay right there. Do. Not. Move."

Only because she didn't trust her legs to carry her up the ramp and away from that dock, she did what he asked her to and stayed put.

He got off the boat and approached the other woman, who'd lit up with delight at the sight of him. Julia wanted to claw her eyes out. "Sherri, what're you doing here?"

"I came to see you, silly." She threw herself at him, but Deacon didn't react. He kept his hands by his sides. "I missed you so much!" She kissed his cheek. "Say something, will you?"

He took a step back from her and moved toward Julia. "Sherri, this is my girlfriend, Julia. Julia, this is my friend Sherri from Harwich."

Sherri looked from him to Julia and then back to him again. "You... You have..."

Deacon put his arm around Julia. "A girlfriend. A very serious girlfriend who I love more than anything."

While Julia tried not to swoon from hearing him say the L word for the first time, Sherri stared at him in disbelief.

"You *love* her? You were with me two months ago."

"We hooked up, Sherri. We had some fun. I was never 'with' you. I'm sorry if that hurts your feelings, but it's the truth, and you know it as much as I do."

"You... You fought with Roger."

"I did, and I'd do it again if I saw another woman about to get beat up by a man. Please don't make that into more than it was. You and I are friends. That's all we're ever going to be."

"You gave me money."

"Because I felt bad about you losing your job after the fight. I'm sorry if you came here expecting something else, but the fact is I'm crazy in love with Julia, and I plan to spend the rest of my life with her. If she'll have me, that is."

Julia wanted to say something cute and witty and profound, but words escaped her as she wallowed in the realization that nothing was going to go wrong, not even an ex-lover, or whatever she was, showing up to stake a claim on him. He was as true blue as he'd seemed from the beginning. For once, she'd gotten it just right.

Sherri broke down into sobs. "I feel so stupid. I thought, when you gave me the money, I thought that meant you were, like, you know... into me."

"I'm so sorry, Sherri. I just wanted to help you get back on your feet after you lost your job. That's all it was."

She nodded. "I get that now. I, um, I'm going to go."

"Do you have somewhere to stay tonight? The last ferry is long gone."

"Yeah. I'm at the Beachcomber. I, uh... Bye, Deacon."

"Take care, Sherri."

She pushed past them and rushed up the ramp, disappearing into the murky darkness.

Deacon turned to face Julia, seeming adorably uncertain. "Hi."

She wanted to hug him and kiss him and tell him she loved him, too. "How's it going?"

"Um, well, you tell me."

"It's going rather well, actually. Better than it has in, well, ever."

He stepped closer to her, seeming to sense that she wasn't going to let Sherri's sudden appearance screw things up for them. A month ago, before he'd shown her that she could truly trust him, something like Sherri's appearance would've ruined her. But everything was different now, and he was the one who'd changed the game for her. "I'm sorry about that."

"I assume you have nothing to be sorry about."

"Technically, no, but that had to have been upsetting for you."

"It was a little shocking when she told me she was waiting for her boyfriend, Deacon, but since I knew there was no possible way you could be her boyfriend when you spend every minute you aren't working with me, I decided to breathe and stay calm and wait to hear what you had to say about it."

His gorgeous eyes sparked with amusement and happiness and so much love that was all for her. "That's highly evolved of you."

"I know, right?"

"I'm very proud of you, darlin'."

"I'm rather proud of myself."

"You should be."

Puppy jumped up and down at their feet, wanting Daddy's attention after a long day without him.

Deacon bent to pick him up. In a few more months, he'd be too big and too heavy to carry around like a baby. They were enjoying being able to carry him while it lasted. Holding the dog in one arm and putting the other around Julia, Deacon escorted them up the ramp to the pier.

"I got a lot more than I bargained for when I set out to meet you after work tonight."

"I got a lot more than I bargained for when my brother made me come to Gansett for the summer. I've got my own little family now, and I love you both with my whole heart."

Julia had kept it together during the episode with Sherri, but hearing him say those words again had her choking up from the swell of emotion.

"I'm sorry you had to hear that for the first time when I was talking to someone else."

"It's okay."

Deacon stopped walking and turned so he was facing her. "It's not all right. I should've told you that weeks ago, because I've felt it for a long time. The only reason I didn't tell you was because I didn't want to freak you out with too much too soon."

"Who're you kidding? You've been freaking me out with too much too soon from the day you kidnapped me from my sister's wedding."

That smile. That dimple. Those eyes. The scruff on his jaw. She wanted to look at that face every day for as long as she lived. "It's not a kidnapping if the bridesmaid comes willingly."

Julia laughed. "I was rather easily led that day."

"For which I'll always be thankful. That day was the start of the best thing to ever happen to me."

"Put down the baby," she said.

Deacon put Puppy down and ignored his whining protest.

Julia flattened her hands on the ridiculously sexy uniform shirt and gazed up at him. "In case you were wondering, I love you, too."

"You do? Really?"

"You honestly have to ask?"

"I was hoping…"

"Deacon, my God, I'm so crazy in love with you, I can't see straight —and I definitely can't walk straight, thanks to you."

His cocky grin lit up his face. "Is that right?"

"You know it is. I love you. I love everything about you, especially the way I feel when I'm with you and even when I'm not."

256

He cupped her ass and brought her in tight against his erection. "How do you feel?"

"Happy, healthy, joyful, amused, aroused, entertained, hopeful."

"All those things?" he asked in the gruff, sexy tone that got to her the same way it had from the start.

"All those things and so much more."

"I'm so glad you decided to blow your dick diet on me."

Julia laughed so hard, she had tears in her eyes, a regular occurrence with him around. "Me, too."

"Let's take our little boy home." Deacon took the leash from her, put his arm around her and directed them toward his place. "I want to get naked with Mommy."

"Mommy would be all for that."

He kissed the top of her head and held her tight against his side. "I love you so much, Julia. It's such a relief to finally be able to tell you."

"I'll never get tired of hearing it."

"That's good, because I plan to tell you every day for the rest of our lives."

"I'm all for that, too."

EPILOGUE

The week after the July Fourth holiday, the McCarthy family finally had the party they'd been planning to celebrate the successful opening of the Wayfarer. The family and their closest friends had gathered on the back patio that faced the ocean to toast the reopening of one of the island's most beloved landmarks.

Maddie McCarthy was reclined on the ever-present lounge chair that allowed her to attend social events but stay off her feet. Her belly was so big that she said she could no longer see her feet. Julia couldn't fathom how she could still have ten weeks to go before the twins were due to arrive.

Working for Mac was fun and interesting and never boring. With every passing week, he relied more on Julia, which she welcomed. She loved being busy and productive, and she was both in that job. And she got to bring Puppy with her every day. That was the best part of a great job.

He was growing so fast that she feared he'd outweigh her by the time he was a year old.

She loved him madly, and thankfully, he allowed her to hug and kiss and snuggle him whenever she wanted. Deacon said Puppy knew exactly who'd saved his life, and she was his person.

As she visited with people who'd become friends, Julia found herself watching the door, waiting for Deacon to arrive. He'd had the afternoon off from work and told her he had something he needed to take care of, but she had no idea what he was up to.

Stephanie came over to her, holding a glass of amber liquid that she handed to Julia.

"I was hoping that wasn't for you."

"Haha, very funny. No bourbon for the pregnant lady, but I know how much you love it." A tiny bump had emerged in Stephanie's abdomen over the last two weeks. The only other sign of pregnancy in her was a slightly fuller face. "I hope this family is ready for the baby boom that's about to happen. Maddie, me, Grace and Abby. All pregnant."

"It's going to be a big year for the McCarthy family."

"Sure is. Did you hear that Mallory and Quinn have set their wedding date for October?"

"Mac told me. That's great news. They're an awesome couple."

"They really are. What they're doing out at the elder care facility is such a blessing for this community. Alex and Paul are so relieved to have their mom back on the island."

"She's doing well?"

"By all accounts, it's been a smooth transition."

Tiffany came over to say hello, carrying Addie. "Ladies."

"What's up?" Julia loved Tiffany and her irreverence. It was probably a good thing that they'd met as adults, because she had a feeling they could've gotten into some big trouble together as kids.

"Not too much. Did I hear you girls talking about the baby boom?"

"You did," Steph said.

"Add me to the list. Number three is on the way."

Julia hugged her. "That's awesome!" Deacon would be thrilled to have another niece or nephew to love. Watching him with Ashleigh and Addie, as well as her niece and nephews, had shown her what an amazing father he would be someday.

She still couldn't believe that it was finally safe to think about someday and future children with a man who loved and respected her and treated her like a queen every single day. He made all the trials and tribulations she'd endured before him worth it.

"When are you due?" Steph asked Tiffany.

"February. What about you?"

"Late December. Grace is due in mid-January, Abby in late January."

"It's gonna be one hell of a winter for the McCarthy family," Julia said.

"No kidding. I heard Big Mac and Linda are sticking around this winter rather than taking off to somewhere warmer like they'd planned to."

When she saw Deacon come through the main door to the Wayfarer, Julia felt her heart do the same crazy backflip it did every time she laid eyes on him.

"Our girl has it bad for the harbor master," Tiffany said.

"Seriously bad," Stephanie said. "It might be a terminal case."

"Haha, very funny." Julia kept her gaze fixed on him as he made his way toward her, stopping to greet friends along the way.

When he reached her, he put his arm around her and kissed her cheek.

Julia leaned into him, always relieved to see him again after long hours apart. She wanted to hug him and kiss him and hold him, but she managed to restrain herself in light of the fact that they were in public.

His hand slid down her back to cup her ass with a light squeeze, letting her know she wasn't the only one who wished they were alone.

Blaine joined them, bringing a second beer that he handed to Deacon.

"Thanks."

The brothers had settled into a cordial, friendly relationship that still included a lot of ball-busting, but it came from a place of humor rather than anger these days, a development that both men seemed to welcome.

"Got an update for you on that boat you were tracking," Blaine said.

"Oh yeah, what's that?"

"Turns out they've been on the DEA's radar for a while now, and you were right. They were using the Salt Pond as a meeting point to bring heroin into Southern New England. The Coast Guard and DEA waylaid them offshore today, apprehended them and seized their latest shipment."

"Wow," Deacon said, grinning widely. "That's awesome news."

"The DEA agent in charge asked me to let you know that your work was instrumental, and I couldn't agree more. Congrats, bro."

"Thanks."

Knowing how much his brother's approval meant to Deacon, Julia was thrilled for him.

"We have a full-time, year-round position coming open at the end of the summer if you're interested."

"Seriously?" Deacon asked.

"Dead seriously. You're a great cop. You'd be an asset to our department. I discussed it with the mayor earlier today, and he agrees."

"I, uh, well… What about my knee?"

"We don't do a lot of perp chasing on the island like you did in the city. You should be fine to work here."

"Could I continue as the harbor master in the summer?"

"I'm sure we could work something out to make that happen."

Deacon glanced at Julia, and she smiled up at him, delighted that he'd be able to stay on the island and do the work he loved once again. When Deacon raised a brow, silently asking if she approved of the idea, she nodded.

"I accept," he told Blaine. "Thank you."

Blaine shook his hand. "You earned it, and we're lucky to have you."

Big Mac McCarthy stepped up to the microphone and asked for the attention of his guests. "I want to thank you all for being here to celebrate the opening of the Wayfarer. It took a little longer than we expected to have this family get-together to celebrate our new business, but the extra time gave us a few weeks to work out the kinks.

We've got a major hit on our hands here, people. Nikki has reported receipts for the first few weekends that far exceeded our most optimistic projections."

He led an enthusiastic round of applause.

"There're so many people to thank for making this big idea of mine a reality. First and foremost—my son Mac, who oversaw the renovations with the help of my nephews Shane, Riley and Finn, as well as our business partner, Luke Harris. Gentlemen, I think everyone will agree that you did brilliant work here, and we couldn't be more thankful."

Julia and the rest of the crowd clapped for Mac and his team.

"Nikki, where would we be without you and the incredible group you've assembled for our first season? Thank you so much for taking on the management of the Wayfarer and for diving into the details the way you have. We appreciate you so much."

More applause followed for Nikki, who seemed mortified by the attention. Next to her stood her identical twin sister, Jordan, who was spending the summer on the island. While the two women looked exactly alike, Nikki glowed with happiness, while Jordan seemed sad and lost.

Julia knew that feeling all too well and hoped that maybe Gansett Island would work its magic for Jordan, too.

After Big Mac raised a beer bottle in a toast to family and the Wayfarer, Owen and Evan took to the stage to perform. When they played a slow, acoustic version of Maroon 5's "She Will Be Loved," Deacon led Julia to the dance floor and wrapped his arms around her, changing the words to "she *is* loved" as he whispered in her ear.

With her arms linked around his neck, she held on tight to him until he flinched. "What?"

"I hurt my back earlier."

"How?"

"I'll tell you about it when we get home."

"Let's go soon."

"I'm ready when you are."

A short time later, they said their goodbyes and headed to

Deacon's place behind Tiffany and Blaine's house, the same place Maddie had been living when she met Mac.

Julia followed Deacon up the stairs and into the apartment where they spent most of their time, so much so that Cindy had suggested Julia just move in with him already. She was thinking about that.

Puppy came running out from the bedroom to greet them with kisses and unconditional love. No one had ever been as happy to see her as Puppy was, as if he knew, like Deacon had said, exactly who'd saved his life and would spend the rest of his life thanking her.

Deacon took the puppy outside to pee, and when they returned a few minutes later, he flipped the lock on the door. Ashleigh liked to come over to visit, and they didn't want her walking in on anything that couldn't be unseen.

With Puppy settled in his bed, Julia looked at Deacon. "What did you do to your back?"

He flipped on the closest light, pulled off his shirt and turned to reveal a new tattoo in the middle of his back.

When she realized what it was, she gasped and blinked back tears.

A turtle shell.

"Deacon…"

"It's supposed to match yours." He gazed at her over his shoulder. "What do you think?"

Julia went to him, put her hands on his shoulders and placed kisses to the left and right of the tattoo. His skin was red and angry looking, and knowing he'd endured that kind of pain for her was almost more than she could process. "I think," she said slowly, "that you're the best thing to ever happen to me, and I love you more than you'll ever know."

He turned to face her, gathering her in close to him and kissing her. "I'm glad you like it."

"I love it, and I love what it stands for."

"I'm your shell, darlin'. Come what may, I'll protect you from the storm."

"And I'll do the same for you." She looked up at him. "Congrats on the big bust and the new job."

His smile revealed the dimple she loved so much. "Thanks."

"I hope it feels good to have Blaine's approval and support."

"I hate to admit that it does. It's been nice finding out that he's not a complete asshole."

Julia laughed, having come to expect nothing less from him when he referred to Blaine, who talked the same way about Deacon. Whatever worked for them. At least they talked to each other and seemed to enjoy spending time together, which was a major step forward for them. "Tiffany told me she's pregnant."

"Is that right? Wow, that's great news."

"It seems like everyone is pregnant around here."

"Are you feeling left out?"

"No. Stop. Of course not."

"Not even a little? Because it would give me great pleasure to knock you up, if that's what you want."

"Don't say things like that."

"Why not?"

Julia stepped out of his embrace and went to get a glass of water, surprised to find her hands shaking ever so slightly.

He followed her to the sink and embraced her from behind, kissing the tattoo on the back of her neck. She wore her hair up more often these days, letting the world see the tattoo she'd once kept hidden. "Don't you know by now that there's nothing you could want that I wouldn't give you if I could? Including babies?"

Julia took a deep breath and let it out slowly. "Sometimes I'm still afraid to believe this new life of mine is real."

"It's so real, darlin'. Our life together is as real as it gets, and it's only going to get better from here on out." He kissed her neck until she trembled from desire for him and everything that came with him. "You want a baby, love?"

"Yeah, I really do." After the disaster with Mike, she'd begun to accept that maybe she wasn't going to find a man she could build a life and a family with. She'd begun to let go of her dream of having a baby someday.

"How many?"

"I'd be thrilled with one."

"So then two would be even more thrilling."

"Only if it's what you want, too. Don't say it just to make me happy, Deacon."

"I would never do that to you. I want you. I want kids with you and a life and everything there is with you."

Julia wished she could control her emotions better, but she couldn't contain the tears that spilled down her cheeks.

He turned her to face him and kissed away her tears. "You're going to have everything you ever wanted, sweet Julia. I promise."

"Thank you."

"For what?"

"For being everything I need and more than I ever dreamed possible."

"Being what you need is the most important thing to me." He framed her face with his hands and kissed her with tenderness she felt everywhere. "Remember when I told you my mom's theory about things happening for a reason?"

She nodded.

"You're the reason I blew out my knee and had to leave the force. You're the reason I got into a fight and tossed in jail, so Blaine would make me come here to find you. It was all about you. You're my reason."

"And you're mine. All the crap that happened before was bringing me to you."

His smile lit up his gorgeous eyes. "So you think we should have a baby?"

"I really do." She held on tight to him, thankful now for every painful, agonizing twist and turn in the difficult journey that had led her home to him.

∾

Bonus Epilogue
A Gansett Island Wedding

THE INVITATION WAS SENT AS AN EMAIL TO JUST ABOUT EVERYONE ON
Gansett Island:

Tobias Fitzgerald "Slim" Jackson Jr.
and
Erin Elizabeth Barton

Request the honor of your presence at their wedding festivities on
Saturday, June 29, at 2 p.m.
At the Southeast Light
Come ready to party the night away!

As SLIM SHOT THE FINAL APPROACH TO GANSETT ISLAND'S TINY
airport, he couldn't wait to land and get to Erin as quickly as possible.
The two weeks since he'd last seen her had dragged interminably. The
separation had reminded him of the months they'd spent apart after
they first met and confirmed what he'd known for more than a year
now—he never wanted to spend another night away from her.

Of course, as a professional pilot who flew people around for a
living, that was an unrealistic goal. His job had kept him in Florida for
two additional weeks after Erin returned to the island to oversee the
final details for their big day. With two of his best customers booking
him for late-June dates, he'd put her on a commercial flight, reminded
her to breathe when she was scared and waited for her to text him
that she'd landed in Providence, where her parents had met her for
the trip to the island.

She'd come a long way from the years when she'd been unable to
get on an airplane after her twin brother, Toby, had been killed in the

9/11 attack on the World Trade Center in New York. Erin now flew regularly, in Slim's plane and on commercial flights, even if it would never be her favorite thing to do. He'd been teaching her the mechanics of flying as part of his effort to make her less afraid of it. She was becoming a competent pilot in her own right, but still, she battled the fear on every flight.

Slim thought about the text he'd sent her that morning before leaving West Palm Beach:

I can't wait to marry you;
I can't wait to live with you forever;
I can't wait to have the baby that only we know about;
I can't wait to give that baby a brother or sister or maybe both;
I can't wait to finally get that dog we've been talking about;
I can't wait for everything with you!!!!!!

And her witty reply: *I'll overlook the semicolons because you finished strong. Oh, and ditto on everything else. Get your sexy ass to our island, will you?!!!*

On my way, love. And everyone knows that ?!!! is not acceptable punctuation.

She'd replied with the laughing emoji.

With his airplane secured, he jumped on the motorcycle he kept on the island year-round and headed for his house on the west side, where Erin was staying until the wedding. She didn't know that he'd arranged for them to spend their wedding night at the lighthouse. It seemed only fitting to spend that night in the place where their relationship had begun.

As he navigated the familiar twists and turns of the island that was home to him, Slim thought about those early days together. He remembered every second of how they'd begun the night he'd found her limping along dark island roads after getting a flat tire on her bike and then spraining her ankle. He'd helped get her and the bike home, spent the night tending to her, had attended Jenny and Alex Martinez's wedding with her and then had to leave for months of commitments in Florida before he could see her again.

They'd reunited over the holidays last year, when they'd spent twelve days together that had cemented the certainty that he wanted forever with her.

As he drove past the spot where he'd found her hobbled on that long-ago night, he thanked his lucky stars and fate for putting him there when she needed help. His heart beat fast as he took the final curve before the left-hand turn that would bring him home to her. He roared up the dirt driveway and skidded to a stop, leaving a cloud of dust in his wake. After killing the engine, he parked the bike and tossed aside the helmet that Erin made him promise to always wear when he would've preferred to go without. For her, he wore the helmet.

As he headed for the house, she came out and ran toward him. They met halfway.

He lifted her into his arms and spun her around, overcome with elation and relief and the kind of joy he'd only ever found with her.

She clung to him, her face buried in the crook of his neck. "Thought you'd never get here."

"We're never spending two weeks apart again." He put her down and gazed at the gorgeous face of the woman who was the center of his world. "Did you hear me buzz the house?"

"I heard it." Smiling, she reached up to place her hands on his face and drew him into a slow, sexy, tongue-twisting kiss.

"Where're your folks?" he asked, his lips hovering just above hers.

"They went to lunch with Jenny and Alex." Jenny had been Erin's brother's fiancée when he was killed a short time before they were due to be married. Slim had first met Erin's parents the night Jenny married Alex Martinez.

"How long ago?"

"They left about a half hour ago."

Slim lifted Erin right off her feet.

She let out a surprised squeak. "Where're we going?"

"To get reacquainted."

She laughed. "We don't need that. We're *very* well acquainted."

"We do need that. I need it."

"What about Jack and his family?" she asked of his brother.

"They're on the three o'clock boat. We've got time."

As he carried her inside, she laughed at his impatience and kissed every part of his face she could reach. He walked them straight to the bedroom and put her down only long enough to help remove her T-shirt and jeans while she unbuttoned his shirt.

"I couldn't wait to see you," he whispered against the smooth skin of her neck. "Every minute without you felt like a year."

"Same. Total torture."

"It's a good thing we're getting married."

"It's a very good thing."

He rested a hand on her still-flat abdomen. "How's the peanut?"

"He's better now that he's let up on the queasiness." They had no idea what they were having and weren't planning to find out, but Erin had a feeling they were expecting a boy, who would arrive in March.

"I'm so glad you're feeling better for Hawaii."

"Me, too, although I'm still not sure how you talked me into twelve hours of flying."

"I'll be there to make it go by fast, and you'll be so glad you did it when you see how beautiful Hawaii is. Besides, we both know there's nothing to be afraid of when you're flying first class."

"That's very true."

"This is gonna be quick," he whispered when they landed together on the bed in a tangle of arms and legs and desperate kisses.

"Quick is good."

When they were first together, he'd had reason to wonder if she would find the courage to give them a shot, but once she'd decided to go for it, she'd been all in. And all-in Erin was the best thing to ever happen to him.

He slid into her and threw back his head, needing a minute to get himself together before he made this *too* quick. "God, *Erin...*"

"I know. Me, too. Me, too."

For the longest time, he only held her, not moving as he breathed her in. The press of her breasts against his chest and the squeeze of her internal muscles around his cock made him crazy. Being with her, making love to her... If there was anything better than that, he'd yet to find it. "Love you so much. You can't ever leave me. I'd never get over it."

"I love you just as much, and I'm not going anywhere without you."

"Promise?"

She nodded and smiled, caressing his face and running her fingers through his hair.

Everything about her just did it for him. Slim wished they had time to do nothing but this for the rest of the day, but his brother's family was due to arrive in an hour, and her parents would be back at some point. He would spend the rest of the day looking forward to being alone with her again later. In the meantime, he picked up the pace.

She was right there with him, in perfect sync as they raced toward a finish that had them straining and clinging and gasping from the sweet pleasure they found together.

After, he closed his eyes and slipped into the blissful state that always followed sex with her. "You've wrecked me."

"I've wrecked *you*? I was minding my own business until a hot guy on a motorcycle showed up."

"Mmm, it's all your fault."

"I'm so glad you're here. I was worried."

He hated to hear that. "What about?"

"You. Flying. You know how I get…"

He knew all about the many ways past trauma manifested itself in her daily life. He'd grown accustomed to her OCD rituals and accommodated them because he knew they brought her peace of mind, but he wished she didn't suffer the way she did. "I'm sorry you were worried and I wasn't here to tell you everything would be okay."

"It's much easier when you're around to keep me calm."

"I'm here, and everything is perfect. This is going to be the best weekend of our lives."

THEY SCORED A PERFECT SUMMER DAY FOR THEIR WEDDING, WITH bright sunshine, low humidity and not a cloud in the sky.

Erin had thought this day would never arrive. They'd set the date months ago, sent the email to their friends, made arrangements with the town to use the lighthouse grounds and reserved a block of rooms at the Sand & Surf for their out-of-town guests. Yesterday, Slim had overseen the digging of a pit on the beach that he'd lined with seaweed for the New England clambake they would serve their guests.

And now it was show time, and Erin couldn't have been more excited. The only thing that would've made this day better was having her beloved twin brother there to share in her joy. Over the last few days, she'd thought of Toby more than she had in a long time. He was always on her mind, but he'd been more present than usual as she counted down to the biggest day of her life.

She'd relived the last time she saw him repeatedly. They'd been at odds that weekend in the Hamptons, which was rare for them. He'd come right out and told her that Mitch, the man she'd recently moved in with, wasn't good enough for her. "Someday," Toby had said, "you'll know what I mean."

When Erin thought about how she'd wanted to punch him for saying that, she could only laugh now at how right he'd been. She was so glad she hadn't married Mitch. He was a good man who'd tried his best to support her after the devastating loss of her brother before giving up on their relationship a year later. It had taken meeting Slim for Erin to finally understand what Toby had wanted for her.

Her Toby had sent Tobias Fitzgerald Jackson Junior to find her the night she sprained her ankle. Of that she had no doubt, and the thought gave her comfort that her brother was always close by.

She heard voices on the floor below the bedroom where she'd gotten dressed. The new lighthouse keeper was due to arrive in the next week, but for now, the magical place where she'd fallen in love with Slim was all theirs.

"Knock, knock," her mom, Mary Beth, said. "Are you decent?"

"I am. Come on up."

Her parents came up the spiral stairs into the room that held so many special memories for Erin, most of them involving the man she was about to marry.

"Oh, honey," Mary Beth said, fighting tears. "You look so beautiful."

"Sensational," her dad, Tom, added, blinking back tears of his own.

Erin had gone with a simple halter-style white dress with a small train and had left her hair down the way Slim liked it best. "Thanks, guys."

"We're so very happy for you and Slim," Mary Beth said. "In case you haven't noticed, we adore him."

"He loves you, too." They'd spent quite a lot of time with her parents after her dad suffered an aneurism that had required emergency surgery. He was almost completely recovered now. Giving her away at her wedding had been one of his primary goals during rehab.

Erin held out her hands to them. "I don't want to make us all into wrecks before the ceremony, but I just want to say... I'm so thankful to both of you for everything."

"We're just as thankful to you." Mary Beth held Erin's hand and her husband's. "We say all the time that we never would've survived losing Toby if it hadn't been for our sweet girl."

They shared a tearful group hug that ended when Jenny arrived. "Hello up there! Is anyone ready to get married?"

"Come on up," Erin said, dabbing at her eyes with a tissue her mother provided.

Jenny bounded up the stairs, bringing bouquets for both of them. She stopped short at the sight of the bride. "Oh, Er... You're *gorgeous.*"

Jenny should've been her sister-in-law, and Erin's bond with her had deepened during the years of grief and disbelief that had followed Toby's death. They referred to each other as sister-friends, and there was no one else Erin would've asked to be her matron of honor.

The two women embraced carefully so they wouldn't crease Erin's dress or smash the colorful bouquets.

"Toby would be so, *so* happy you chose Slim."

"I think so, too. He'd also be very smug about how right he was."

Jenny laughed. "Yes, he would." She pulled back from the hug to hand Erin her bouquet, which was made up of white lilies and hydrangeas.

She'd told Jenny to wear whatever she wanted and loved the lilac-colored dress she'd chosen and the bouquet of purple hydrangeas she carried. "We clean up pretty good, huh?"

"You certainly do," Mary Beth said, beaming at both of them. Jenny was like a daughter to Mary Beth and Tom, who were doting extra grandparents to Jenny's son, George.

Somehow, someway, the four of them had survived and thrived and found a way forward through the darkness and back into the light.

It was what Toby would've wanted for them. He would've been devastated if his death had ruined their lives, too. Erin was comforted knowing that he'd be proud of them for carrying on when it would've been so much easier not to.

"Slim is waiting for you," Jenny said. "He told me to tell you to hurry up."

"The man has no patience."

Jenny crooked an eyebrow. "I think he's proven otherwise, wouldn't you say?"

Erin laughed at the question and the raised eyebrow. "You're right. He has. Let's do it."

She followed the others down two spiral staircases to the mudroom, where she glanced at the wall against which she and Slim had once had wild sex. Life with him was never boring, that was for sure.

In the yard, where Jenny had thrown tomatoes at Alex, who was now her husband, Erin's parents escorted her to the spot at the edge of the property where she and Slim had chosen to exchange vows.

They'd asked retired Superior Court Judge Frank McCarthy to officiate, and every one of the hundred and fifty chairs they'd borrowed from the Wayfarer was filled with family and friends from Gansett, West Palm Beach, Pennsylvania and California. Everyone who mattered to them had come, but Erin saw only Slim.

Tall and broad-shouldered, he was devastatingly handsome in the navy suit he'd bought for the occasion. He wore a white dress shirt without a tie, per her request because she knew how much he hated them, and a white rose on his lapel. His dark hair ruffled in the light breeze, and his warm brown eyes were fixed on her as she made her way toward him.

Owen Lawry played an acoustic version of the song "Please" that they'd fallen in love with while watching *The Voice* together on the phone during the months they'd spent apart after they first met. The song had come to mean so much to them, and hearing it now brought tears to Erin's eyes.

She'd promised herself she wouldn't cry, but now that the moment was upon her, she realized she was fighting a losing battle with her emotions.

Slim's brother, Jack, stood by his side, along with Slim's two young nephews, who'd wanted to help their dad be their uncle's best man. Slim's parents were there, as were several of his half siblings and cousins, some of whom Erin had met for the first time the day before.

Everyone from Gansett had come, or so it seemed, including the entire McCarthy clan, the Martinez family, Slim's friend Seamus O'Grady and his wife, Carolina. So many people had become family, first to Jenny when she'd come to Gansett to be the lighthouse keeper and then to Erin when she took over for Jenny. The two women owed that beautiful beacon so much for providing a place for them to finally heal amid the wild beauty of Gansett Island.

Erin and her parents reached the spot where Slim stood waiting for her. Mary Beth and Tom kissed Erin and hugged Slim. It meant so much to her that they adored him. Although, how could they not? He was perfect for her, and they'd seen that even before she'd been willing to admit it to herself.

She handed her bouquet to Jenny and took the hands her groom extended to her.

He kissed her cheek. "You're simply breathtaking."

"Likewise."

They shared a warm, loving smile that filled her with elation. She'd gone years without experiencing a fraction of what he made her feel simply by existing.

Frank welcomed them and their guests and led them through the traditional recitation of vows before turning to Slim, giving him the floor.

They'd debated about whether they wanted to write their own vows. Slim had insisted on it. "I have things I need to tell you," he'd said.

Now that the moment was upon them, he gazed down at her with his heart in his eyes and a smile on his face. "I'll never forget the night I picked you up by the side of the road."

"*Slim!*"

He laughed, as he did every time he said it that way. "My beautiful bride will want me to clarify that she'd sprained her ankle, and I was the lucky one who found her, along with her bike, which had a flat tire. I picked up her and the bike, drove her home and stayed with her that night so she wouldn't be alone. I've wanted to be wherever she is ever since."

He took a pause to wipe away the tears that spilled down her cheeks.

"My beautiful, sweet, brave Erin, I admire you more than anyone I've ever known. You've survived things that would've ruined a lesser person. I never had the chance to know your beloved Toby, but I have no doubt that you've made him so proud with your fortitude, your resilience and your grace."

Oh Lord. He's bringing the big guns.

After he'd wiped away more tears, Slim cupped her cheek. "I promise to never use semicolons and to overuse exclamation marks every chance I get. I promise to never use the word *moist* unless I absolutely have to. I promise to *occasionally* eat a veggie pizza, even though that goes against everything I believe in as a carnivore, and I promise to keep you in Thin Mints year-round."

Erin laughed even as more tears filled her eyes as she recalled discussing their likes and dislikes for the first time.

Slim wiped away her tears. "More than anything, I promise to love you forever."

Judge McCarthy turned to her. "Erin?"

"How am I supposed to follow that?"

Everyone laughed, including her beloved.

"You did good."

His broad smile lit up the kind eyes that looked at her with so much love.

"You're the best thing to ever happen to me, Tobias Fitzgerald Jackson Junior. For the rest of my life, I'll never forget the night you told me your real name. The realization that my Toby had sent a new Toby to me is something that's meant so much to me, especially because I know, without a doubt, that he would've loved you as much as I do. He once told me that I was with the wrong man, and oh, how that made me mad. That was the last time I ever saw him, and I left angry with him, even if he'd tried to fix it by telling me someday I'd know what he meant. It wasn't until I met you that I figured out what he was trying to tell me and that he was right, as always. There was someone better waiting for me, and that someone was you."

Now Slim had tears in his eyes as he listened to her.

"I once told you how I'd been spinning for years by the time I met you, and only after we were together did the spinning finally stop. Before I met you, I would've said I was perfectly content with the life I'd figured out for myself after everything went sideways. But I would've been so wrong. I was merely existing before I had you and your love and your laughter and the joy you bring to each day. Not only did you get me back in an airplane after fifteen years, but you've also taught me how to fly so I won't be scared. You've taught me to fly in so many ways. Thank you for being just what I need and more than I ever allowed myself to dream possible. I love you and our life together more than anything, and as long as you forsake the word *moist* and semicolons, I can't wait to spend forever with you."

Slim laughed and kissed her, his tears mingling with hers.

"Not quite yet, folks," Frank said, making everyone laugh. "Jack, could we have the rings, please?"

Slim's brother handed over the rings, which they exchanged.

"*Now* I can pronounce you husband and wife, Mr. and Mrs. Jackson, and Slim, you may kiss your bride—again."

Slim wrapped his arms around her and kissed her face off. Erin kissed him right back as their guests cheered and whistled and cried right along with them.

He held her for the longest time, mindless of the guests and the photographer and the party that awaited them. "We did it," he whispered.

"Yes, we did."

He extended his arm to her.

She hooked her hand through his arm and stepped with him into their new life as Mr. and Mrs.

THANK YOU FOR READING *TROUBLE AFTER DARK*! I HOPE YOU ENJOYED Julia and Deacon's story as well as Slim and Erin's long-awaited wedding.

Keep in touch with all things Gansett Island by LIKING the NEW Gansett Island Facebook page here https://www.facebook.com/GansettIsland/. Join the Trouble After Dark Reader Group, https://www.facebook.com/groups/TroubleAfterDark/ to discuss the details of the new book with spoilers allowed.

My profound thanks to my reader, Nicole, for her insight as the adult survivor of childhood abuse. Julia's turtle without its shell description came from her. Thank you to my friend Dr. Kate Reynolds, DVM, for her help with rabies information, for sharing some of her personal story with me for this book and for doing an early read of the book.

Huge thanks to my crack editing team of Linda Ingmanson, Joyce Lamb and Anne Woodall as well as my Gansett Island beta readers: Kelly, Amy, Jennifer, Gwendolyn, Katy, Doreen, Trish, Judy, Leslie, Kelly, Jaime, Melanie, Lynanne, Tammy, Betty, Michelle, Laurie, Andi, Mona, Juliane, Betty and Marianne.

As always, a big thank you to the amazing team that supports me every day: Julie Cupp, Lisa Cafferty, Holly Sullivan, Nikki Haley and Ashley Lopez, as well as my husband, Dan, and my "kids," Emily and Jake, who went and became adults on me.

To all the readers who've supported the Gansett Island Series over 21 books, all I can say is thank you, thank you, thank you. And—there's much more to come! Turn the page for read an excerpt of book 22, *Rescue After Dark*, out next summer.

Xoxo

Marie

RESCUE AFTER DARK

Chapter 1

Summertime, and the living was... not easy for Gansett Island Fire Chief Mason Johns. During the seemingly endless winter, year-round residents on the remote island counted down to the summer season. For Mason, Memorial Day weekend signified the end of peace and the start of insanity.

His department went from three to five calls a week to five to ten calls per day, and it went on that way for months. Summer on Gansett was an endless cycle of moped crashes, alcohol-related incidents, sun poisoning, falls from the bluffs, near-drownings, bicycle accidents, surfing accidents, unauthorized bonfires and the occasional house fire. At least once a week, they evacuated someone to get trauma treatment on the mainland via a life flight helicopter. On the island, the saying went, *If you see the chopper coming, someone is in big trouble.*

The drama never ended during the summer, and while he enjoyed helping people and being part of the Gansett Island community, he found himself craving time away from the madness.

Mason rarely took a day off until after Labor Day, which meant he had to make the most of the free time he did have to get in a workout.

Exercise was critical to keeping the stress of the season under control. As he rode his mountain bike over rugged trails on the island's north end, he tried not to think about the piles of paperwork he'd left behind or the long night he still had ahead of him as he tried to stay caught up.

Two weeks into another summer, and it was living up to its reputation thus far. He'd stolen a rare hour to ride his bike and get away from it all before he returned to the office with a takeout dinner to finish the endless paperwork that went along with the uptick in calls.

The sun inched closer toward the western horizon, giving him about another hour of daylight before it became unsafe to be riding on the trails, even with the headlight he'd installed on his bike. After dark, he stayed on the road, but he preferred the trails that wound through some of the most scenic real estate on the planet.

Or at least he thought so. Despite the madness that descended this time of year, he loved this island and all its wild beauty. He wouldn't want to live anywhere else. When he'd first come to Gansett, he'd feared that island life would be too confining, too limiting, but he'd discovered the opposite to be true. Island residents were masterful at keeping themselves entertained, even in the dead of winter, and he'd come to love everything about living there.

This was his favorite part of the trail, the top of a hill that always sent him airborne down an embankment that veered off to the left. More than once, he'd nearly ended up in the seagrass that grew along the trail, but he always managed to right the bike at the last second. He laughed out loud at the thrill of flying through the air on the bike and landed hard, still on the trail. But just barely.

He got his thrills from exercise these days after kicking booze thirteen years ago. A binge-drinking habit from his college days hadn't aged well, and he'd had the choice of giving up drinking or finding another line of work. Since he'd longed to be a firefighter his entire life, giving up his new job as a probationary firefighter in Providence hadn't been an option. The department had sent him to thirty days of rehab with the edict to kick it or find another job. So he'd kicked it, which had been the hardest thing he'd ever done, hands down.

Staying sober had been his primary goal ever since, and fitness had played a huge role in making that happen by giving him a more productive way to spend his time away from work. He pushed himself until he was so exhausted, he would fall into a dreamless sleep when he finally went to bed at the end of every long day.

Sobriety was a daily challenge. He'd never lost the desire to drink, but he'd learned to control the desire, to channel it into other more productive things. AA meetings helped, and he tried to never miss a day, although that became more difficult this time of year.

Mason completed one lap around the giant land conversancy Mrs. Chesterfield had deeded to the island upon her death and, after gauging the sun-to-horizon ratio, decided to take a second loop around the four-mile path. As he approached the jump, he sped up, looking for even more height this time, and as he cleared the incline, he noticed a plume of smoke that took his attention off the landing— only for a second, but that was all it took. He landed wrong and flipped over the handlebars, landing hard on his left side several feet from the path.

The impact knocked the wind out of him for a full minute. He lay on the ground staring up at the sky, watching as daylight began to fade into night and wondering if he was actually hurt or only momentarily stunned.

And then he remembered the smoke and forced himself to move, to breathe, to shake off the crash. Standing, he glanced in the direction of the smoke and found the plume had doubled in size in the time he'd been flat on his ass. He found his phone in the pocket of his jacket and called dispatch.

"It's Mason. There's a fire on the west side. Dispatch all units. I'm on my bike but heading there now."

"Right away, Chief."

He ended the call, stashed the phone in his pocket and fished his bike out of the tall grass, groaning when his left elbow protested being used. "Crap." The last freaking thing he needed right now was an injury, so he gritted his teeth and pretended his elbow wasn't messed up as he pedaled hard toward the smoke.

Something was wrong. Jordan Stokes didn't know what or where or how she knew that something was wrong, just that it was. The sleeping pill she'd taken hours ago had made it so she couldn't move to do anything about it. Her chest hurt like it had during the first major asthma attack she'd suffered as a child and every one she'd endured since.

That'd been the first time she'd thought she was going to die, but it hadn't been the last.

Don't think about that night or him...

She was so tired—mentally, physically, emotionally. She'd taken the pill out of sheer desperation for some much-needed rest. While the pill had made it so she couldn't move a muscle, her mind was wide awake, as always. With her identical twin sister, Nikki, and Nikki's fiancé, Riley, off-island for a few days, Jordan was home alone in the house that Nikki and Riley had restored over the winter. Technically, it belonged to their grandmother, but Evelyn had all but given the house to the happy couple.

Jordan had come to Gansett for the grand opening of The Wayfarer, where her sister was the general manager. After all the years of support Nikki had given to Jordan and her career, such as it was, the least Jordan could do was come to be there for Nik during her big weekend. Two weeks after the grand opening, Jordan hadn't worked up the initiative to return to her so-called life in Los Angeles.

Things were a mess, and the last place in the world she wanted to be was in that massive, empty house on the West Coast. So she'd stayed on Gansett, even if she felt out of place in the house that had always felt like home to her and Nik.

Nikki and Riley were so ridiculously happy that being around them was almost painful for Jordan to watch after the disastrous end to her horrible marriage to Zane. The one-name rock n' roll wonder had beaten the crap out of her in a hotel room last year and then pleaded with her to forgive him every day since.

Even after she'd blocked his number, he'd popped up again and again using other people's phones to plead with her to talk to him, to beg for another chance. She'd read online that he was taking "time away" from the tour to deal with "personal issues" and had checked himself into a facility to contend with substance abuse and mental health concerns.

Jordan was glad he was getting the help he needed, but wished he would stop contacting her. Each message she received from him further lacerated her already shredded heart. She'd put everything she had into that relationship, and the failure of her marriage weighed heavy on her heart.

Her chest hurt all the time, but it hurt worse than usual now.

She wanted to rub her aching breastbone but couldn't seem to make her arms cooperate with the directive from her brain.

Something was wrong.

Alarm flooded her system, reminding her of the panic that came with asthma attacks.

A piercing noise sounded, adding to her anxiety.

Jordan struggled to find the surface, to open her eyes, but her eyelids felt like cement weights.

Pounding footsteps came toward her, a shout that sounded like concern. Then she was flying through the air, more loud noises, a rush of cool air over her face, the press of warm lips to hers, a flood of air to starving lungs. The lips were soft against hers. She tried to get closer, to keep them there, to open her eyes to see the face that belonged to the lips, but her eyelids wouldn't cooperate.

Her chest hurt so badly, it was almost all she could feel, except for those lips against hers.

A panicked shout, more loud noises, the lips were gone, something covered her face, a sharp pain in her arm and then, blissfully, nothing.

"Is she breathing?" Mason asked Mallory Vaughn, a nurse practitioner who filled in periodically on the rig.

Mallory held a stethoscope to the stunning young woman's chest and nodded in response to his question. The woman had long, silky dark hair and exotically beautiful features. Something about her was familiar, though he couldn't recall having met her. "But her respiration is labored, and her heart rate is through the roof. Let's get her to the clinic. I'll call David on the way."

Dr. David Lawrence, the island's only doctor, was always on call.

"Do we know her?" Mason asked.

"She's Nikki Stokes's sister, Jordan. They're identical twins."

That was why she'd seemed familiar. She looked like Nikki, but he saw subtle differences.

Mallory moved with precision to stabilize Jordan while Mason's guys extinguished the blaze that had started in the chimney. "Good thing you saw the smoke. It's possible she's having an asthma attack."

Adrenaline coursed through Mason's system, making him feel amped up the way he always did after a rescue.

Mallory glanced at him and did a double take. "What'd you do to your face?"

"Huh?"

She pointed to his left temple.

He reached up, felt wetness and winced at the flash of pain. "Fell off my bike."

"You need to get that looked at."

"I'll come by the clinic after we finish here."

"Let's roll," Mallory called to the firefighter driving the ambulance.

They took off with lights flashing and sirens screaming.

Jordan was in good hands with Mallory and David, so Mason turned his attention to the smoldering remains of Mrs. Hopper's chimney. Jordan's sister, Nikki, and her fiancé, Riley McCarthy, had done a ton of work to the house over the winter. Hopefully, there wouldn't be too much damage from the fire that'd been contained mostly to the chimney.

He tried to shake off the jitters that followed the rush of running into a burning building and bringing someone out alive. The amped feeling stayed with him as he supervised his firefighters, inspected the damage and tried to pinpoint the source of the fire as his mind raced, trying to process a strange occurrence.

When he'd put his mouth on hers to blow air into her lungs... The craziest thing had happened. She'd moaned and moved her lips as if to kiss him. That'd certainly never happened before, and it was for damned sure that he'd never felt a current of electricity zip through his body while administering mouth-to-mouth resuscitation to anyone else.

What the hell was that about?

Read *Rescue After Dark,* available on June 23, 2020.

OTHER BOOKS BY MARIE FORCE

Contemporary Romances

The Gansett Island Series

Book 1: Maid for Love *(Mac & Maddie)*

Book 2: Fool for Love *(Joe & Janey)*

Book 3: Ready for Love *(Luke & Sydney)*

Book 4: Falling for Love *(Grant & Stephanie)*

Book 5: Hoping for Love *(Evan & Grace)*

Book 6: Season for Love *(Owen & Laura)*

Book 7: Longing for Love *(Blaine & Tiffany)*

Book 8: Waiting for Love *(Adam & Abby)*

Book 9: Time for Love *(David & Daisy)*

Book 10: Meant for Love *(Jenny & Alex)*

Book 10.5: Chance for Love, *A Gansett Island Novella* *(Jared & Lizzie)*

Book 11: Gansett After Dark *(Owen & Laura)*

Book 12: Kisses After Dark *(Shane & Katie)*

Book 13: Love After Dark *(Paul & Hope)*

Book 14: Celebration After Dark *(Big Mac & Linda)*

Book 15: Desire After Dark *(Slim & Erin)*

Book 16: Light After Dark *(Mallory & Quinn)*

Book 17: Victoria & Shannon (Episode 1)

Book 18: Kevin & Chelsea (Episode 2)

A Gansett Island Christmas Novella

Book 19: Mine After Dark *(Riley & Nikki)*

Book 20: Yours After Dark *(Finn & Chloe)*

Book 21: Trouble After Dark *(Deacon & Julia)*

Book 22: Rescue After Dark *(Mason & Jordan)*

Sex Machine

Sex God

Georgia on My Mind

True North

The Fall

Everyone Loves a Hero

Love at First Flight

Line of Scrimmage

Erotic Romance

The Erotic Quantum Series

Book 1: Virtuous *(Flynn & Natalie)*

Book 2: Valorous *(Flynn & Natalie)*

Book 3: Victorious *(Flynn & Natalie)*

Book 4: Rapturous *(Addie & Hayden)*

Book 5: Ravenous *(Jasper & Ellie)*

Book 6: Delirious *(Kristian & Aileen)*

Book 7: Outrageous *(Emmett & Leah)*

Book 8: Famous *(Marlowe)*

Romantic Suspense

The Fatal Series

One Night With You, *A Fatal Series Prequel Novella*

Book 1: Fatal Affair

Book 2: Fatal Justice

Book 3: Fatal Consequences

Book 3.5: Fatal Destiny, *the Wedding Novella*

Book 4: Fatal Flaw

Book 5: Fatal Deception

Book 6: Fatal Mistake

ABOUT THE AUTHOR

Marie Force is the *New York Times* bestselling
author of contemporary romance, romantic
suspense, historical romance and erotic
romance. Her series include the indie-
published Gansett Island, Treading Water,
Butler, Vermont and Quantum Series as well
as the Fatal Series from Harlequin Books.

Her books have sold more than 9 million copies worldwide, have
been translated into more than a dozen languages and have appeared
on the *New York Times* bestseller list 30 times. She is also a *USA Today*
and *Wall Street Journal* bestseller, a Speigel bestseller in Germany, a
frequent speaker and publishing workshop presenter.

Her goals in life are simple—to finish raising two happy, healthy,
productive young adults, to keep writing books for as long as she
possibly can and to never be on a flight that makes the news.

Join Marie's mailing list on her website at marieforce.com for
news about new books and upcoming appearances in your area.
Follow her on Facebook at www.Facebook.com/MarieForceAuthor
and on Instagram at www.instagram.com/marieforceauthor/.
Contact Marie at marie@marieforce.com.